Surprised by Love

by

May Paddock

TELEMACHUS
PRESS

Cover Designed by Jefferson Eliot

Published by Telemachus Press, LLC
http://www.telemachuspress.com

ISBN: 978-1-937698-04-1 (eBook)
ISBN: 978-1-937698-56-0 (Paperback)

Version 2012.01.11

Printed in the United States of America

10 9 8 7 6 5 4 3 2 1

In Memory of

Joan Tuckerman Dick
and
Anne Dick Eliot

Acknowledgements

First of all I want to thank my editors, Melissa Hermans and Winslow Eliot. Without them, this book would not exist. I want to thank Jefferson Eliot for the photograph and design of the cover.

Friends and relations have read this book in various drafts and have been very helpful with their criticisms as well as encouragement, especially Kendell Shaffer, Jefferson Eliot, Lisa Hunt, Annie Newman, Liberty Winter, King Harvey, Marianne Rannenberg, and Alexander Eliot, who came up with the title.

I also want to thank Neil Smith and his writing group who spurred me on, year after year, as well as art therapists, Bea Birch and the late Anne Stockton, who gave me experiences of color that I have tried to pass on in words.

Although this is a work of fiction, I wouldn't have been able to write it without having traveled to Nicaragua with the Columbia County, Malpaisillo Sister City Project. I want to thank the project's organizers both here and in Malpaisillo, and the many people who made me welcome there, especially the Navarro family.

Last of all I want to thank Fred Paddock, for supporting me all along the way.

Surprised by Love

Chapter One

JOAN'S HUSBAND, CHARLES, died when their daughters were twelve and fourteen. He and Joan had been making breakfast on a snowy morning in Boston. "Hell's bells, we're out of coffee!" he'd said. "I'll go get some."

"Great!" Joan called as he headed for the door. "Could you pick up The Globe as well?"

"Sure," he'd answered as the door closed behind him.

Newspapers were sold on the opposite side of Massachusetts Avenue. He'd been hit by a bus as he tried to cross.

The day after Charlie's funeral, Joan's mother called her to say, "My dear, I really do think the very best thing would be for you and the girls to move in with me on Beacon Hill. I have plenty of room and I'll hire an excellent governess for the girls. And I'll see to it that you're invited to gatherings where you'll meet some of your own kind of people. Charles was a good man of course," she continued, "and he was a good father in his own way. But he wasn't, I have to say it, all that I'd hoped for you. His dying was a terrible tragedy, of course, for you and the girls, but it also means that now you'll be able to meet people with standing in the world. Won't it be nice to have the coming out parties for the girls that you missed by eloping with Charles?"

"Mother, for God's sake," Joan said, feeling about eleven years old rather than thirty-eight.

"I know you're upset," her mother said. "Now why don't the girls stay with me on the Cape while you pack up? They'll be just fine with me."

Joan took a deep breath. "Thank you, Mother, that's very good of you. I'm sure the girls would love to be at the Cape for a while."

"That's the spirit," her mother said cheerfully. "I'll send the car over for them before tea. They always like having tea with me."

"That will be lovely. I'm very grateful."

"Don't mention it, dear. Good bye!" And she hung up.

The next day Joan drove to New York City and found a one-bedroom apartment on West 97th street. She decided she could put the girls in bunk beds in the bedroom and she would sleep on the sofa in the living room. She spent the following week sorting their belongings, giving or throwing away everything that wouldn't fit in their new apartment. Two weeks later, she drove out to her mother's house on Cape Cod.

"Mother, the girls and I are going to try living in New York City," she said, hating hearing her voice shake a little. "Charlie grew up there and we always planned on going back some day. So in a way I'm doing this for him as well as for us. In any case," she quickly continued, "we're doing it. Come on girls, get your things. We have a long drive."

And, amazingly, it had all worked out. Joan found a job teaching four-year-olds in a "Head Start" program on the Lower East Side. Angelica was accepted at the prestigious Music and Art High School and then went on to Cooper Union. Sarah, while still in high school, got a small part in a television commercial. Instead of going to college, she enrolled in acting, dancing, and singing classes, while working short-term secretarial jobs.

Joan was complacently proud of how well her daughters were doing, until one February night of Angelica's third year at Cooper Union, when she was found curled up and bleeding in a doorway near the college after cutting her wrists with a broken bottle. This led to a series of hospitalizations for terrifying depressions interspersed with periods of energetic creative work. Despite her instability, Angelica's talent and hard work, when she was well, had finally led to her being represented by a mid-town gallery.

Chapter Two

IT WAS ANGELICA who'd invited her mother to a family gathering in a Chinatown restaurant on a cold February night.

"What are we celebrating?" Joan asked.

"Life itself," Angelica answered, smiling as though at an inside joke.

"How nice," Joan responded vaguely. She was grateful for Angelica's good spirits, and sighed with pleasure as she looked at her older daughter whose eyes were bright and cheeks rosy from the winter cold. Two months before, Angelica had been ashen and haggard, battling a depression that had landed her in St Vincent's hospital.

Joan's younger daughter, Sarah, arrived late. Her face was pale except for dark circles under her eyes. She wore black jeans and a black sweater and looked, Joan thought confusedly, as though she were in mourning.

They talked first about politics. Would President Reagan take away funding from all the social service agencies?

Then Sarah asked about Joan's students in the Head Start Program—Chinese, Black, and Puerto Rican children. Joan loved to talk about their idiosyncrasies, their friendships, and the fun they had learning words in each other's languages.

Angelica described a retrospective of Ad Reinhart's paintings that she had seen the day before. "Everything black. Black on black. Absolutely stunning!"

"Didn't he kill himself about fifteen years ago?" Sarah asked.

"Yes, he did," Angelica confirmed sadly. "A tragedy! But," she continued, "he'd already changed the future of painting. We can never go back now."

At the end of the meal, as Joan reached for a fortune cookie, Angelica grabbed her hand. "Talking about the future, Mother, Sarah has something to tell you." Joan turned toward Sarah, but Angelica pulled on her hand and continued, "Please don't interrupt her, Mother, until she says it all. And don't forget," she added imperiously, "We're in a restaurant that I like a lot, so don't make a scene."

Joan wanted to say, "You're the one who makes scenes!" Instead, she turned to Sarah and asked, "What's up?"

Sarah was clutching her teacup so hard that her knuckles were white. Angelica still held one of Joan's hands. Joan put out her other hand to cover Sarah's, but Sarah pulled away.

"Mom, I'm going to ask you a big favor," Sarah said quietly but clearly.

"If I can do it, I will."

"The favor is not to ask any questions about what I need to tell you."

"It's none of your business anyway", Angelica interrupted.

"Angie, please, no need to get Mom upset," Sarah smiled wanly at her sister, "before I even tell her."

Then she looked directly at Joan and said, "Mom, something has happened."

"Something bad?" Joan asked anxiously.

"Well, yes, I guess so. I know you'll think so." Sarah looked down at the table.

Angelica interposed loudly, "I call that a fucking question." The Japanese tourists seated at the next table, peering at a guidebook, looked up somewhat startled.

Sarah turned to her sister. "Angie, please—I need to…"

"Mother," Angelica interrupted, raising her voice even further and speaking rapidly, "Sarah is going to have a baby and it's none of your business who the father is because he's flown the coop."

The Japanese tourists quickly gathered their cameras and guidebooks and headed for the cashier.

Joan watched the Japanese pay their bill. Her eyes followed the group out the door and up the stairs to the sidewalk. She heard Angelica light a cigarette and, after a pause, she heard Sarah crunch open a fortune cookie. Finally, Joan turned toward Sarah and asked, "Have you gone to confession?"

"Oh honestly, Mother…"

But Sarah interrupted her sister, "Yes I have. I went to Father McGinley."

"That's good." Joan stood up a little unsteadily. She put some money on the table and reached for her coat. "I think I'll go home now. You know I love you," she said to Sarah, "both of you," she continued, looking at Angelica, "but I need to go home now. We'll talk some other time." She headed for the door, carrying her coat under her arm, bumping into chairs and tables, but finally reaching the darkness outside.

She breathed deeply, feeling much better in the cold air. She walked north, crossed Canal Street and continued along the dark empty streets lined with factories. She was too unhappy to be afraid.

Chapter Three

JOAN DID NOT call ahead to St. Vincent's to ask if Father McGinley could see her. She was afraid that Nora, the church secretary, would ask what it was about. Father McGinley was eighty-seven and Nora was very protective of him. Instead of asking for an appointment, Joan went to early Mass. As she shook hands with Father McGinley afterwards, she whispered, "Would you have a few minutes Father? I'd like very much to talk with you. It doesn't have to be this morning but…"

"Sure, Joan, I'd be delighted. I'll ask Nora to fix us up with coffee and something to nibble. I could eat a bear. I'll be in my office in five minutes."

When he joined her, he had taken off his cassock and wore a black shirt with a priest's collar and black slacks. He was tall and thin. Nora followed Father McGinley into his office. She carried a tray with two mugs of coffee, and two buttered corn muffins.

"Thank you, Nora. How lovely they look, and how hungry I am. Help yourself please, Joan."

Then Joan sat back in her chair.

"Now, Joan, what can I do for you?"

Joan knew that Father McGinley would never mention that Sarah had spoken with him, so she told him the information as though for the first time. "Sarah is going to have a baby, and there's no father in the picture at all."

Father McGinley smiled at Joan and reached his hand out over his desk. Joan, not understanding why, put her hand in his. He gave it a friendly shake and said, "Congratulations, you're going to be a grandmother."

"I've been such a bad mother to both my girls. This would never have happened if…"

Father McGinley interrupted a little sharply, "You've been a good mother, Joan, and now your girls are young women. Sarah's present situation has nothing to do with your way of mothering. And Angelica's illness was not caused by how she was brought up. You know that, Joan. You need to pay attention to your own life, now that the girls are grown up. If your daughters need you, they need you to be strong and happy, a good role model."

"But Sarah needs my help now. If only I'd…"

"Sarah may need practical help now," Father McGinley interrupted again, "But try to keep it practical. I'm not saying don't pray for her," he added. "Prayers are extremely practical. But, Joan, try not to burden Sarah with your personal judgments, either about your own mothering, or her situation."

After a moment, Father McGinley continued, "Sarah is warm-hearted, intelligent, and strong. You've raised a terrific daughter, Joan, and she'll be a fine mother, no matter what the circumstances. You may even enjoy being a grandmother. Many people do. God bless you, my dear."

"Thank you, Father," Joan mumbled automatically as she stood up, bumping hard into the side of his desk. She gathered her purse and coat, eager to get out of his office and into the air. Her thoughts came in a rush of irritation. It was all very well for Father McGinley to be cavalier about Sarah having a baby. Not being allowed to marry meant that priests were really ignorant about some things. If she had done better by Sarah, this never would have happened. In any case, she would make it up to her—somehow. Of course she wouldn't be judgmental. Who did Father McGinley think he was talking to? The only person she was judging, beside the baby's father, whoever he was, was herself for somehow leaving Sarah vulnerable to this disaster.

Chapter Four

WHEN JOAN CALLED Sarah that evening, Sarah sounded as though she'd been crying.

"Hello, dearest, I want to apologize for…"

"That's okay, Mom. It was my fault. I should have told you before—just the two of us."

"Well perhaps we can talk now. Are you in touch with…?"

"No, Mom," Sarah interrupted. "He's really left. His phone's been disconnected. I wrote him a letter, and it came back. He's gone and… Oh Mom, it's such awful timing. I've been auditioning for a film being made here next fall, and I got the part! But the baby is due early August! Even if I can get myself back into shape by September, how can I possibly take the job—I can't bring a baby to the set!" She began to sob. "This was going to be my big break, and I blew it, blew it clear out of the water."

"Listen, Sarah," Joan said firmly, "How about if we live together and I take care of the baby while you're at work?"

"But you'll be working too."

"I'll retire early," Joan responded, more cheerfully than she felt. "I'll have a bit of a pension. But it would be easier if we had only one rent."

"Oh, Mom, would you? Would you? That would make everything okay. But are you sure? You wouldn't mind too much giving up your job and all those kids you love so much?"

"Yes, dear, I'm sure. This is an important time in your career. If this would be of help to you, I'd be glad to do it."

"You're an angel, Mom! I can't thank you enough. I'll call my agent right now."

After three months of searching, Joan and Sarah found a large but inexpensive loft on Canal Street in the old factory district. Once Sam was born, Sarah stayed home for six weeks, exercising religiously on the stationary bike and rowing machine she'd set up in one corner of the loft. Often she carried Sam in a backpack during her workouts. She said the extra weight helped her work on her abs, and there was nothing like it for putting him to sleep.

Joan felt as though she was carrying extra weight as well. While Sarah worked out at home, Joan was at Head Start training the teacher who would take her place. She hated giving up the teaching job she'd loved for so many years. And it had been hard as well to leave her rent-controlled studio apartment with its view of the Hudson. "Stop complaining," she told herself again and again. "This was your idea. This is what it means to be a good mother."

Sarah was back in shape in time to keep her role in the film. She left for work before dawn and often got home after dark. The film was a hit. Although Sarah had only a small part in it, the film's success led to parts for her in made-for-television films. And the television work, in turn, led to auditions for Off Broadway productions.

Joan was surprised by how much she enjoyed taking care of Sam. When he was a baby, she carried him against her chest, and they spent hours gallery-hopping and museum exploring. Sam seemed happy enough wherever they went, as long as she stopped every few hours to give him a bottle and a clean diaper. When he became too heavy to carry, she bought a stroller and they walked the streets of New York City, in and out of ethnic neighborhoods, window-shopping and people watching. When Sam began walking, Joan found playgrounds to take him to. After he had swung on the swings, crawled through the cement tunnels, and slid down the slides for a few hours, he was happy to sit back in his stroller and explore the city with his grandmother.

Chapter Five

ONE MORNING IN early April, when Sam was with his mother, Joan decided to go on her own to the Museum of Modern Art. She meandered slowly up Fifth Avenue until she heard someone playing "Luck Be a Lady" on an oboe. She quickened her pace. The musician was standing on the corner of Fifth Avenue and 53rd street in front of St. Thomas' Church.

He was tall, with dark brown hair cut very short, wearing jeans and a button-down shirt with the sleeves rolled up. He had wire-rimmed glasses, but he played with his eyes tight shut. By the time Joan reached him, he was playing "Take Back Your Mink."

Joan stood for a while, entranced. Then she climbed the stone steps of the church and sat down to listen in comfort. In between songs, the musician opened his eyes, looked around for a minute and grinned. The church steps began to fill up, and people leaned against parked cars to listen.

After a while, the musician switched to songs from "Annie Get your Gun." Joan, disappointed by his choice, realized that the coldness of the stone steps had seeped through her skirt. When she got up, she was too stiff to stand upright. She slowly and carefully descended the church steps, afraid of tripping over a listener's outstretched leg, or stepping on someone's hand. At one point she put her hand on somebody's shoulder to steady herself. The young man turned in anger. Joan was about to apologize, but when he saw her, he said, "Let me help you, grannie." Joan smiled ruefully as he held out his hand to guide her down the last crowded step.

On the sidewalk again, Joan stood for a minute trying to straighten her back. When the oboist finished "I've Got the Sun in the Morning," she dropped a dollar into his open oboe case.

The musician smiled at her and winked. Then he closed his eyes and began "Anything You Can Do, I Can Do Better." Joan walked west on 53rd street humming. She couldn't remember the last time a man had winked at her. By the time she reached the museum, she found that she was standing more or less straight again.

Later that afternoon, Joan, with Sam's help, set the table, while Sarah made macaroni and cheese for their supper. Sarah had a solo in "The Three Penny Opera" and she was singing softly to herself.

Despite her daughter's singing, or perhaps thinking her daughter would like a distraction, Joan told Sarah about the oboist that afternoon. "It was such fun to hear those songs. Street musicians are a sign of spring don't you think?"

"That sounds nice, Mom," Sarah said vaguely as they sat down to eat. "How do I look? Does my hair look shinier to you? I used a new conditioner."

Joan stopped eating and looked at her daughter. Her short brown hair was wrapped around pink curlers. Her eyes sparkled under green eye shadow that seemed to glitter.

"Well dear, I…"

Just then Sam tipped over his glass of milk. He began to cry and Sarah got out of her chair to hug him and hold him close while Joan sopped up the spill. Sarah noticed the wall clock over Sam's shoulder and gasped, "I'm late for rehearsal." She gave Sam a kiss on the top of his head, and grabbed her jacket. She was almost out the door when she remembered that her hair was still in curlers. She grabbed her mother's long silk scarf from the coat tree near the door and wrapped it around her head like a colorful turban. Then, in a rush, with a "Wish me luck!" and a banging door, she was gone. Joan heard her running down the stairs toward the street door, and sent up a prayer that she wouldn't trip and turn her ankle.

Chapter Six

AFTER SAM WAS in bed, Joan hummed some of the songs from "Guys and Dolls" as she did the dishes. Then she sat down at the kitchen table to work on a large jigsaw puzzle. Angelica had given the puzzle to Sam, but it was much too hard for him. He was just learning to recognize pieces with straight edges be used for the borders.

It was past eleven when the doorbell rang. Joan wasn't surprised; she'd seen Sarah's forgotten keys on the kitchen counter. When Joan opened the door, there was the oboist from 53rd Street, shaking hands goodbye with Sarah and turning toward the stairs. Joan opened the door wider and said, "Come on in. Sam and I baked some oatmeal cookies." She smiled at them both.

Sarah, instead of seconding her mother's invitation, asked, "Do you know each other?"

"Sort of," Joan said, looking at the oboist. "I heard you play this afternoon on 53rd Street. I enjoyed it a lot." She held out her hand, "I'm Sarah's mother, Joan Fitzpatrick. It's nice to meet you."

He shook her hand, with a warm friendly grasp. "You do look familiar. Pleased to meet you. My name is Joe Wilson. I'm in the Three Penny Opera pit."

"Come on in." Joan repeated.

"Okay, do, if you want to," Sarah mumbled.

They went into the kitchen. Joe looked at the puzzle for a minute and picked up a piece and fitted it in.

"Thank you," Joan said. "What will you have? Can I interest you in a cookie and a cup of coffee? We have a little espresso-maker."

"That sounds perfect," Joe said, and sat down at the kitchen table. "I'm going to go check on Sam," Sarah announced. "I have a three-year-old son," she called, almost defiantly, over her shoulder.

"How nice," Joe said, and smiled at Joan. "Are you a musician, Mrs. Fitzpatrick?"

"No, Sarah gets her voice from her father. He was the lead tenor at Saint Paul's in Boston. Please call me Joan. Have some cookies. Coffee will be ready in a sec."

"Thank you, I will."

"Have you played in many orchestras?"

"Just a few. I'm also in a chamber group. 'Wind in the Reeds.' Have you heard of us?"

"No, but I'd like to hear you play."

"Well, we don't have a gig scheduled right now, but I'd be happy to let you know when we do."

"Let Mom know what?" Sarah asked as she came back into the kitchen. She poured two cups of espresso which she brought over to the table, giving one to Joe. She sipped from the other, after dipping a piece of oatmeal cookie into it.

"The next time my chamber music group has a gig."

"Oh, Mom's not interested in music," Sarah retorted.

"Why, Sarah!"

Sarah looked at Joan and shrugged. "You always say how much you enjoy a quiet evening at home with a good book."

"That's true," Joan agreed, "but I love going to concerts and would do it more often if I had my evenings free." Looking at Sarah's face, Joan regretted her words immediately. "In any case" she went on, "when 'Wind in the Reeds' has its next gig, please let me know, and if Sarah is working, I'll get a baby-sitter. Have another cookie."

"No, thank you," he answered as he gulped down the coffee. "They're delicious, but I think I'd better go. It's been a pleasure to meet you." He shook Joan's hand again. "And I'll be sure to let you know," he added with a wink. "Good night, Sarah," and he was off.

Sarah closed the door too quietly and locked it. Still facing the door, she said, "I didn't realize I was keeping you from concerts."

"I shouldn't have said that. I'm sorry. It's just that you embarrassed me by saying I wasn't interested in music, when in fact I am. Or at least I used to be," Joan added, surprised by the bitter tone of her voice. "Oh well, I'm just tired. Good night dear, I'm going to bed. I like your friend."

"He's not my friend," Sarah called after her mother, as Joan left the kitchen pretending not to hear.

Chapter Seven

THE NEXT MORNING, Sarah and Joan sipped coffee and munched bagels while listening to the news on the radio. Sam arranged cheerios into patterns on his place mat. Suddenly, Sarah said casually, "I think I'll put Sam in nursery school."

Joan's hand shook and she spilled hot coffee onto the table. Sam got down from his chair and climbed into her lap. Sarah continued, as she got up for a sponge to wipe up the coffee, "Of course there is nobody who can take care of him like you, Mom. But I feel guilty about how tied down you've become." As she took the sponge back to the sink and rinsed it out, she said, "Actually, I think it's time Sam experienced other children. I don't plan to have any more, and he needs to learn how to socialize. You give him everything he wants…" Despite Joan's attempt to break in at this point, Sarah continued very quickly, "I don't mean that you spoil him, not at all. What I mean is that he needs to start playing with other children so he can experience the give and take involved."

Sam got down from Joan's lap without a word and moved to a chair near the jigsaw puzzle where he began to move the pieces around.

"How can we afford it?" Joan said, finally able to speak.

"I'm not sure yet. But I bet we, I mean I, can cut back on something. Also, it's not that expensive," she went on. "Anyway, I'll look into it and then we can talk about it further." With that, she picked Sam up, almost hiding behind him as she said, "Let's go get dressed, snukums, so Gran can drink her coffee in peace."

Joan watched them go, trembling with fury. In response to Sarah's cries of desperation, Joan had let go of the job she loved to take care of Sam. And now, when it was too late for Joan to get back into teaching, Sarah had decided she wanted Sam to have more 'give and take.' Joan promised herself that she wasn't going to pay for someone else to take care of Sam. She needed her money for the monthly stipend she sent Angelica to help with the rent.

After a few minutes Joan followed Sarah into the large bedroom she shared with Sam. She spoke to Sarah's back as she dressed Sam. "I think I'll visit Angelica. I'll be back before five. I hope you both have a lovely day."

"Maybe I'll order a pizza so you won't have to cook," Sarah answered, not looking around.

"Whatever you decide," Joan replied, as she turned away. "I wouldn't want to impose my cooking on your son against your wishes," she added before she could stop herself.

"Oh, Mom!" she heard, as she closed the door on her daughter's words.

Chapter Eight

ANGELICA LIVED IN a loft on Prince Street where she had room to paint. She had no phone and there was no doorbell on the street door, so to get her attention Joan needed to yell up from the street below to her third floor window. Then, if Angelica wanted company, she would throw the keys out the window. Joan went through this routine every time she visited, even though she had her own set of keys given to her by the landlord during one of Angelica's hospitalizations

It was embarrassing and infuriating to have to stand there yelling, "Angelica!" again and again while people passed by. Joan was almost ready to give up when the keys came flying down, just missing her head and landing very close to a pile of dog droppings. She carefully picked them up, unlocked the door, and climbed up three flights of stairs.

"Hey, Mother, did you come to look at some real art, instead of the crap in the galleries these days?" Angelica shouted down the stairwell.

"I did indeed, dear," Joan answered, panting a little. "How are you?"

"I'm great. Come have a look!" When Joan entered the studio, Angelica pointed to a huge canvass resting on two easels. The entire canvass, perhaps five feet by five, was painted an intense black, almost like velvet. But on a diagonal, in the right-hand corner, was a long slash of blood red.

The huge painting made Joan uncomfortable. She offered to take Angelica out to lunch, but was refused, "Sorry Mother, but some of us have to work. I'm getting ready for a show."

"That's wonderful" Joan said, wondering if the show was real or simply hoped for. "Sorry I interrupted. You look radiant, darling, and the painting, well, it's very powerful." She felt ridiculously hypocritical as she trooped back down the stairs and out into the street. Would she ever be able to have a real conversation with Angelica? The trouble was, she was afraid that if she said the wrong thing she could cause Angelica to get sick again. She wasn't sure if she was afraid of Angelica herself, or of her illness. They seem to have become inseparable.

Once outside in the sun and the warming spring air, Joan felt heavy with depression. She walked north, crossing Houston into Greenwich Village. Usually the boutiques, cafés, and little bookstores made the Village a joy to wander in. But today, all she could see was the broken glass, discarded newspapers, and dog droppings on the sidewalks. She kept walking north, surprised and frustrated by her tears. She entered Washington Square Park, where she and Sam had had many good times at the playground and wading in the large central fountain. Now she was conscious only of the homeless people, in their layers of dirty clothes, dragging their garbage bags of belongings while searching one wire trash can after another. How could she have brought Sam here to play? Maybe Sarah was right. Maybe Sam would be better off in a nursery school. Why had she thought she was a good grandmother? She knew she hadn't been a good parent.

She sighed as she went through the huge archway out of the park and onto Fifth Avenue. Here, there was nothing but apartment buildings with uniformed doormen. As she walked further north, the apartment buildings were replaced by expensive stores with large plate glass windows extolling their wares. She trudged up the avenue for a couple of miles until she arrived at Saint Patrick's Cathedral, where she decided to sit for a while and catch her breath.

Inside the cathedral, busloads of tourists were wandering around, talking, laughing, and deciding where to go for lunch. Joan tried to avoid them by going into a small chapel to the right of the altar to kneel in front of the image of the Virgin of Guadalupe. When her knees ached, she sat back on the bench and continued to pray with her eyes closed. She heard people sit or kneel beside her. Some prayed aloud in Spanish, some in languages she didn't recognize. Some were silent. Somebody in the pew in front of her began to sob. Joan opened her eyes to make sure the person was all right. The young woman in front of her stood up, blew her nose a few times, and left, with her high heels making a quick staccato rhythm. Joan stared at the image of the Virgin. The image stared back at her. The Virgin seemed to understand everything. Joan could feel the heaviness of her depression lift.

After a prayer of thanksgiving, Joan stood up, nodded good bye to the Virgin, and moved quickly through the tourists to the nearest door. She was eager to catch a bus back to the loft so she could look up a recipe for a fancy dessert to make as a surprise for Sarah.

Chapter Nine

A FEW WEEKS later, Joan asked, although she knew it might be better not to, "How is that nice young man, Joe, I think his name is, the one who plays the oboe so well? Is he still in the orchestra?"

"Yes, I guess so. I haven't really noticed."

"You haven't noticed if he's in the orchestra where you perform every night?"

"I think he is, Mom. But he doesn't interest me."

"I don't know what you mean by 'interest.' I heard him play, and therefore he interests me. Please remind him, if you get a chance I mean, that I'm looking forward to hearing his chamber group. 'Wind in the Reeds' I think he said it was called."

"Okay, if he's there, I'll tell him."

"I admit," Joan went on, "I enjoyed thinking that he was walking you home at night. I know it's a wonderful neighborhood, but even so…"

"I don't want you worrying about me at night and I won't worry about you and Sam during the day. You, Sam and I, we're all street-wise."

"Yes, I know. But he seemed very nice, and he's a fine musician."

Sarah turned to face her mother, "It was you who taught Angelica and me that we didn't need men. After Daddy died, you never went out with a man, not even once, despite all of Grandma's harangues. You focused completely on us, and we three had a lot of fun, at least until Angie got sick. So, when Sam's father wandered off, I remembered how you'd been with us and I decided that I too could be happy with just my child." After a minute she went on, "Not that it's come up much. Joe was the first man in a long time who's suggested walking me home. It made me kind of uncomfortable, especially the way you invited him in."

"Why did it make you uncomfortable?"

"Well, for one thing, he's so good-looking. I know a lot of the girls in the show have noticed him. So, I didn't know why he'd picked me to walk home with. And for another, I just told you, I decided not to need a man. Just like you, Mom…" Sarah began to cry.

Joan took her daughter into her arms, "Sarah, when your father died, we'd been married for eighteen years. We'd had a wonderful life together. You're too young, dearest, to let Sam's father's idiocy keep you from getting married. In any case, Sam is such a joy that we can only be grateful, don't you think?"

"Of course I'm grateful about Sam, but you're missing the point…" Then she was silent for a moment. "By the way, it turns out nursery school is expensive, just like you thought. I guess we'll have to go on the way we've been, if it's okay with you."

"It's more than okay with me," Joan said, looking away in case she cried.

A few nights later, Sarah called home from the theater around eleven. "Hey, Mom, did I wake you up?"

Joan realized with surprise that she had been sleeping, sitting upright on the sofa, with the book she'd been reading on the floor beside her feet. "No, what's up? Forget your keys?"

"No, Mom. Listen, Joe asked if he could walk me home and I was wondering if we had something there we could offer him to eat or drink. And, if you're not in your night-gown, well, then I'd invite him in."

"That would be nice," Joan said, sitting up straighter. "Sam and I made some fudge for the Church fair. We've got plenty."

"Mom, don't make a ta-doo, okay? He may not even want to come in."

"Of course not," Joan said. Why did the girls always act as though she were the one who had tantrums or fussed? "Only invite him in if you want to," she added. "You're not doing this to entertain your old mother are you?" But immediately Joan wished she hadn't said that—nobody likes to be seen through.

"No, of course not," Sarah responded quickly. "He lives on Lispenard, so he passes by us anyway. Is Sam asleep?"

"Like a log. See you soon. Have a good walk."

Joan got the espresso machine out of the cupboard. Around midnight she heard them coming down the street. They were singing "Mack the Knife," making it sound melodramatic and frightening and then laughing at their parody. Joan felt a thrust of joy hearing her daughter's full-hearted laugh.

Chapter Ten

AFTER THAT, JOE came often. Sam and Joan sometimes baked cookies for their "After the Play Parties." Sam often woke up when he heard Joe's voice, and Sarah would let him join them in the kitchen. He would point to the cookie Joe was eating and say, "You like?" sounding just like the baker around the corner who gave Sam gifts of broken cookies or crumbled cake slices.

"You're my favorite baker." Joe always replied, giving Sam the high five.

Then one night Sam asked Joe, "Can we go to the zoo?"

"I'd enjoy that very much. Maybe your mother would come."

"Oh no, I've too much to do. But maybe Mom would…" she turned to Joan.

"Gran won't go. She doesn't like animals in cages," Sam reminded her.

"You're right. I'd forgotten that." Sarah said. Then after a pause, "Okay, let's all three go together."

"How about next Monday?" Joe suggested.

"Yeah!" Sam answered for them both.

The three began to make a habit of weekly excursions. Sometimes Joan joined them, but usually not. At first they let Sam suggest the places: the carousel, the model-sailboat pond, the dinosaurs in the museum. Then Sarah and Joe took turns: the Cloisters, Fulton Fish Market at dawn, a walk across the Brooklyn Bridge.

One Monday, Sam had a bad cold. The plan had been for all four of them to take the Circle Line around Manhattan. Joe had heard that one of the tour guides was exceptionally good, a 'stand-up comic' his friend had said, so Joe had procured tickets.

Joan told Sarah, she'd be happy to stay home with Sam. "Why don't you go with Joe? You hardly ever get to be alone with him." But, Sarah called Joe to suggest they put off the trip to another Monday.

"I don't think the tickets are refundable," he'd said wistfully, so she'd agreed to go with him, and they would try to sell the two remaining tickets at the dock.

That night, after Sam had been put to bed, Sarah and Joan sat in the kitchen. "So what happened?" Joan asked. She'd been aware all evening of a pent up excitement in Sarah. When Sarah didn't respond right away, she continued, "How was the tour guide? I wondered about you in the rain. Were you able to see from inside?"

"It was just a light rain. Most of the people went inside, but we didn't. The city is amazingly beautiful from the water. A lot of lights were on because it was such a grey day, and everything shimmered, in the buildings themselves, and in their reflections in the water. We talked about the city and how much fun we'd been having exploring it. We talked about Sam and planned some Monday trips that he would enjoy, places like the Firemen's Museum, that I would never have thought of. Joe has a real feeling of what it's like to be a young boy in the city. Then, near the end of the trip, when we were coming back to the dock, the sun came out and we saw a double rainbow. Did you see it?"

"No. I wish I'd been looking. I've never seen a double rainbow."

"It was wonderful. We stared at it together, not saying a word. We just stood next to each other and stared. It felt as if we were one person. I've no idea how long it lasted. Everyone else got off the boat, but we didn't move until it had faded completely."

Joan waited, knowing something else was coming.

"Then, Mom, Joe asked me to marry him. Right out of the blue. But it wasn't really out of the blue somehow, because we'd been seeing something, something like the future, in the rainbow." There was a moment or two of silence while Sarah seemed to see the rainbow again.

Joan could barely contain her excitement.

"Well?" she prompted urgently.

"Well," Sarah said, looking at her mother in a sort of dazed way, "I said yes!"

"Oh my darling!" and Joan hugged her daughter so hard she could hardly breathe. "I'm so happy for you, for you and for Sam, for all of us."

Angelica moved to Boston before the wedding, in spite of Joan's protests. "I'm tired of this filthy city. I have a friend who works in a gallery on Park Street. She's going to Europe for three months and wants me to stay in her apartment and take care of her cat. By the time she gets back, I'll have found a studio. She'll be able to introduce me to other gallery people. They don't pay as much up there, but they're not so faddish about art. She thinks I'll do fine."

"What if you…?" But Joan didn't know how to ask, "What if you get sick and I'm not there?" So she said, "What if you don't find a studio? Will you keep your place here in case? Could you sublet it to someone?"

Angelica stared at her mother for a moment and then shouted at her, "Mother you're so…oh I don't know. You're such a worry wart, a spoil sport, a wet blanket. I'll find a studio. I have a place to live, rent free! God damn it, get off my back! Can't you be happy for me?"

Chapter Eleven

SARAH AND JOE were married in August at St. Vincent's. Sarah wore a white silk sheath, a present from Joan, and held a bouquet of irises. Joe wore a tuxedo, an investment, he said, for future concert gigs. Father McGinley beamed all through the service. The reception was back at the loft. Joe's musician friends played dance tunes and everyone, including Joan and Sam, danced up a storm. Then one of Sarah's friends began to sing "I've Grown Accustomed to Her Face" and they were off, singing all the Broadway hits they could remember, which were many. Angelica sent a small painting as a wedding present, and her regrets. This was a relief because Angelica was unpredictable at parties, especially when there was alcohol. Joan felt proud of her beautiful daughter and her handsome and talented son-in-law, and proud of their friends, such terrific musicians and singers. She only wished that Charlie could have been there. Sam stayed close to her throughout the reception. Joe and Sarah were taking him with them on the night train to Mt. Desert Island for their honeymoon. This would be Sam's first trip outside of New York and he was excited but a little frightened as well. He took hold of his grandmother's hand whenever he had a chance. Joan was delighted that they wanted Sam to travel with them, but she would miss him and was glad to feel his hand in hers.

Around nine that evening, Sam, Sarah and Joe left the loft in a taxi to catch the train. Soon after that, their guests left for their respective lofts and apartments. By ten, Joan was by herself collecting glasses and wrapping up leftovers. Suddenly, she sat down at the kitchen table, put her head on her arms and began to sob. When there were no more tears, she got up a little shakily, blew her nose and made herself a cup of tea. With the tea mug warming her hand, she tried to think about where the tears had come from. Surely she was happy about Sarah and Joe? She had longed for this day. And now Sam had a father. Surely she was happy about that? Were her tears because she was exhausted? She didn't think so. They'd felt like the tears of a child who'd been abandoned. Joan looked around her at the debris she'd been collecting. She felt that she herself was debris, left by the family who'd once needed her with them to be happy. Neither Sarah nor Sam needed her now. Joe was going to move in with them and he and Sarah had decided to put Sam in nursery school. The tears flowed freely again. There was no reason to stop. Nobody would care how long she cried.

While preparing for the wedding, Joan hadn't had time to think about what all this meant for her. Now, as she blew her nose noisily and drank some more tea, she did have time, and it didn't look pretty. Nursery school was probably just half days. Both Joe and Sarah would be working in the evenings. They would still need her. On the other hand, who wants to live with newly-weds, and what would her days be like without Sam to teach and have adventures with? She was sixty-two years old. She knew the school system wouldn't take her back. What should she do now?

The next morning Joan walked over to St. Vincent's for early Mass on the chance that Father McGinley would be free to see her afterwards. He was. "Come on into my study, Joan. What a lovely wedding that was. Didn't Sarah look beautiful? As did you, my dear; and the reception was lovely. Did you really make all that food? You're a marvel, Joan. But," he continued after looking at her for a minute, "you look very tired. No wonder. Come sit down and I'll make us a cup of tea. Nora's away for a few days." He soon came back from the kitchen saying, "I hope you take it black. I forgot to get milk last night."

"That's fine Father, thank you." Joan reached for the cup and put it down on her side of the desk untouched.

"Now what can I do for you," he said as he settled back in his chair.

"I'm feeling somewhat lost," Joan began. "With Sarah and Sam away and even when they get back, and with Angelica in Boston, I'm not sure what I'm supposed to do next."

"In what sense, 'supposed to do'?"

"What do you mean?"

"You say you don't know what you're supposed to be doing and I'm wondering who's giving the orders. Who's making the decisions about what you should be doing?"

"That's why I'm coming to you. I'm hoping you'll know what God wants me to do."

"I don't know what God wants *me* to do from moment to moment." After a while, seeing her blank look, he went on. "That's one of the reasons for prayer, to ask at each turning, 'Which way do I go now?'"

"And does God tell you?"

"Sometimes I feel a nudge or, at times, a kick in the butt. But when the question is difficult or complicated, I find it hard to be sure whether I'm being nudged or whether I'm following my own desires or habits without knowing it."

"What do you do then?"

"I pray. I ask for more help, more guidance."

"Are you saying that you can't help me, that it's up to me to do my own praying and see what happens?"

"I think that's a good place to start."

"I know we're here on earth in order to help people. I've spent too much time thinking only of myself and my family. Now that they don't need my help, I don't know what to do."

Father McGinley waited a minute to see if she would say more. Then he sighed and said, "What we Jesuits say is that we're here to give glory to God. That, of course, can be interpreted in many ways. There is nothing wrong with helping people, Joan. It's a fine vocation when it comes from an overflowing joy in God's love. But you don't need to help people out of expiation for earlier mistakes. We have the sacrament of confession for that. You need to trust the absolution that God has given you." He watched her for a minute to see if she understood. Her face looked both stony and blank. He sighed again before he went on, "But, as I said, there is no harm in helping people. What about volunteering at a hospital or teaching literacy?"

Joan stared at him. What did he mean, "There's no harm in helping people?" Helping people, wanting to help people, doing what you could to help people—wasn't that the whole point of being Catholic? Wasn't that what 'giving glory to God' meant? How could Father McGinley make it sound as though he were indulging a whim of hers by thinking of places she could volunteer?

"Thank you, Father," she finally said. "And thank you for the tea." she added, as she got up to go.

"Oh, Joan," Father McGinley said, as he also stood up, "I'm sorry." She stared at him for a minute, thinking he was going to say how wrong he'd been. But he just smiled and took her hand, "Thank you for coming," he said, as though it had been a tea party.

"You're welcome," she said, realizing almost immediately how foolish she sounded. "Thank you," she amended weakly, and left.

Outside, the weather was hot and sticky. Joan's tears quickly dried and turned into sweat. She decided it was too hot to go anywhere but home. On the way, she stopped at a convenience store and got a New York Times and a pack of Camels. She decided she would read about the troubles of the world, and, since nobody needed her, she might as well smoke.

Chapter Twelve

BACK UPSTAIRS IN the kitchen, puffing away, which she hadn't done for years, Joan found she had no interest in the news. Her head ached. She stubbed out the third cigarette. She was nauseous and found it hard to catch her breath. "Maybe I'm having a heart attack," she thought. "They'll find me in a few weeks, when I smell really putrid." She put her head down on her arms on the kitchen table and let the blackness envelop her. "Is this what death will feel like?" she wondered.

Just then the phone rang. If it hadn't been hanging on the wall, right next to her head, she would not have answered it. But it was so loud and went on for so long that she felt she had no choice. "Hello?"

"Hi, Joanie. It's me. Were you asleep?" Joan's sister asked.

"Hello Marianne. No, just daydreaming. How are you? We missed you at the wedding though of course we understood. It's an awful trip. It was beautiful though. I'll send you some pictures."

"Maybe you could bring them."

"Bring them?"

"Yes, maybe you could bring them here."

"Definitely, some day. But, I'd better send them first— by the time I get there, the pictures could be faded."

"Joanie, could you come soon? I really want, well actually I need…I mean with Sarah married and Angelica in Boston, I was wondering, we were wondering, if you could come out here for a bit."

"Marianne, you're amazing. I was just bemoaning my solitude when you called. I'd love to visit, sweetie, but not just now. I have to figure out my next step, where I'm going to live and all. I don't want to hang out with these love-birds."

"Joanie, distance wasn't the reason we didn't come to the wedding. We really wanted to, but…"

"But what? Marianne what is it?"

"I'm starting chemo on Monday. They say it can be really rough, especially at first; so Caleb and I were wondering if perhaps you could come out here and look after me and maybe cook for Caleb. I really don't want anyone else around, especially in the beginning."

"Marianne," Joan spluttered. "What's happened?"

"It's gone into the liver. Please come," Marianne said, almost in a whisper.

"I'll be on a plane tomorrow," Joan said. "I'll call you later to tell you which one. No need for Caleb to meet me, I'll take a cab to your house."

"Thank you," Marianne sighed.

"I love you," Joan said a little fiercely, "and I'll call you later. Bye."

Marianne and Caleb lived in Venice, California. They had a house on a walkway a block and a half from the beach. Joan had visited two or three times before. She loved to stroll along the boardwalk. It went on for miles and was lined with cafés, boutiques, little hotels, second hand bookstores, and a bar or two. On the boardwalk itself across from the shops were people sitting, sometimes at tables, sometimes under makeshift tents, ready to tell your fortunes, massage your back, sell you photographs or paintings, read your palm, read your Tarot cards, explain your astrological chart, explain the meaning of the bumps on your head, or draw your portrait in charcoal or pastels. Joan had loved looking at them all.

This visit was different. Marianne wanted Joan to be with her as much as possible. On weekends when Caleb was home, Joan sometimes slipped away. She'd cross the board-walk and head across the sand down to the water with its gentle rolling waves curling themselves onto the beach. She'd listen to them as though to music, and stare out to the horizon. Joan's other trips out of the house were inland a block or two to buy groceries. Every time she returned, Marianne would call from the bedroom, "Who's that!"

"It's me dear," Joan learned to answer right away. One time she waited too long and Marianne began to cry with fear. She didn't have the strength to leave the bedroom, and not being able to see the front door made her very uncomfortable.

"Please sing," she would call out to Joan when she couldn't see her. "You have such a nice voice. I love to hear you sing." So Joan sang as she cooked the meals, washed the dishes, swept the floors, and folded the laundry. She knew that her singing was often off key, but it helped Marianne to know what part of the house she was in.

Marianne was a nurse who had traveled all over the world with Catholic Relief Services. She spoke Spanish like a native because she'd worked in El Salvador during the guerrilla war. She'd also worked in the jungles of the Congo. She was the bravest woman Joan knew. Joan reminded herself of this when she found Marianne's present fears irritating.

Things were much easier in the evenings when Caleb came home. "Where are the two most beautiful women in the world?" he would call out as he entered the door.

"Here's one of them." Marianne would call from their bedroom.

"Oh, thank goodness," he might say, as he went towards her. "I thought you might have decided to leave me for Michael Cain. I saw that look you gave him last night."

Caleb was a surgeon. Joan could only imagine the horror of his impotence as he watched Marianne become weaker. They never talked about it. He spent all his energy while at home trying to comfort and entertain Marianne. After kissing her ardently, he settled into his favorite chair beside her bed and told her his news of the day. He told her about his patients, giving them made-up names, and about the other doctors and nurses, some of whom she knew. Joan brought in their supper on two trays. When they suggested that she join them, she told them she preferred to eat outside in the cool of the evening. She took her tray to the porch at the front of the house. Sometimes, when she had finished eating, she'd put her tray down on the floor of the porch, and simply walk down toward the beach without telling them she was going. It was such a relief not to have to account for herself.

Chapter Thirteen

AFTER SIX MONTHS of chemo, Marianne was given a respite. She felt a little stronger and was able to putter around the house. Sometimes she sat outside on the porch in the sun, but usually she sat in the living room, writing letters to her friends all over the world and to her three sons. Jonathan was a doctor in Nigeria; Ethan was building houses in South Africa; and Young Caleb, recently married, with a new baby, was living in Chile where he gave English lessons and played in a band.

After three months of Marianne's feeling more and more energy, her doctor told her that she was in remission and might live to be a hundred. Marianne quoted the doctor when she came back into the waiting room where Joan sat leafing through a magazine. "That's wonderful," Joan said. "How shall we celebrate?"

"Let's go someplace where we can hear jazz."

"Great idea."

Joan remembered her mother's horror when she discovered that her teenage girls had been to a nightclub with their father to listen to a jazz quartet, while she was at a fundraiser for the Boston Symphony. After that night, jazz had become a favorite treat for the sisters.

"I think there's a place on the boardwalk that has jazz in the afternoons," Marianne said. "Let's take a taxi."

They found the little place, tucked between a tattoo parlor and an art gallery. There was a trio playing, piano, guitar and drums to an audience of about twenty people. Joan and Marianne sat at one of the small tables, ordered mineral water with lime and leaned back to enjoy themselves.

When the set was over, Marianne asked, "So, dear, now that I'm better, what do you think you want to do? Have you been looking forward to going back to New York?"

Joan stared at her. She hadn't considered this aspect of Marianne's improvement. It was true that Marianne had begun to do some of the cooking for the three of them, but Joan still did all of the shopping and the vacuuming and the dish washing. Surely, Marianne wouldn't want to take on everything right away.

Marianne looked at her younger sister, who'd become a little pale. "You've been such a help," she said. "Who knows what would have happened to me, let alone Caleb, if you hadn't come out? You're always helping people. What you've done for Sarah! And look at Angelica, living on her own in Boston. You really know how to help people get back on their feet."

Joan smiled and said, "I didn't have any choice when it came to the girls."

"But you did. You could have continued teaching, which I know you loved, and let Sarah care for Sam. You could have let Angelica live in a protected half-way house situation so that you wouldn't be the one called in the middle of the night for her emergencies. You had choices, but you always chose to give up what was best for you in order to help the other person."

"You should talk, traveling all around the world in dangerous situations, exposing yourself to diseases no one knew how to cure."

"Yes, that's true, and isn't it ironic I end up with plain old cancer. Sometimes I think I did all that traveling just to get back at Mother. I mean I'm glad I did it. I enjoyed the adventure of it and I love nursing. But I have a feeling that my real motivation was to make Mother angry. Do you remember what she said when I told her I was going to nursing school? 'Well if you want me to pay so you can learn how to empty a bedpan, the least you can do is marry a doctor and live the life that I've brought you up to appreciate.' Three years later, when I fell in love with Caleb and he was a god-damn doctor, I made him promise that we'd never get rich and complacent. When he suggested we go overseas with Catholic Relief Services, I knew he was the one for me."

"Yes," Joan said with a laugh. "I remember Mother's fury at that decision."

"Imagine what your life would have been like if she'd convinced you and the girls to live with her in Boston after Charlie died!"

"It's hard to imagine."

"She'd have bought you all expensive clothes and loaned you her pearls and paraded the three of you in front of one widowed or divorced CEO after another until you finally gave in and married the one with a vacation house on Mt. Desert."

"You're right. That's the one." Joan smiled at the image, and then went on, "On the other hand, he might have paid for some extraordinary doctor for Angelica. That's the only thing I wish I'd had money for," she sighed.

"That's what I mean about you. Imagine being willing to marry someone just so Angelica could have a good doctor."

"But I didn't do that," Joan said a little glumly. "I took the girls to New York—no pearls, no CEO, and dealing with Angelica's illness the best I could."

They looked at each other in silence for a minute. The musicians were heading back to the stage. "Actually, it would be wonderful if you could stay on for a bit," Marianne said. "You're a much better cook than I am. And I still don't feel like shopping. If you could…" here she had to raise her voice to be heard over the music, "if you could be in charge of all the food stuff, then I could work in the garden and on my journal."

Joan knew that Marianne had been writing a journal since her diagnosis. She was hoping it would be helpful to other people with cancer and their families. Caleb had promised to write a preface.

"If it would really help, I'd love to stay," Joan said quite loudly for the music was in a crescendo.

"Terrific!" Marianne said, putting out her hand to shake on the deal. Then they settled back to listen.

Joan tried not to recognize her feeling of relief. Sarah and Joe were about to have a child and there wouldn't be room for her at the loft. Angelica was still in Boston, sharing a studio with another painter. It was a large loft and the two women lived together in one end of it and worked in the other. Joan had never seen it or met the woman, but Sarah had been up to visit and said that the other woman was older and rather well to do and had, it seemed, taken Angelica under her wing, including finding a "perfectly wonderful" therapist for her.

Now that Marianne felt better, Joan moved out of Caleb's study and upstairs to a studio apartment that was used for visitors. Joan asked about the boys visiting, but Marianne said that she did not want them to come "until I feel really strong."

Joan began experimenting with macrobiotic cooking. Sarah had sent her a book that extolled macrobiotics as a cure for cancer. Marianne was willing to give it a try. Caleb ate meat and potatoes at the hospital and manfully ate Joan's experiments in the evening. Marianne began to put on weight, for which they were all grateful. Now that Marianne could be left alone for hours during the day, Joan took longer walks on the beach and explored second-hand bookstores and cafés along the boardwalk.

In June, Sarah's daughter Kari was born. They sent lots of pictures. Joan felt a little hurt that they hadn't asked her to be at the birth, the way she had been when Sam was born. "But of course, they don't realize how much better Marianne is and that I could have gone," she told herself.

In September Marianne's symptoms returned, and she needed to go back on chemo. They were all heartbroken, although they kept up a good front for each other. Joan brought back inspirational books from the local bookstores, but she could only take walks now when Caleb was home, which she noticed was more and more often.

In April the doctor suggested hospice, but Marianne didn't agree to that until June. As soon as she did, hospice sent a visiting nurse once a week and a home health aide every other day. Joan still cooked, but Marianne could no longer eat. Caleb hardly ate as well, so Joan began making finger food that could be given to the many visitors who came to say goodbye. In July the boys came home. Joan offered to move back down into Caleb's study but the boys insisted on staying in a small hotel on the beach, three blocks away. Young Caleb brought his wife and baby, but Jonathan had to leave his family of four at home, and Ethan's partner, William, wasn't able to leave South Africa. Jonathan and Ethan shared a room, and Young Caleb and his family were next door. They told Joan later that it had been a great help to be together.

Marianne died in her sleep on August 28, two years after she'd begun her first chemo treatment. A few days later the boys returned home and Caleb went back to working very long hours at the hospital. At first he came home for supper with Joan once or twice a week, but after that, he almost never got in before Joan had gone to bed and always left in the morning before she was up.

Chapter Fourteen

EARLY ONE SUNDAY morning, when Joan came down for a cup of tea before going to Mass, Caleb was sitting at the kitchen table, drinking coffee. "Sit down a minute, won't you, Joan? I need to go the hospital but I wanted to have a word with you first." His tone was friendly but determined.

"Of course," Joan said, half knowing what was coming.

"You know there is no way we, or rather I, can thank you for what you've done for us," he began.

"I was grateful for the opportunity," Joan said softly.

"The thing is, Joan, I think I am going to sell this house and get an apartment near the hospital."

"Oh," Joan said, trying not to sound disheartened. "Won't you miss the beach and all?"

"Yes," he sighed, "but there are too many memories here. I just can't face these same walls. Maybe I'll rent this place and share an apartment in town. I don't know, but I do have to get away from here. Ah," he paused uncomfortably, "you don't want to rent this from me do you? I'd make it as low as possible."

For a moment Joan felt the joyous possibility of having a place to stay and with the beach nearby. But then, reality overshadowed the image and she said, "Thank you Caleb. You're an absolute dear, but I know how much these houses go for. No, I think I'll go back East. I seem to miss winter," Joan lied.

"Will you go to the cottage?" he asked casually.

"The cottage?" Joan questioned.

"The one Marianne left you. I've never seen it, but she always made it sound very nice."

"What cottage?" Joan said completely confused.

"That's right. You weren't at the reading of the will. I meant to tell you about it, but with everything else, I guess I forgot. Marianne left you her cottage."

"What do you mean?"

"It's a cottage that one of her patients left her a few years ago. It's part of a large estate in Ipswich, northeast of Boston. I think it was the chauffeur's cottage. The rest of the estate stayed with the family, but this cottage was left to Marianne. Marianne went out and saw it, and said it was nice. She arranged to have it managed and rented by a local real estate agency. And now she has given it to you."

"But what about you and the boys?" Joan spluttered.

"The boys and I are in fine shape. Don't worry about us. This is her way of saying 'Thank you.' It has a new roof and a new furnace. It's in good shape. And we had it cleaned and painted after the last renters moved out."

"The last renters?"

"Yes, they moved out a few months ago. That's when Marianne decided to give it to you. She told the agent to leave it empty until you decided what you wanted to do with it. Joan, she changed her will so she could do this. It's yours."

"It sounds like the perfect place for me to go, northeast of Boston you say. That means I'd be near Angelica if she needs me. I can't thank you both enough." Joan got up and kissed him on the cheek. She could feel him flinch slightly and realized he was still too raw to be touched casually. "After church I think I'll go for a walk and say good bye to my favorite haunts."

"Good," Caleb said. "But be back before seven tonight. I want to take you out to dinner."

"You're on." Joan said as she headed out.

Chapter Fifteen

THE LAST THING Joan wanted, she thought, was to be stuck way out in the country like an old geezer. She loved living in cities. She loved being with people from all over the world—being surrounded by the possibilities of museums, galleries, lectures and concerts. She couldn't imagine living away from all that. On the other hand, cities were expensive. She still needed to send money to Angelica, who seemed to be doing well in Boston.

Joan had called Angelica when Marianne died, but Angelica had refused to fly out for the funeral. "I'm sorry Mother. I'm in the middle of moving. My roommate was getting bossy and possessive, a little like you if you know what I mean, so I've found a studio I can live in, but it's a little high. Do you think you could up your check by a hundred? Just until I begin selling my paintings. Then I'll pay you back. I'll pay you back with interest, Mother. Don't think I won't."

"I'm sure you will, dear," Joan had said. "And I think I can manage. I've saved up some while I've been out here. I'd love to see your studio. Shall I come visit when I come back East?" At that point Joan had no idea how soon that would be.

"No, Mother, please," Angelica had answered quickly. "You know I love you and all that. But, I can't explain it…you give me the willies. I know you don't mean to. And I'm grateful for your help. But please don't come visit."

"How soon do you need the money?" Joan asked coldly, her anger softened only by the pain of Marianne's death. "Can you wait until next month?"

Angelica ignored her mother's tone. "Yes, I can wait. Give my love to Caleb," she added, "and to the boys of course. I wish I could see them. Tell Ethan he owes me a letter, okay?"

"Okay," Joan said. "Take care of yourself." She wanted to add, 'because I'm not going to,' but she knew she always would, so she held her tongue.

"You too Mother," Angelica said quickly, "Bye."

Sarah had come out for the funeral, leaving the children with Joe. She had shared Joan's bed in the upstairs apartment and had told her mother how happy she was with her new family. She'd announced that Kari was going to share Sam's room, so Joan could have her old room back, but there was no pleasure in her voice. Joan told Sarah that she might stay with Caleb for a while "to cook for him and so forth."

Sarah tried not to sound relieved when she said, "I'm sure you're a great comfort to him, Mom. You do like it here don't you?"

"I do indeed," Joan had responded.

"Well that's good then," Sarah declared. Joan said nothing, but she felt as though she'd been disposed of, rather like a difficult teenage being sent off to boarding school.

Joan remembered all this as she walked along the boardwalk. She could hardly see through her tears. She told herself that she was crying about Marianne, but at the same time she knew that she was crying because now that Marianne had died, nobody was left who wanted her around. After a while, the sun dried her tears and she began to take herself in hand, talking out loud as she thought things through, causing some of the other boardwalk walkers to make wide detours around her. "There is nothing more beautiful than New England in the fall," she said aloud. "If I move to Ipswich now, I'll have all of October there, which will be okay, and then I can think about my next move. Perhaps I'll sell the cottage and find a studio apartment in New York. At least I don't give Sarah 'the willies,'" she added so bitterly that an elderly couple stopped to stare at her.

She stepped off the boardwalk and headed down towards the water. Her sandals slid around in the sand, so she took them off and carried them in one hand. Standing at the edge of the water, she stared out towards the horizon.

Then she heard herself shout to the incoming waves, "God damn it Charlie, why did you leave me?"

The waves continued coming toward her.

She was completely alone.

Caleb took Joan to a bang up dinner that night, and then put her in a taxi to go home because he had to return to the hospital. That night she called Sarah. Joe answered, "Hello, Joan. How nice to hear from you! I was so sorry that the kids and I couldn't get to the funeral. Kari's better now, but the doctor said with an ear infection you can't be too careful."

"I completely understood. And so did Caleb. I remember when the girls used to get ear infections. It's so hard when they're too young to talk. They can't tell you where it hurts, and you can't tell them it will get better. How's Sam?"

"He's doing great. He's really got the big brother thing down. He keeps all the things he really cares about too high for her to reach, and lets her play with the toys he's grown tired of. Actually, I think he's beginning to like her a little. And she adores him, follows him wherever he goes. It's beginning to go to his head, especially since he can climb to the upper bunk of their bed when he wants to be alone"

"Good. Please give them both a kiss for me. Listen Joe, I want to ask you for a favor."

"Of course. Shoot."

"Well, I'm planning to move to a town north of Boston, called Ipswich."

"You are? I thought you were coming back here. We've kept your room for you. I mean, I practice in it for a few hours, but all we've put in it is my music stand. The rest is just as you left it. The children are looking forward to your coming back, especially Sam."

"Thank you, I am coming. I mean, I'm taking the plane in a couple of days. But my plan when I get there is to pack up my stuff and rent a 'Uhaul' and take everything, including my bed and desk and a few chairs, anything you're not using, up to Ipswich."

"Well, that's fine. My furniture hardly fits in here, so we have plenty between us."

"I was wondering if you could help me move. I mean, if we could go up on a Monday, that is if you don't have a gig, and you could return on the Tuesday morning train. I know it's asking…"

"Of course I can," he interrupted her. "I want to see where you're going to live in any case."

"So do I," Joan said, a shade bitterly. "See you soon!"

Chapter Sixteen

TWO WEEKS LATER Joe and Joan drove to Ipswich; he, in a rented Uhaul truck, and she, in a second-hand Ford that she'd bought in the city. Sarah stayed home to take care of the children. Joan wondered if she was making a mistake moving into the cottage sight unseen. On the other hand, since this was going to be her home, like it or not, she thought it might feel less alien filled with her belongings.

She was in for a surprise. The cottage was a delight. It was a chauffeur's house for a mansion that could just be seen at the end of an elm-lined gravel drive. It had four rooms, two of them with large windows onto a little garden. Joe and Joan grinned at each other as they examined it before bringing in the furniture and boxes. Behind the cottage was a red barn and a field. Joan felt as though she'd stepped into an English novel. The trees edging the field and lining the driveway to the big house were aflame with autumn colors, and she sighed deeply, realizing that she was truly glad to be back in the east.

After they lugged in the furniture and boxes from the Uhaul, Joan, impressed by her own strength, but exhausted to the point of trembling, sat at the kitchen table while Joe made them a cup of tea. She sighed with pleasure as she stared out the kitchen window and saw a picnic table on the grass under an oak tree next to a tilled patch of earth with some daisies, Queen Anne's lace, and what looked like tomato plant stalks. As she warmed her hands with the cup of tea Joe handed her, she realized how generous Marianne and Caleb had been.

That evening Joe and Joan drove into town and had supper at The Clam House. It was ostentatiously casual, with red checked cloths on the tables, clean sawdust on the floor, and a large shiny many-colored antique juke box in one corner that was playing an Elvis Presley song when they entered. It was crowded. Some of the people were tourists with their cameras and maps. Some were bird watchers with binoculars around their necks and long lists in front of them. Some teenagers were dancing near the juke box, plying it with quarters.

"I think Ipswich clams are famous," Joe said as they found a table and sat down. "I don't mean they're just good. I mean that I've heard about them in New York City. Something about 'for oysters you go to Boston, but for clams you go to Ipswich.'"

Joan laughed. Perhaps she wasn't so far out of the loop after all. They ordered a bottle of wine and Joan realized that she was having more fun than usual. Maybe she would keep herself from being lonely in the evenings by sipping wine and remembering old times. She wondered about Joe's old times and realized she knew very little about him besides that he was a wonderful musician and made her daughter and grandchildren remarkably happy.

"Did you grow up in New York?" she asked. Joe had invited lots of musician friends but no family members to his wedding. "Are your parents still alive?" she went on, not waiting for him to answer her first question.

"I'm not sure about my father," Joe said. "My mother died of liver cancer."

"Oh, I'm so sorry."

"It was a long time ago." Joe smiled a little wistfully as he added, "I was nine and didn't know what was happening. All I knew was that Mom started to complain about the noises I made when I chewed my food, coughed too often, or laughed when reading a comic book. One day she told me the noises I made were going to kill her."

"Where was your father?"

"He was in Korea. He'd met someone there during the war and decided to stay."

"How did your mother manage?" Joan asked, horrified.

"She didn't really. She began spending all day in bed. She'd give me money to go to the store to get bread and peanut butter and tomato soup. But when I'd heat up some soup for her, or make her a sandwich, she'd push it away whispering, 'Leave me alone. Are you trying to kill me?' Then she would start coughing, hacking really, which convinced me that I had hurt her in some way. I would tiptoe back into the kitchen, sit as quietly as possible at the table, eat the food myself and then start my homework. I knew she was in pain because she groaned and cried out, especially at night. One night, when I went into her room to ask if I could help, she whispered, 'Just you wait till this happens to you! Now get the hell out of my life and never come back.' After that, I put a pillow over my head all night to muffle the sounds."

"How awful for you! You must have been terrified."

"It was worse than that. She'd convinced me that I was causing her suffering, and I didn't know how to stop whatever I was doing to hurt her."

"I can't imagine how dreadful that must have been for you. How long did it go on?"

"A year and a half."

"And there was no one to help you, no one to help her?"

"No, she never went to a doctor, so no one knew what was happening. And since she'd convinced me it was my fault, I never told anyone."

"What happened when she died?"

"That morning, when I couldn't wake her at all, I told my teacher that my Mom wouldn't wake up. She asked me a lot of questions and then made me sit in the principal's office almost all day. Finally, she took me home; my Mom had been taken away by then. Some police asked me questions about who else there was in my family. I told them I didn't know anyone except my father and I didn't know where he was. Then my teacher packed my clothes and took me in a cab to the orphanage. I assumed it was a prison because I'd killed my mother. I lived there until I was eighteen."

"What about your father?"

"I never heard from him."

Neither of them said a word for a while. Joan refilled their wine glasses. Joe turned in his chair and stared unseeing at the teenagers dancing to Frank Sinatra's 'Young at Heart.' When he turned back toward Joan, she said, "It's so wonderful to see how good Sam is with Kari. Sarah wrote me that Sam taught Kari to walk. How old was she when she took her first steps?"

Joe sighed and relaxed a bit as he described in detail Kari's first steps and Sam's new ability to throw and catch a ball from quite far away.

Chapter Seventeen

JOE TOOK THE train back to New York the next day, and suddenly Joan was on her own. She remembered how irritated she'd been by Marianne's fear of being alone, but now she could sympathize.

It was one thing living alone in New York City when her daughters had moved out. She'd had her teaching which involved lots of evening meetings and her friends, colleagues usually, who were happy to go to a movie with her in the evening, or a museum on a weekend. But here in Ipswich she knew nobody, and the movie theater was half an hour from her cottage and what would she do if she had a flat tire driving home at night?

She called Angelica, as soon as she got back from the train station, to invite her to Ipswich for a weekend.

"Mother, listen. I want you to really listen. I don't want to visit you. I mean, I love you, you know that, but I don't want to be near you. I've been better since I've been living far away from you. Admit it, Mother."

"Angelica" Joan replied, carefully holding on to her temper, "You know how happy I am that you've been so well. And I didn't move here to be near you."

"Yes, I know; the cottage was empty and Aunt Marianne gave it to you. I hope it works out. I hope you like it there; I hope you make friends. But, if you don't, please don't decide you need to come visit me in Boston because you think I'm not well, or for any reason at all. Okay?"

"Okay, dear. You know if you change your mind, or if you need…"

"I know Mother; you're the best. But please don't come. Promise?"

"I promise." Joan answered. After she hung up, she thought what a sad awful promise that had been. Her anger at Angelica's rudeness was made worse by momentarily wondering if what Angelica had said might have some truth in it. Was it at all possible that she used Angelica's illness as an excuse to spend time with her because she herself was lonely? No, of course not, that was the illness itself talking. Every mother likes to spend time with her children.

That night she called Sarah, "Hi, dearest, I just want to thank you both for helping me buy the car and pack every-thing, and Joe was so wonderful coming up with me. Did he tell you how nice it is here? I'm hoping you'll all come for a visit sometime soon."

"Of course we will, Mom. Only not just now because of school, and work and everything. Joe is playing over Thanksgiving weekend so we'll have to wait for Christmas. Maybe you'll come here for that. What do you think?"

"Of course I'll come to you if that's easier than your coming here. Depending on how Angelica is of course. But I was so much hoping to see you before then. Christmas seems ages away. The trees are absolutely at their peak now. And there are horses. Did Joe tell you about the horses? I'm sure Sam would love to see them, maybe even feed them a sugar cube, although I'm not sure how good that is for their teeth, maybe a carrot or something like that. Don't you think Sam would enjoy that?"

"I'm sure he would Mom. Look, I have to go. Kari's crying. Call me if you need anything. Love you," and she hung up.

During the day, Joan tried to make herself take a walk, at least up the driveway to the mansion and back. The owners were away. Her only neighbors were the two horses who lived in the barn. Twice a day a teenager sped into the driveway, left the motor running and radio blaring, while he was in the barn for a few minutes, and then sped off again. Joan had seen the horses once, when she walked down to the barn while the teenager was there, to introduce herself and say hello. He'd barely returned her greeting, but did introduce the horses, Starlight and Sundance. She thought of visiting them other times when he wasn't there, but the barn was private property so she decided against it. Also, she wasn't sure it would be good for the horses — perhaps they would think she was going to feed them and become agitated.

On Sundays Joan went to Mass at St. Bridget's in Ipswich. She had hoped to make friends there, but the older parishioners, struggling with canes and walkers, were too intent on their difficulties to give Joan more than a cursory glance or nod. The younger parishioners were surrounded by small children and never noticed Joan's presence. The priest, elderly and haggard, showed no sign of wanting to get to know Joan better.

The leaves fell from the trees, covering the path up to the mansion with a long Persian carpet of color. Joan, as she walked, told herself it was a magic carpet and could take her anywhere she wanted to go. Where was that? She imagined herself in the Van Gogh museum in Amsterdam, or sitting on the hill above the ruins at Delphi staring down through the ancient olive trees at a glimpse of the sea beyond, or on the boardwalk of Venice beach, watching a painter do a quick but insightful portrait of a tourist. But it wasn't places she was missing, it was people. Sometimes in the evenings, as she made her supper and ate it at the kitchen table, seeing her own reflection in the window, she wished she could join Marianne and Charlie wherever they were.

Toward the end of November the snows began. It snowed two or three times a week and Joan became frightened that she would be snowed in. She hated driving in snow, especially on unplowed roads, so whenever there was a sunny day and the roads were clear, she would rush into town and buy enough food for the next week. She bought large bags of bird food that she spread out on the picnic table outside the kitchen window for the neighborly birds and squirrels. On snowy days she would go out every few hours, sweep the snow off the table and cover it again with sunflower seeds. She made friends with the spider in her bathroom and carefully removed it from the tub each time she took a shower.

Perhaps because of the bird seed, she started seeing mouse droppings in the kitchen. One horrible morning as she approached the gas stove, coffee pot in hand, a mouse peered up at her through the circle around the burner. She screamed and dropped the coffee pot, sending glass shards throughout the kitchen, as she ran from the room. Ten minutes later, when she forced herself back into the kitchen to sweep up the glass, she decided to get a cat, a full-grown one who would already know how to catch mice. So instead of going into Ipswich that day, she drove in the other direction to Hamilton where there was an animal shelter. There she found a tabby tomcat named Bruce. He was a little scruffy and was missing a piece of one ear. The lady at the shelter told Joan that Bruce had been badly hurt in a fight and urged her to keep him indoors. "Yes, of course" Joan said, thinking of her birds.

"Bring him back in a month and we'll give him his rabies booster."

"Okay," Joan agreed, and took the cat home.

Bruce seemed to enjoy his new home. He went from room to room exploring all the corners. Then he jumped up onto the kitchen chair next to Joan's, curled up, and went to sleep. That night, as though he'd been doing it all his life, he jumped up onto Joan's bed and curled himself against her lower back. She was thrilled. She stayed as still as possible, and then she fell asleep.

Chapter Eighteen

AT FIRST JOAN called Caleb at his office once a week, to thank him for the cottage and tell him how well she was getting on, and to ask how he was doing. Caleb was always polite, even friendly, but often seemed distracted. Finally, in early December, Caleb said, "Joan, I'm so glad that the cottage is working out for you and that you're doing so well. I'm also doing well. I'm making friends in a grief support group. It's really important for me at this moment in my life to be going forward. Sometimes, when you and I talk, I feel as though I'm going backward, backward towards the paralyzing grief and depression I felt in the beginning. You know, my dear Joan, how fond of you I am, but I think it would be better if we didn't talk together for a while..."

"But..." Joan tried to interrupt.

"Joan, I'm serious. That depression was very frightening, both to me and to my colleagues. I could have lost my position. I really must go forward with new friends and new experiences. Joan dear, let me call you next time," he continued quickly, fearful that she would interrupt him, "I wish you all the best. Thank you for being so understanding. God bless." And he hung up.

When Joan put the silent phone back in its cradle, she pulled Bruce into her lap and hugged him as she wept. She felt as though she had lost Marianne all over again.

Joan called Angelica weekly as well, until Angelica said, "You know, these calls are long distance for you. Do you think you should be spending your money on them?"

"I love to hear your voice and your news and know that you're fine."

"The thing is, Mother, sometimes you call when I'm painting and it really interrupts."

"Oh, dear, I'm sorry," Joan said keeping her voice calm. "When's a good time to call?"

"I think the best thing is to let me call you."

"But you won't," Joan said to her own surprise.

"Look, Mother, how about if I swear I'll call you if anything goes wrong. Will you, can you, leave it at that? You say you want me to be fine. Well, these calls make me jumpy. How about if I call you once a month for sure. Would that do it?"

"Yes," Joan answered crisply, "You can call me when you receive my check, so I know you got it safely."

"It's a deal, Mother, and thanks. Bye." She hung up before Joan could answer.

So that was that. Sarah or Joe called every Sunday around teatime, always putting Sam and sometimes Kari, on the phone to say hello. They sounded happy. Sarah had begun teaching acting classes part time. Sam loved kindergarten, and Joe had gigs lined up for months.

One morning, Joan woke up to a heavy snowfall. There was no electricity and the phone was dead. The furnace was out, as was the electric pump that brought the water up from the well. She knew that she had only the water in the pipes and in the toilet tank. There was no driving somewhere for help because the road hadn't been plowed and her car was under a mountain of snow.

She wondered what would happen to the horses, but late in the morning the teenager appeared on an ATV and dealt with them and left before she could figure out what to ask him to do.

She felt as though she and Bruce had been thrown into solitary in a third world prison. She made a fire in the living room fireplace and then stood in front of it trying to get warm while munching bread and butter. Later she got the idea of taking a pot outside and filling it up with snow and then bringing it in by the fire to let it melt to give her and Bruce something to drink. She was amazed by how little water a pot full of snow made. Every hour or so she put on her boots and took out her broom to sweep the snow off the picnic table outside the kitchen window. She then poured birdseed on the table, hoping the birds would get to the seeds before the snow covered them again. Then she brought more firewood in from the garden shed. She was grateful that the last tenant had left a big stack.

As dusk was falling, she checked her cupboards. She had half a loaf of bread, some butter and peanut butter and three cans of soup. She also had a pound of rice, but she didn't know what she could do with that. Her biggest worry was that the pipes would freeze and then crack open. She had no idea how to stop that from happening. Bruce spent the day on the couch in front of the fire except when Joan went outside. Then he would jump up onto the kitchen table and watch her every move through the window.

By the time darkness came, Joan had made a huge pile of wood beside the fireplace. She laid the pillows from the couch on the floor in front of the fire and then brought all her blankets and her winter coat, rolled herself up in them and stared at the fire. Bruce curled himself up behind her knees. She promised herself not to sleep soundly so she could keep the fire going. She read a little by the light of the fire, but the letters began to blur so she closed her eyes. The last thought that ran through her brain before she slept was, "Well, this has been sort of fun." Another part of her brain answered, "Are you kidding?" but before the first part could reply, she was asleep.

The next day was sunny and surprisingly warm. The electricity was back on by late morning, and the roads were plowed. Joan drove into town for more food and birdseed. Everyone was smiling in the sunshine and trading stories about their evenings in the dark. A store clerk asked Joan how she had managed, "living so far out of town and all," and Joan felt very pleased by his concern and assured him that she had done just fine.

The phone took another day to get reconnected. Sarah called early the next morning to make sure Joan was okay. Joan found that she enjoyed telling about keeping the fire going and feeding the birds every few hours. It had been sort of fun, she realized, to have to think about how to survive instead, of feeling lonely.

Chapter Nineteen

CHRISTMAS WAS A week away. Joan sent some extra money to Angelica with a note saying she was going to be with Sarah and Joe for a few days at Christmas and asking if Angelica wanted to join them. Angelica's reply was an unsigned Christmas card saying, "Thanks for the $. Much rather stay here." Joan couldn't tell if that sounded depressed or not, but she kept to their bargain and didn't call. She would talk with Sarah over Christmas, she decided. Maybe Sarah would know how Angelica was doing.

Christmas in New York was cold and glittery. Joan and Sam walked along Fifth Avenue after dark to look at the shop window decorations. They watched the skating at Rockefeller Center and marveled at the size of the tree. They walked over to Park Avenue to look north along the long line of decorated trees and on Christmas Eve they went to St. Patrick's Cathedral. Sarah stayed home with Kari who had a cold. Joe had to be away the entire week, playing a gig in Tucson.

To her surprise, Joan wasn't sorry to leave them the day after Christmas. She felt a little under the weather, having caught Kari's cold, and she was concerned about Bruce, whom she had left alone with heaps of food and four big bowls of water. But more than that, she found she was looking forward to simply being by herself a bit. She'd enjoyed Kari and Sam a lot, but they started the day very early and by the time they were in bed, neither she nor Sarah had much energy left. Also, to her surprise, she found New York City itself rather tiring—the exhaust fumes hurt her eyes and the noises made her a little jumpy.

When she got back to Boston, she called Angelica from the train station, to see if she'd like her to drop in. "I'm in Boston on my way home, and I've brought an apple pie that Sam and I made—local apples from Ipswich you know—and I was wondering if you'd like me to come by to give it to you. I wouldn't stay if you didn't want me to, but I thought it would be a way for you to share Christmas with us. Every-one missed you and they all send love. We really did miss you, dear."

"Thank you, Mother. Actually I'm very busy—it would not be a good idea for you to come now. Please enjoy it for me."

"I wouldn't stay but a minute. You're just a few metro stops from Back Bay and…"

"Please don't come. I'm happy. I'm doing fine. Please don't spoil it. How can I say it more clearly?"

Joan sighed. "You've said it clearly enough. I wish things were different. You know that I love you."

"Yes, I know that. I just don't know what I need to do to make you feel, not paid back exactly, but quits."

"Quits?"

"Mother, I thank you for your love. I thank you for the monthly allowance. I owe you a lot. But I can't get sick for you."

"What are you saying?"

"I'm saying please don't come over. I'm working hard. I need to be working hard. Please don't come."

"I know, but I just wanted…"

"Listen to me. I don't want my mother hovering over me. That's completely normal. In this particular way, I am completely normal."

"But I don't hover."

"I've got to get back to work. Good bye, Mother."

Joan heard Angelica put the phone down before she could reply.

Despite that, Joan's first day home was lovely. Bruce wove round and round her legs in greeting. It was cold but sunny out and she walked up to the "big house" and then past it and down the slope to the Ipswich river, beautiful with twigs along the shore coated with ice and sparkling in the sun. So much nicer, she thought, than all the glitter of New York. By evening though, she missed the children and Sarah and the city itself.

Chapter Twenty

THE NEXT MORNING, Joan took Bruce to the Animal Shelter for his rabies booster. Bruce wasn't pleased with any of it, but she managed to hold him still while Dr. Nesbit injected him. "You have a real good way about you Mrs. Fitzpatrick," Dr. Nesbit told her as he put Bruce back into his carrier. "I'm shorthanded today and I wonder if you'd be willing to help me with my next patient. He's a little Scotty that was abandoned in September when his owners returned to the city. We're still hoping to find him a family."

"Sure," Joan said, "I'd be happy to."

"We've got heavy gloves here, if you're afraid of being bitten, but it's actually better without because you can feel what the animal is doing. Do you want the gloves?"

"No, thanks," Joan said, although she hadn't thought of the possibility of being bitten.

"He's a good dog," Dr. Nesbit went on, as he lifted the slightly trembling Scotty onto the table. "He's never even growled at anyone, pretty desperate to please in fact."

He showed Joan where to hold the dog and as soon as she put her hands on the Scotty, the dog seemed to relax. Dr. Nesbit's injection was over in a minute, and Joan patted the dog with pleasure as he wagged his tail before Dr. Nesbit took him back to his cage and disappeared back into the lab.

Joan put on her coat and hat, picked up Bruce's carrier bag, and went out to the reception desk to pay for the rabies shot. As the office manager gave her a receipt, she said, "Dr. Nesbit says you have a way with the animals, Mrs. Fitzpatrick. It's too bad we can't have you here more often."

"Are you looking for people to work here?" Joan asked.

"We always need volunteers," the office manager said. "We'd love to pay you of course," she went on, "but we just don't have any money in the budget. I'm only paid for working part time, though I'm here all day. Would you consider it?"

"What does it involve?" Joan asked.

"It's mostly walking the dogs, cleaning out the cat boxes, and once a month, when Dr. Nesbit comes, holding the animals that are getting shots or being euthanized."

"I don't know if I could do that," Joan said.

"Well, of course you wouldn't have to. Although, I think it's important for them to be held by someone when it happens."

"Well, I am free tomorrow," Joan said. "What time would you like me to come in?"

"We're open nine to five every day of the week, and any time you could give would be terrific. We could sure use your help," she added a little wistfully.

Joan went to the shelter around ten the next morning. It was an unusually warm day and so walking the dogs, one by one, turned out to be a real pleasure. And the dogs were so grateful, so glad to get out of their cages, so happy to spend time with her, to be petted and appreciated and then to be allowed to wander down the driveway and around the grounds, with her following wherever they wanted to go. Most of them had learned that the longer they put off "doing their business," the longer their walk would last, so Joan found that she'd had some good exercise by the time all the dogs had been walked. The office manager, whose name was Mary, had brought in a sandwich for Joan as well as herself, "Just on the off chance that you'd decide to stay through lunchtime," she said. After lunch they fed the dogs and then Joan walked them all again, while Mary cleaned the cat boxes, swept the halls and dealt with paper work at the desk. Joan and Mary left together at five. Mary showed Joan how to turn down the heat, turn off the lights and lock up, "Just in case you're on your own here some afternoon."

"Are the dogs able to manage not being let out until the morning?" Joan asked.

"No," Mary assured her. "We have two volunteers who give them a bed-time stroll every evening. They live right down the road and they say they enjoy the excuse to get out under the stars."

When she arrived home, Joan felt she had earned her tiredness. She couldn't imagine how Mary managed on her own during the days when there were no other volunteers around. Joan decided she would go in three or four days a week, or perhaps even more if Mary needed help.

After that, most mornings Joan left mountains of bird-seed on the picnic table, gave Bruce a big hug and extra-large bowls of food and water, and set off toward Hamilton. Chores such as food shopping and house cleaning were all left to Saturday. Sundays meant church in the morning and then sometimes an afternoon back at the shelter.

With this busy schedule, January, February and March went by quickly. Joan hardly worried about the snowy roads because she was so eager to get to the animal shelter. She felt needed, even essential, and it gave her energy and great pleasure. She was learning more about the animals, even trying to teach some of the dogs tricks to impress the people coming to look for a pet to take home. She had come to trust Mary's decisions about which animals to euthanize, and Dr. Nesbit found her a great help on his monthly visits.

Spring came slowly during April, with lots of rain and alternately wintry and warm days. But May brought more warm days, and suddenly daffodils, irises and tulips broke through the earth in the garden plot behind the cottage. Joan was enthralled and stopped at a nursery almost every after-noon to buy seeds that she planted after a quick supper. Bruce watched her from the kitchen window and once, thinking that he was really sad about not being out, Joan opened the kitchen door for him. He shrank back and ran into the living room. After that she decided he simply liked to watch.

Then one night, Joan was woken by a phone call. It was Angelica.

"Mother!"

"Yes, dear?"

"Call me a taxi!"

"Are you at home? Where do you want to go?"

"I'm at a bar downtown, and I need to go to the loony bin."

"The only thing to do, dearest, is to call 911."

"Will you call them?"

"Do you know the name of the bar?"

"Oh, go to hell! What kind of a mother are you?" and Angelica hung up.

Joan didn't go back to sleep. She tried to figure out if there was anything she could do in the middle of the night. She imagined calling the Boston police and giving them a description of Angelica. But she worried that such a phone call might give Angelica some sort of a police record. In the morning, she called all the hospitals listed in the Boston phone book, but no one of Angelica's description had been seen that night.

After breakfast, Joan took the train into Boston and the subway to Angelica's loft. She prayed over and over that Angelica would be home. To her great relief, Angelica was there. And even more wonderful, she had a friend, Jessica, with her. It was Jessica who let Joan in. Angelica was lying on the couch in a sort of stupor. She said nothing to Joan, but mumbled to Jessica, "Look what the cat dragged in."

While Jessica made coffee for them, Joan sat in a chair across from the couch, knowing that anything she said would be rebuffed. As they drank their coffee, Jessica offered to drive Angelica out to the emergency room at Danvers State Hospital, which was well known for its psychiatric wing. Another possibility was to ask Angelica's doctor to have her admitted to a hospital in Boston. But Angelica didn't want her doctor called, claiming that this was all his fault anyway.

Joan asked Jessica if she wanted her to come too. "No, thank you. If you could just help me get her into my car, I can take it from there."

"Hell, yes. Fuck off, Mother. Nobody wants you."

"Well, if you're sure..." Joan said to Jessica, who nodded.

Then, one on each side, they stood Angelica up and, almost carrying her by her arms, walked her downstairs and put her into Jessica's Chevrolet. Joan promised to visit her "as soon as they let me." Usually hospitals kept Angelica in seclusion for a few weeks before they would let Joan visit. Joan had the suspicion that Angelica told the doctors such terrible things about her mother that it was a wonder Joan was ever allowed to visit. Jessica took off, with Angelica curled up in the back seat. Joan sighed in relief and went back upstairs to get her coat and pocketbook, but then decided to deal with the dirty dishes, dirty laundry and rotting food in the refrigerator.

That night she called the fourth floor of Danvers. "Yes, Mrs. Fitzpatrick, I was told that I could confirm that your daughter has been admitted. No, I am not able to give you more information than that. We are very strict here about our patients' privacy. No, your daughter is not in a position to receive phone calls or visitors at this time. We will call you when the situation changes."

Chapter Twenty-One

IN JUNE, SARAH came up with the children. Joe had been able to obtain a chair in the Tanglewood Orchestra, so he commuted between Lenox and Ipswich, spending Monday through Wednesday with the family and then going to Lenox for Thursday through Sunday. Most mornings, when Joe was in Lenox, Joan dropped Sarah and the children off at the beach before going to the shelter for her morning shift. The shelter had found a veterinary student to cover her afternoon shifts, so at lunchtime, Joan drove back to the beach and shared the picnic Sarah had packed for them all. Then Joan and Sam took long walks, looking for shells and colored glass worn smooth by the sand, while Kari slept and Sarah read.

When Joe was in Ipswich, he and Sarah took Sam with them for afternoons of exploring. They came home with descriptions of the lobster boats in Gloucester, a horse show in Hamilton, the House of Seven Gables in Salem. Joan would tell them about Kari's laughter when she snuggled with Bruce, of her excitedly reaching out to a flock of starlings when they landed in the grass near her, and of her paddling joyfully in the plastic wading pool that Joe had set up near the garden.

In the evenings Joe and Sarah sometimes went to a movie together, or out dancing. After putting Kari to bed, Joan would play checkers with Sam before reading him a chapter from "The Jungle Book."

The only shadow over that summer was Angelica. Joan called the hospital every week and was told that Angelica was doing "as well as could be expected, but was not yet ready for visitors." At Joan's urging, Sarah called the hospital when she and the children arrived for the summer. A week later Angelica called back and told Sarah she would like her to visit but that she was not yet ready to see her mother. Sarah began visiting on Saturdays. After the first visit, the hospital told her she could bring her children, so she did. They were a subject of conversation and at times a distraction from Angelica's moroseness. Angelica seemed to enjoy holding Kari on her lap or playing checkers with Sam.

A month later a nurse at the hospital told Joan she could visit once a week but could not stay longer than an hour. "Your daughter's relationship with you is very intense, Mrs. Fitzpatrick. This is an experiment. We'll see if it works out."

Joan went every Wednesday afternoon even though Angelica almost never spoke to her. Angelica liked to sit in the solarium and play classical music on her portable radio and Joan would bring her knitting and join her there. Sometimes Angelica would have a pad and pencil with her and she would sketch Joan, making her look haggard and hideous. When Joan saw the sketches, she tried to smile encouragingly although she felt embarrassed and angry.

Before leaving the hospital Joan almost always bought herself a pack of Camels at the gift shop, and smoked as she drove home. She had given up smoking when the girls were toddlers because they were always tipping over her ash-trays. But ever since Angelica's first hospitalization, Joan had allowed herself to smoke while Angelica "went through her bouts," as she put it to herself.

One night after a visit to the hospital, Joan said to Sarah, "I wonder if I tried too hard with Angelica. After your dad died, I wanted so much to make up for that awful loss. Per-haps I didn't leave her quite free enough. Although," she quickly added, "they say that schizophrenia just comes, that they have no idea of its cause, that it's all a mystery."

"It's a terrible mystery," Sarah said. "The worst part is that it comes and goes. It's almost more painful to be with her when she's clear-headed and witty and painting like crazy, because you know it won't last. I don't know how she can bear it." Sarah's eyes filled with tears. "But you know, Mom, it's nobody's fault. You and I didn't do anything to cause this. It just happened."

Chapter Twenty-Two

ON LABOR DAY weekend, Angelica came to Ipswich for the first time that summer. The hospital had given her a weekend pass which Joan had managed to extend through Monday so that Angelica could see Joe. In one of their few conversations in the hospital, Angelica had said to her mother, "Joe and Kari are the only fucking family I have. They don't judge me. Maybe it's because Joe doesn't think of me as family, so he doesn't care how I am. And Kari, thank God, is too young to care. Even Sam stares at me in horror sometimes. At least he looks at me though, not like you and Sarah, too repulsed to look me in the eye."

It was partly true. Joe was always gentle and considerate of Angelica. They seemed to enjoy a banter that was somewhere between teasing and flirting. Also Joe, an ambitious and hard-working musician, understood Angelica's ambition to be a well-known artist.

Labor Day was warm and sunny. Joan and Sarah planted iris bulbs while Kari slept in a tiny hammock that had been rigged up in the center of the garden. Then Sarah and Sam picked the lettuce, tomatoes and cucumbers needed for lunch. Angelica spent the morning on a lounge chair behind the house with her portable radio and three or four packs of cigarettes. She listened to "Morning Pro Musica" and smoked. Joan took her a cup of coffee and was discouraged to see cigarette stubs all around her chair. She then brought out an ashtray, but even while she was putting it on the grass beside the chair, Angelica stubbed out a cigarette and flicked it over her mother into the grass.

Joe arrived just before lunch. When they heard his car crunch the gravel near the barn, everyone, even Angelica, stopped what they were doing and went to greet him. As Joe hugged Sarah and lifted Kari toward the sky, Joan noticed that he looked exhausted, almost desperately so. But his words were cheerful as Sam and Kari pulled him to the back of the house where lunch was laid on the picnic table under the oak tree.

That evening, after he put Kari to bed, Joe said he would drive Angelica back to the hospital. Sam begged to go with him. Sarah tried to reason with him. "Dad will be back soon and we're leaving tomorrow morning; don't you want to spend the evening with Gran and me?" Sam smiled at his grandmother but said, "Dad just got here. I never see him. I've been with Gran and you all the time. Please!"

Angelica flopped down on a chair in the front hall, looking rather angrily at Sam. Joe also sat down. He didn't flop but sat almost carefully and looked at his son without a word. Joan noticed how grey his face looked and how his eyes seemed surrounded by dark bruises. His mouth was squeezed shut as though he were trying to keep in a cry of pain or anger. Finally Sarah asked him, "What do you think. Joe?"

But it was Angelica who answered first, "Come on, Sam, don't be ridiculous. Your dad and I aren't running away, we just want to spend some time together. I haven't seen him in a long time."

Joe sounded exhausted as he said, "It might be a good idea. Sam can keep me company on the way home."

"Yeah!" shouted Sam.

"Get your jacket Sam," Sarah reminded him.

"Well, lover, I guess we won't elope tonight," Angelica drawled, southern belle style, and then as she got to her feet, she said to Sarah, "Good bye, sis. Thanks for the chaperone. Don't know what I would have done otherwise."

Joe still sat there until Sam came back with his jacket on. Sam reached for his father's hand and helped to pull him up, "Thanks, old man," was all Joe said in reply and then he kissed Sarah full on the mouth, strong and long, and went out the door without another word.

Joan and Sarah played a game of Scrabble. Joan was already feeling a little bereft knowing that everyone would be leaving in the morning. They went to bed early, Joan because she wanted to read in bed rather than talk. It had been exhausting having Angelica in the house for two nights.

As she turned off the light, Joan heard Joe's car crunch into the driveway.

By the time Joan got up the next morning, Joe had left again. "He had to go to Boston, Mom," Sarah told her. "Something about a job possibility."

When Sam and Kari came into the kitchen, Kari in pajamas that covered her feet with Sam, who had dressed in shorts and a tee shirt, carefully holding her hand, Sam asked, "Where's Dad?"

"He needed to go into Boston early this morning. He'll be back about eleven and we'll pack a lunch for the car. He told me he knows of a good place for a picnic and maybe even a swim. Could you please get your bathing suit out of your bag and put it in here?" She held out a plastic bag, "and also get four of the old raggedy towels," she added. "You don't mind, Mom, do you?"

"Of course not," Joan said, but she followed Sam to the linen closet to find the worst towels.

After breakfast, Joan and the children walked up the grassy path along the elm-covered driveway to the big house, and around to the back and into the woods to say good bye to the Ipswich River, which was only a wide shallow stream at this point. Kari was in a stroller that was a little hard to push once they were off the path, but Sam enjoyed helping his grandmother with the harder places. While the children said goodbye to the stream, Joan said a silent goodbye to them. It had been a wonderful summer and she was going to miss them hugely.

They were back at the cottage around ten forty-five, a little out of breath from hurrying. But Joe hadn't arrived yet, so they all went inside to see if Sarah wanted help with last minute packing. She didn't. So Sam led them around to the picnic table where he and Joan played pick-up sticks while Kari fell asleep in her stroller. "This is a good spot," Sam said, "because we'll be the first to hear Dad's car."

"Yes," Joan agreed. "You found a good spot."

At eleven thirty Sarah brought out their luggage and sat it down next to where Joe would park when he returned. Next to the suitcases she put a wicker basket filled with cucumber sandwiches, a thermos of iced coffee, another of orange juice, hard boiled eggs, and the oatmeal raison cookies that Joan had made for their trip. She covered the basket with a gingham cloth on top of which she laid their bathing suits wrapped in four large somewhat frayed towels. Her idea was to insulate the picnic from the hot sun. After a while she moved the picnic basket back into the kitchen, which was cool, for fear that the mayonnaise in the sandwiches would go bad. Around 1:00 she unpacked the basket and they ate most of its contents at the picnic table behind the house.

As they munched, Joan asked Sam, "How was the ride to the hospital last night? Did you have fun? Did you play twenty-questions?"

"No," Sam said, "Dad pretty much talked with Angelica the whole way there."

"Oh?" Sarah asked, very casually, "What sort of things did they talk about?"

"I think Angelica was crying. They had the radio on and they talked pretty softly. After a while I fell asleep," Sam said. "Where's Daddy? Why doesn't he come get us like you said?"

"I don't know sweetheart. I think he must have gotten held up in Boston in some way."

After lunch, Sam wheeled Kari in her stroller down to the barn to say goodbye to the horses. He had made friends with the teenager who had said he was always welcome in the barn when the wide doors were open.

When the children were out of hearing, Joan asked Sarah, "Are you sure he didn't mention anything about the job he was interviewing for? Or even what part of Boston?"

"I've been trying to think. All I remember is that he said it rather quickly as he was getting dressed. I asked him what time he thought we should leave today and he said something like. 'Well, about 11:00, I think, because I have an errand to do in Boston first.' Then I asked 'What sort of errand? Can't we all do it together on our way?' And he said something like, 'No, it's work; it's about a job. I think it would be better if I go alone. I should be back by 11:00.' So I said, 'Who are you seeing?' And he seemed to hesitate a minute. His back was to me and he was buttoning his shirt. What I think he said was, 'It's about next summer.' Then he quickly started talking about having a picnic and a swim in Stockbridge on the way home."

When the children came back from the barn, Sarah told Sam that since he had been out so late the night before, he should take a nap with Kari now. She dug into their bags for Sam's favorite book and Kari's 'blankie' and put them together into the hammock while Joan went inside to call Angelica at the hospital. At first, they said she could not speak to Angelica so soon after her weekend pass, but when

Joan explained what had happened, they 'made an exception.'

"Hey, Mother, what's up? Did I burn down the house with some cigarette butts?"

"Hi, Sweetie. No, it was lovely having you. But something's happened and I wondered if you could help us."

"Not from the loony bin I can't."

"Joe went to Boston early this morning to see someone about a job. He hasn't come back yet and we don't know how to get in touch with him. Did he perhaps tell you anything about where he was going?"

"Fuck off, Mother. I've got to go."

"Please dearest."

"Couldn't you tell how terrible he looked? What's the matter with you?"

"What do you mean 'how terrible he looked'?"

"You're impossible. No wonder I'm so fucked up."

"What did he tell you Angelica?"

"I'm hanging up Mother."

"Please, dearest."

"Well, unlike you nitwits, I asked him if he felt as shitty as he looked."

"And what did he say?"

"'Worse.' That's all he said. But he kissed me Mom. You can tell that to the good daughter."

"What do you mean?"

"If you don't know, I can't explain it. But maybe Sarah will know. He probably kissed her like that once long ago."

"I don't believe you, Angelica."

"I didn't think you would. Why bother to talk with me at all? Ask him." And she hung up.

Chapter Twenty-Three

AROUND SIX O'CLOCK, Sarah unpacked their suitcases. Joan drove into town with Sam and they brought back five servings of fish and chips for supper. Sam had stopped asking when they were leaving and whether Dad would call soon. In fact, there was nothing left to say.

Sam and Joan played checkers while Sarah gave Kari a bath. After her bath Sarah brought Kari in to say good night and she put her on Joan's lap. Then Sarah took Sam onto her own lap. "We're not finished with the game, Mom," Sam complained. Sarah held him a little tighter and said. "You and Gran will finish it tomorrow. It's time for bed, but before we go, let's take a few minutes to pray for Daddy to be fine and to come home later tonight. But even if he doesn't, tomorrow we need to go back to the city without him."

"But Mom…"

"You're supposed to start school tomorrow, Sam, so you'll already be missing the first day. Kari has day care, and I've got classes to teach."

"I don't want to go to stupid school," Sam lamented.

"Gran will be here if there is a call that Dad has been hurt or something."

"If he's been hurt, we'll come back, right?" Sam said.

"Yes, Sam, of course. We'll come back as soon as we know anything, anything at all."

"Mom, do you think he's hurt?"

"I don't know, son. While you and Gran were buying supper, I called all the hospitals. I called the police."

"You called the police?"

"Yes, in case there was an accident or something that they would know about."

"What'd they say?"

"They said we should call back tomorrow. It takes a day before they can start looking."

"Does Daddy know I'm not his son?"

"What do you mean Sam?"

"Angelica told me I look like my father. I said I wished I had black hair like him and she said, 'Oh, not Joe. I mean your real Dad. He had blond hair and looked like Robert Redford.' Do you think Daddy found out and that's what made him leave? Do you think Angelica told him?"

"Sam, Daddy is your father in every possible way. Angelica was wrong to talk like that…"

"Do you think she told Daddy that and that's why he hasn't come home?"

"No, my dearest. There is nothing that Angelica could say to Daddy to make him not want to come home to you. Daddy loves you and Kari with all his heart. You know that."

"Well, where is he then?" Sam said as he began to sob.

"I don't know, dearest. Perhaps he will come home later tonight. If he does, he'll wake you up to give you a hug and tell you he's home. Let's pray now. Our father who art in Heaven…"

"Hallowed be Thy Name…" they all continued to the end.

"Now I lay me down to sleep" Sarah began the next prayer.

"I pray the Lord my soul to keep…" the others responded.

"May God bless Daddy and bring him home now." Sarah prayed.

"Please Daddy come back. Come back tonight. Please!" Sam was sobbing.

"May Daddy be safe wherever he is and know that we love him with all our hearts and we'll do everything in our power to find him," Sarah prayed aloud as she hugged Sam.

"Amen" Joan said, but her prayer continued silently, "Oh Lord," she prayed, "Please bring him back. If you need one of us, please, I beg you, take me."

Chapter Twenty-Four

JOE HAD KNOWN there was something wrong. He'd had tests done in Boston on his last visit home. He hadn't told Sarah. He didn't want to frighten her.

The doctor called him at Tanglewood to make an appointment to discuss the results. He suggested 8:30 Tuesday morning. Joe said, "That'll be fine. I'm leaving for New York the same day."

On Tuesday morning Joe told Sarah he was going to a job interview. He'd taken his oboe with him to substantiate the lie. As he drove into the city, he felt bad about the lie. "But," he told himself, "it's for her sake. There's no point worrying her until I know what's going on."

Now he knew. The doctor had taken Joe into his office, pointed to a comfortable arm chair and then sat down across from him in a similar chair instead of behind his desk. They talked about the weather — it was warm for September — and then the doctor said, "I'm sorry to have to tell you this, Mr.

Wilson, but I'm quite certain that you have a carcinoma of the liver."

Joe didn't say anything. How had his mother punished him with this so long after her death? How had he thought he could live a good life, after his mother had cursed him? She'd said, "Wait till this happens to you!" And now it had. He longed for the earth itself to open a wide crevice that he could disappear into. He imagined himself falling into the welcoming darkness.

Finally, shaking himself slightly under the florescent lights of the office, Joe whispered, "Do people survive that now?" His mother hadn't.

In the doctor's answer there was no emotion, except that he spoke a little too quickly, as though he himself didn't want to hear the words he was saying. "The statistics for survival are not good," he said. Then he sighed, and continued more slowly, "On the other hand, we must never give up hope. You may be one of the rare lucky ones. Miracles happen."

"How long?" Joe asked, ignoring the doctor's change of tone.

The doctor sighed again before saying, "You have a few months before you'll need hospitalization. I can certainly give you a few months."

In the silence that followed this assurance, Joe heard his mother's voice loud in his head, bouncing off his eye sockets, his inner ear, the crown of his head, 'Your turn. Your turn. Let's see how you treat your wife and kids while the cancer eats you alive!'

Joe gasped as he imagined Sarah and the children living through the horrors of what was coming. He had to protect them somehow.

Perhaps he could hide in a hospital now and wait to die, surrounded by professionals who wouldn't care how much he groaned and cursed. But he knew no hospital would take him in, until the very end.

He stared at the doctor who was complacently making notes in Joe's chart. Finally, the doctor looked up. "Talking about miracles," he said, "there is a clinic in Mexico. They're doing a combination of alternative therapies down there. There's nothing scientific about what they're doing, I mean nothing they can prove, but I've heard a couple of stories of people going into remission. I'm not sure about liver cancer though."

"Where is it?" Joe asked dully.

"Outside of Mérida, in Mexico. It's called something like, 'Los Brazos Abiertos.' 'Open Arms' I think that means. Anyway, as I say, I'm not sure they've had any luck with liver cancer. But you never know," he continued. "The important thing is not to give up hope. That's what everyone says. You never know for sure what's going to happen." He stood up and held out his hand to Joe, who slowly got up as well.

"I wish you the very best, Mr. Wilson. Have your doctor in New York call me and I'll send him all the appropriate records. Just sign a release form with my secretary, will you?"

At Logan Airport, Joe left the car unlocked and the key in the glove compartment, hoping it would find its way back to the rental company. He paid for the ticket to Mérida via Mexico City with cash from his last paycheck and then pocketed the change.

He made the trip to Mérida as though in a nightmare. He felt as though he'd already died and was being taken across the river Styx. He sat with his eyes shut, his oboe in his lap and waited for it all to be over.

Outside the airport in Mérida, there was a green minibus parked with its engine running. On its side, printed in large yellow letters was a sign that read, "La Clínica de Los Brazos Abiertos." He got in, and nodded at the driver who had white hair, a wrinkled face and a smile that showed the few teeth he had left. Soon a middle-aged American couple with their very thin bald teenage daughter joined him.

Almost an hour later, the minibus drove through a wide gateway into the clinic's parking lot. The driver did not ask for money, but Joe noticed that the American couple handed him a few dollars. Joe did the same, receiving in return a wild and wonderful smile as well as a wink. Then the driver turned the bus around and headed back the way he had come.

Joe followed the family through the narrow wooden door of a one-story cinderblock building into a sunny waiting room with miniature trees growing in pots. There were chairs around the edge of the room. The family took seats and Joe did too. There were about a dozen other people sitting and waiting. There was no receptionist to give one's name to, but every five minutes or so a nurse appeared and called out a name, and someone got up, and followed her into the doctor's office.

Finally Joe was the last person waiting. The nurse said to him, "I no see your name. Please, you come." He followed her outside into a patio and then under a protruding balcony where a desk and two chairs were screened by five potted trees budding into white flowers. The nurse pointed to one of the chairs for Joe, and then she sat down on the other side of the desk. She held out her hand and said, "Your insurance card please." Joe pulled it out of his wallet and handed it to her. "You have international card?" Joe shook his head. The nurse waited in silence for a minute or two. Then she shook her head and stood up, saying. "You wait. Dr. Appleton you explain," and she walked away.

After a few minutes, a lanky bearded man with grey hair almost down to his shoulders appeared in the entrance of the alcove. He held out his hand as Joe stood up, and said, "Hi, I'm Dr. Appleton."

"I'm Joe Wilson," Joe said, immensely relieved to hear an American voice.

"What can I do for you? I hear you've come here without an appointment and without an international insurance card. Do you have your medical records with you?"

"No, I didn't think of that," Joe mumbled.

"The reason I ask" the doctor went on, as he sat down, "is that although we can't admit you if you don't have insurance or the money to pay the fees, it might be possible to see you as an outpatient if we feel we can be of help to you."

"As an outpatient?" Joe asked, sitting down as well.

"Yes, if you were to find a place to live nearby, perhaps in Mérida, I could give you a regimen to follow, and then I'd be willing to see you every other week, to check on how it was going. I'm assuming you don't need nursing care at the present time; is that right?"

"Yes, I mean, no. But," Joe went on, "I'm not sure how I'd find a place in Mérida, I mean…" Then he caught himself up. "But that's not your concern. I understand that. I thank you very much for your time."

"You're more than welcome," the doctor replied. He opened a drawer in the desk and took out a paper entitled "Basic Regimen Instructions" and a form entitled "Request for Records." "This basic regimen will get you going, and if you'll fill out this release, your doctor can send me your records and we can tune the regimen to your specifics." He handed Joe the form and waited while he filled it out. When Joe gave it back, they both stood up and shook hands.

"Thank you very much, sir," Joe said. Then he pocketed the "Basic Regimen Instructions," picked up his oboe and headed back into the reception room and then out into the sun.

The sun's glare blinded him at first. Near the front door was a stone bench. He sat down on it with his oboe beside him. "Perhaps this is still part of the clinic," he thought. "Maybe I'm not supposed to be here. But what could they do to me? I'm dying." A feeling of exhilaration, of having at last won his freedom, suffused him. For a minute, instead of feeling exhaustion and despair, he felt at peace.

After a while, the minivan drove up and four people walked up the path to the clinic. The driver looked at Joe and called out "Mérida?" Joe nodded. The journey toward death was continuing—all he needed to do was follow directions. He got up from the bench and re-entered the minivan. The driver turned around to face him, "I go to Market before Airport. Okay you wait? Next plane not to three hours. You forget suitcase?"

"I'm not going to the airport" Joe said, although for a moment the longing for Sarah and the children seemed to break in on his nightmare and make him long to live. But then he remembered. People with liver cancer don't live. "I'm dying" he reminded himself, and sank back into his despairing resignation. "I don't know where to go," he said.

"Ah" the driver said. "You want place to stay in Mérida?"

"Yes," agreed Joe. "I need place."

"Mi primo, my cousin, he has good place. I take you there."

"Thank you," Joe said, and from then on they were silent.

Chapter Twenty-Five

THE PENSION LOOKED forbidding at first—tall stony walls, but as they approached, Joe saw an open iron gate. It was just large enough for the minivan to drive through into a patio, at the center of which was a small fountain. The driver ushered Joe out of the minivan and toward a man who was coming out of the office which was just inside the gate. As Joe stood silently clutching his oboe, the driver talked rapidly to his cousin in Spanish, then tipped his hat to Joe, got back into the minivan and left.

Joe looked at the owner, who was dressed in a grey suite, despite the heat, without a tie and with his shirt unbuttoned half way down his chest. He held out his hand to shake Joe's, or to ask for money, Joe was not sure which. Joe put his hand in his pocket and drew out the $25 that he still had. The man then broke into reasonable English.

"You are welcome here. My name is Señor Gomez, at your service." He then handed back $10 along with a key. He looked around for a suitcase but saw only the oboe case that Joe was clutching. He said, "I show you upstairs your room."

It was clean, whitewashed, with a window looking down on the patio. The bed was narrow, but the mattress seemed firm when Joe sat down on it. He sat there and looked around at the empty white walls, the pegs to hang the clothes he didn't have, and a basin and pitcher on a stool. Joe found the bathroom down the hall and then went back to his room and sat again on his bed. He had no idea what to do next. He lay down for a bit, hoping to fall asleep, but sleep didn't come. Was there enough money in the bank account to take care of them until Sarah could find work? Who would pay to have him buried? Where would he go tomorrow since he couldn't afford another night here? Why couldn't he just die now and have it over with? Finally he sat up, got the oboe out of its case and then, standing near the window, staring down into the patio, he began to play. He had no sheet music, so he played some Mozart and Chopin that he knew by heart and then some Brahms. When he ran out of pieces he knew by heart, he reverted to the show tunes he had played on the streets.

After a while, someone knocked on his door. Joe opened it with an apology on his lips for making so much noise, but Señor Gomez interrupted him. "Señor, I hear you play and I need beg from you a favor. Tonight at the restaurant down-stairs I have music. Today the man calls me to say he no can come. So I think—no music. Then I hear you play. I think perhaps you play tonight in my restaurant. I give you room free, meal and wine." He held out Joe's $15.

Joe took the money as he said, "Yes, I can do that." Then he thought for a minute before he said, "Maybe you can give me some money instead of wine."

"Yes, I put out basket. I give you ten pesetas from my pocket." Señor Gomez reached into his pocket and gave Joe a ten peseta bill.

"You come down now, eat with cook, with waiters. One hour restaurant open."

"Señor Gomez, I must tell you that I don't know any Mexican music," Joe said, wondering if he had the energy to eat with, and then play for, people who didn't speak English.

"Señor, I hear you play. You make people very happy," Señor Gomez assured him.

So Joe did as he was bid. He washed his hands and face, and then, carrying his oboe case, he went down into the patio and followed the sound of a radio to the restaurant. The cook, two waiters, and the cook's helper were already sitting around a large table. There was a place setting and a chair waiting for Joe. One of the waiters spoke some English. He was hoping to travel to the States one day and he enjoyed practicing. He told Joe the Spanish names of the food they were eating. Joe's attempts to reproduce the names made the others laugh. Joe realized he was hungry. He had left Ipswich that morning in too much of a hurry to eat breakfast. He quickly ate the rice and beans and stringy meat sauce. The cook's helper winked at him and gave him another portion of everything. Joe wondered for an instant that he felt well enough to eat so much, but then stopped wondering and simply ate.

It turned out that people liked his music. The restaurant and bar opened on to the patio so the loudness of the oboe didn't bother them. There were a few Americans among the guests who knew some of the show tunes and began to sing along as Joe played, and that got some of the locals enthusiastic as well. Joe played until closing, around two in the morning. Mr. Gomez had put out a small basket with a little handwritten sign that said, "por la música" and at the end of the evening, he gathered the money in it, handed it to Joe, and thanked him.

Joe fell into bed and slept until Señor Gomez knocked on his door around noon. Joe stumbled into his pants and shirt before opening the door. He assumed Señor Gomez wanted his $15 for the next night's lodging, but Señor Gomez said, "You make my guests very happy. The man who plays guitar, he finds new job. So I ask if you stay here more and if you play for my guests this night."

"Well," Joe said, "I guess I can play tonight."

"Good. I give you now ten pesetas for this night. Maybe you buy clean shirt. Or maybe my sister wash for you." Joe looked down at his wrinkled and sweat-stained shirt.

"Ok," he said, and then pocketing the offered ten pesetas, he added, "Where can I buy a shirt?"

The narrow streets of Mérida were crammed with trucks, busses, cars and bicycles—all but the bicycles giving off terrible fumes. The sidewalks were narrow and crowded and edged by blank stone or cement walls—no windows, no balconies, nothing except every once in a while a door. Joe coughed, his eyes stung, and he sweated profusely as he looked for the store Señor Gomez had told him about. Joe asked himself again and again, how he could have picked this place to end his days. Señor Gomez had given him an address of a store owned by a relative. He'd told Joe he would call ahead so they would know what Joe needed. When Joe finally found the number and went through the door, he was once again in an airy inner patio with stores opening onto it. He bought new underwear, and socks, as well as two shirts. He felt spiffy when he left the clothes store and found his way to another store that Señor Gomez had told him about where he could buy sheet music. The streets no longer felt so claustrophobic now that he knew that behind each door was an airy patio.

The music store not only had popular Mexican music, but classical music as well. Joe spent the $15 dollars he no longer needed for lodging on sheet music.

When he got back to the pension, he practiced for a few hours and then fell asleep. When Señor Gomez knocked on his door, he went down to eat supper and begin his new gig.

Chapter Twenty-Six

SARAH COULD NOT sleep. She got into bed with Kari and held her tightly through the night sometimes crying into the back of her neck. Kari slept through it all. At dawn, Sarah got up and went into the kitchen. She dug up her mother's Boston phone book that Joan had obtained to be able to call for emergency services for Angelica. Holding a cup of coffee in her hand, she called every hospital in the Boston area as well as the missing persons department of the Boston Police. She then called all the homeless shelters. By that time, they had emptied out for the day, but nobody remembered seeing someone of Joe's description. She called Joe's old phone number at Tanglewood but was told that the number had been disconnected. She called Angelica's hospital but was told that Angelica could not take calls at the present time because it was contraindicated by her doctor. Sarah then asked to speak to the doctor but was told that he was on vacation for a few days.

When the children woke up, Sarah got Kari dressed and then made breakfast. They were sitting around the kitchen table, not saying much, when Joan came in, her eyes puffy with tears or lack of sleep. Sarah didn't know which and wouldn't ask in front of the children. Instead she said, a little too briskly to fool anyone, "Good morning, Mom. I made a new pot of coffee and there's a bunch of pancakes in the oven staying warm for you."

"Good morning, darlings," Joan said and helped herself to coffee and pancakes. Then she joined them at the kitchen table.

"I've made a lot of phone calls," Sarah told her mother. "No news yet," she went on.

"Did you find Daddy?" Sam asked.

"No, sweetheart, not yet. But I think it's best if we go back to New York this morning. Perhaps Gran could stay home most of the day, after she takes us to the station, in case Daddy calls."

"Of course I will," Joan said quickly. "But I hate to see you go…what if…?" Then she caught herself up and said to the children, "I'll miss you, my sweeties. I've enjoyed your being here so much."

"Well, you may see more of us soon," Sarah said.

"We'll come right back if Daddy calls." Sam explained.

"Of course you will" Joan said. "Let's hope he calls today. I'll be right here if he does."

Joan drove them to the train station, holding back her tears. They arrived a little late. The train was making sounds of departing so there was no time for hugs and kisses. Sam grabbed his small bag. Sarah grabbed a bag in one hand and Kari in another and they ran for it, calling over their shoulders, "Goodbye, Mom, and thanks."

"Goodbye Gran, I love you."

As the train pulled away, Joan was crying too hard to drive. She sat in the parked car and allowed the tears to flow. She felt completely bereft and incompetent as a mother and grandmother.

She wondered what Angelica had meant by "How awful Joe looked." He'd looked exhausted, that's all. Angelica must have lied about the kiss, so maybe she was making it all up. But still Joan felt she should have been able to see something was wrong. "Oh Lord, please help us. Please bring Joe home. Please heal this family. I beg you." This time she prayed aloud. The answer seemed to come from the sunny sky, the trees with splotches of color and the high clouds making wonderful shapes in the bright blue sky. God was too busy making beauty to keep an eye on one musician.

When she got home, Joan called Angelica again. Someone at the nursing station told her that Angelica had had a setback and was not able to speak to anyone until perhaps next week. Joan hung up wondering if the setback was real or if Angelica was avoiding her. She considered calling Angelica's doctor, but realized she couldn't face it. He always gave her the feeling that he was trying hard not to blame her for Angelica's illness.

Joan didn't leave the house that day. Sarah had told her that she had given the Missing Person's Bureau of the

Boston Police Joan's number as well as her own in the city. Joan cleaned the cottage, packing up all the clothes and toys that Sarah had not been able to fit into the two suitcases she and Sam could carry. She cleaned up breakfast dishes and pans, grateful for things to do. She knew that if she sat down, she would sink into desperation.

In the early evening, she called Sarah.

"Hi, sweetie. I have no news. I just wanted to hear your voice and hear how your trip went and how the kids are doing."

"The kids are okay. Sam talked almost all the way down about how much he hates school. I think it was just to fill in the silence. When we got home, they both dove into the television, and we had a pizza delivered. I've just put them to bed. I have to get off the phone now, Mom. Maybe he'll call. I love you."

"I love you too. We'll talk tomorrow."

But Sarah had already hung up.

As Joan closed the curtains against the dark, she felt nervous for the first time since she had moved there. She locked the front door and then the kitchen door; she pulled down blinds and closed curtains until all the windows were covered, and then she picked up Bruce, and carried him, squirming a bit, to her bed. As he watched her, she quickly undressed and got into bed herself with "Pride and Prejudice" which she opened at random and read until dawn.

The next morning it was pouring rain, as though nature itself was mourning Joe's disappearance. At seven-thirty

Joan called the animal shelter and told Mary what had happened. "I need to stay right here until he or the police call."

"You take as long as you need to, dear, but remember we want you back as soon as all's well. Perhaps he'll come back today."

"I hope so," Joan sighed. "I'll call you as soon as I know anything."

"You're in my prayers, dear," Mary told her. "And if you want me to…"

But Joan interrupted, "I think I better get off the phone now, Mary. He may be trying to call. I'll talk with you soon. Bye."

After lunch, Joan called the Missing Persons Bureau. "We'll be in touch with you as soon as we know anything, Madam" a tired-sounding detective said. "It's actually better if you don't call us, so that we can have our lines free for leads. You can count on our getting in touch with you as soon as we know anything at all."

"Thank you," Joan said.

Then she called the hospital to ask about Angelica, hoping to get a nurse that she knew. But the receptionist wouldn't put the call through. "Mrs. Fitzpatrick, the nursing station asked me to tell you that there is nothing to report about your daughter. They will call you as soon as there is anything to report. They also said that your daughter will call you as soon as she is able to, which might be in a week or two."

"Thank you." Joan said, gritting her teeth.

She stayed indoors for two more days, waiting for the phone to ring. Not quite trusting the Missing Persons

Bureau, she called every hospital in Boston and Cambridge and in the various towns between Boston and Ipswich. The third hospital in Boston told her they couldn't give out the names of their patients, so after that she simply called and asked to speak to Joe Wilson. The first time she was told, "He must have checked out." she asked excitedly "Where'd he go to?" "We don't have that information" was the response and after having the same back and forth with two different hospitals she realized that if she seemed to know Joe Wilson was a patient there and they had no record of him, the assumption was that he had come and gone.

Each night she spoke for a few minutes with Sarah. She called at suppertime, and Sarah usually let Sam talk with her for a few minutes. His first question was about his dad, but after that he told her about school or about something he'd done that day.

The third day, Joan allowed herself an hour in the garden planting daffodil and iris bulbs and pulling out weeds around the lavender bushes. By the fourth day, she had to go into town to buy groceries. On the fifth day, she went back to the animal shelter where Mary greeted her with a big hug and some hot chocolate. It was Dr. Nesbit's day so Joan was needed immediately to hold a German Shepherd while Dr. Nesbit shaved around a wound he'd received in a fight.

Chapter Twenty-Seven

JOE FOUND HE could pick up the Mexican songs pretty quickly. The locals, who were there more for the bar than the restaurant, would sing and he would accompany them. Then, one night, a man with a guitar climbed up on the small stage with Joe. He played melodies Joe hadn't heard before, so Joe played harmonies above and below him. The guests sang along with great gusto until way after the usual closing time. At the end of the evening Joe divided the basket of contributions between them.

After that, other musicians came into the bar bringing their instruments, sometimes coming late after their own gigs were over. They taught Joe beautiful old ballads that seemed to go back centuries. Joe taught them Count Basie and Benny Goodman tunes and sometimes they simply jammed with no specific tune in mind. It was a great relief to Joe to be speaking the language of music rather than struggling to find words in Spanish.

Joe spent most of the daytime hours asleep, except for the two or three hours he practiced each afternoon. He was memorizing a Bach unaccompanied cello piece that had been transposed for the oboe. Sometimes he asked himself why he practiced and memorized as though he had a future. He had no answer, but went on playing.

One afternoon as Joe ate breakfast, he pulled a folded-up piece of paper out of his pants pocket. It was Dr. Appleton's regimen which was a series of recipes and times when they should be eaten. Joe had begun waking up in the middle of the night with cold sweats and migraines. Were these symptomatic of what was to come? Perhaps he could now afford a visit to the doctor.

After breakfast he went out to find a Spanish-English dictionary. With that in hand, he showed the cook the doctor's instructions and asked if he could help him with the regimen. The cook said "Claro que sí!" and then explained with the help of his assistant that he had cooked for other clinic patients. Joe remembered that Señor Gomez was a cousin of the clinic's bus driver.

Joe began to eat his meals separately from the rest of the staff. The cook handed him odd concoctions that Joe swallowed without wanting to know what had gone into them. Eating was no longer pleasurable, but he did feel a little more energetic.

Two weeks after he started the new regimen, Joe called the clinic to ask for an appointment with Dr. Appleton. The receptionist said she would arrange for the minivan to pick him up on its way back from the airport.

Dr. Appleton had received the test results from Joe's doctor in Boston. He examined Joe thoroughly and asked how long he'd been on the regimen. "You're doing well," he said. "Next time you come, you'll have an art therapy session. Do you know anything about painting?"

"No, nothing. I'm a musician."

"Good," Dr. Appleton said. "You can often do much better with these therapies if the experience is new to you. We'll keep music therapy to the last. Are you happy at the pension?" To Joe's nod, he continued, "Good. Well, Diego can take you back in about fifteen minutes. No, no charge," he added, seeing Joe dig into his pocket for money, "We'll think of you as part of an experiment. We haven't had much experience with liver cancer. I think it's only fair to tell you that, but I have a feeling that things are going to work out well. See you in a couple of weeks."

Chapter Twenty-Eight

FOR ABOUT TWO months Joan called the Missing Person's Bureau every week. "Hello, Mrs. Fitzpatrick. It's always a pleasure to hear your voice. We have no news yet, Mrs. Fitzpatrick, but you'll hear from us as soon as we do."

The autumn was of extraordinary beauty that year. The trees changed colors during the day, depending on the sun and clouds. It was as though the hills absorbed the colors of the sunrise and then played with them all day. Even people in town commented that it was a special year for the leaves. They were hopeful that the leaf peepers would give a real boost to the economy and help everyone get through the winter.

Then she would call the hospital. "She's not ready to come to the phone yet, Mrs. Fitzpatrick. She's doing well, but she thinks, and the doctor agrees with her, that it's best at present for her not to become involved with events outside the hospital. You can rest assured that her doctor will call you when there is any significant change in her status.

She is receiving the best possible care, Mrs. Fitzpatrick. Thank you for calling."

Almost every evening Joan called Sarah. At first Sarah was so disappointed to hear her mother's voice rather than news of Joe, or Joe himself, that instead of talking with her mother, she'd put Sam on right away. One evening Joan called later, after the children had gone to bed. She said to Sarah, "Darling, how about if I call you at six o'clock sharp or not at all. That way you won't think that the call might be from Joe. What do you think?"

"That's a good idea Mom. You know I love talking with you and I'm really grateful for your calls. It's just that when the phone rings, for a minute I think, well, I feel…"

"Yes, dearest, I know. How are the kids?"

"I think they're okay. I don't know how much Kari realizes. Sam doesn't say much. But, he's liking school. I've got to go—Kari's crying. I love you."

"And I you." But Sarah had already hung up.

When it got too cold for Joan to work in the garden in the late afternoons, she baked cookies and almond squares to send to Sam and Kari. On weekends she sometimes walked on the beach. In November, hers was often the only car in the huge parking lot. The seagulls and the sandpipers seemed to own the beach again. On dark cloudy days the colors of the water and of the wild spiky grasses that grew at the top of the sand dunes seemed to shine with new luminosity. As she walked along the empty beach, she allowed herself to cry. Somehow it seemed less frightening than crying by herself at home. On the beach, the birds, the ocean, the dunes, the sky itself, seemed to be accompanying her.

Joan took Bruce with her when she went to New York City for Thanksgiving. She took the children to the Macy's Parade and did most of the cooking. Sam still enjoyed helping to bake pies. Sarah seemed restless all day, and after the Thanksgiving meal, when the children were asleep, she told her mother why.

"Mom, I made a promise to myself last week."

"What was that dear?"

"I promised myself that if I didn't hear from Joe on Thanksgiving, I wouldn't stay in the city any longer. You know how much he loved Thanksgiving. I figured that if he was coming back on a special day, today would be it. So," she sighed deeply, "I'm going to leave this city where I think I see him around every corner. It's just too painful."

"Will you come up to Ipswich with me?" Joan asked. "I'd be thrilled," she added.

"No, I can't move to Ipswich. I think I have to find a place for myself and the kids. I love being with you, you know that, but I have to start a new life, a life without Joe, and I think I need to start it in a new place, just the three of us. Of course wherever we are, we would want you to visit. And of course we would visit you. But I need to have a home base for me and the kids."

"I can see that," Joan said although she was very disappointed. She had already pictured how much fun it would be to have her house full of family. "Where are you thinking of?"

"Do you remember where I did summer stock when I got out of high school? Carleton, New York—it's southeast of Albany, near the Mass Pike."

"I remember. I came to see you the second summer a couple of times when you had good parts in the shows."

"I saw in the trade magazine that the same summer stock theater, The Globe, is looking for an assistant administrator, someone to keep the books, audition the chorus roles, and maybe even run the children's program. What do you think?"

"I'm sure you could do all that, but wouldn't you miss being on stage?"

"I think it's a way in. If I auditioned for an acting job, it would probably be only for one play, but this is year round, so we'd have enough to live on. And maybe they'll let me act at the same time."

"Have you talked with them?"

"I think the first thing I'll do is go up and look around and see if I still like the place. Also I need to see how much the rents are. What shall we do about the loft? Do you think you'll want to come back here?"

Joan hung fire for half a minute and then decided. "I think I may be getting a little old for the city."

"Maybe I can get some money for it—people pay key money to the last renters when they find a good loft. We'll split it."

"You keep it, Sarah. You'll need it to get started in your new place and to move and everything. I'm all set, thanks to Marianne and Caleb."

"Would you be willing to stay on for a bit while I look around? Could you be here, like the old days, taking care of the kids and stuff? I'd like to go up to Carleton tomorrow and see what it looks like and perhaps contact the theater and look for rentals. I might want to stay there a few days. What do you think?"

"Of course, I'd be happy to." Joan realized to her surprise how thrilled she felt in being needed once again. "I'll call Mary at the Shelter and explain. I'm sure she can get another volunteer for a few days."

"Thanks Mom. I don't know what I'd do without you."

Chapter Twenty-Nine

THE NEXT MORNING Sarah took the train to Carleton. She carried a small backpack in case she decided to spend the night. She felt almost young—the children were safe with her mother; she could do whatever she wanted. Joe seemed to be close to her, encouraging her to make this move. She decided she would look first for a place to live, and then she would look for a job.

It was warm for late November, lots of sun and no wind. Sarah stopped to look in the window of a second hand bookstore called Penelope's Loom. She saw a small wooden sign at the foot of a book display that said 'Café Open' so she went in. The bookstore had two large rooms with floor to ceiling bookcases. One of the rooms was for children, with red bean-bag seats and a rocking chair. The other room had a table with a reading lamp, and two comfortable chairs. Sarah noticed that an older man was sitting at the table with a couple of books open, taking notes as though he were in a research library. Near the door was a high desk with an old cash register. A man sat on a stool behind it reading a book. He smiled at Sarah when she came in and said, "If I can be of any help, please let me know." Sarah thanked him and walked through the children's room to a wooden spiral staircase at the back. There was a wooden sign hanging from the banister that said, 'Café Upstairs.'

She went up the staircase through what seemed to be a large hole in the ceiling and came out into the café. A dark-haired girl, who looked to be twelve or thirteen, was playing an ornate piece by Bach on an alto recorder. She had long blond braids and was wearing blue jeans and a large red sweatshirt. She looked as though she were practicing in her own home. Sarah sat down at one of the four little tables. Behind the counter, a woman with short grey curly hair, wearing a large blue apron, had her back to Sarah as she stirred something on the stove. On the walls were paintings, some of them almost like photographs, others quite abstract, but all seemed to be depicting the Main Street of Carleton that Sarah had just walked down.

When the music stopped, Sarah got up to look at the paintings. The woman from behind the counter came over to her. She was older than she had looked from the back — too old to be the mother of the girl playing the recorder. But her smile was warm and friendly and Sarah stopped trying to guess her age. "These were done by my students," she said. "We're having a sale to raise money for the Library. I have a list of the prices if you're interested."

"I think they're lovely," Sarah said, "But actually I'm here to look around for a place to rent. For myself and my two children," she added.

"Oh," the woman seemed to need to catch her breath at this abrupt change of the subject. Then she said, "A friend of mine is looking for someone to share her house…did you say you have children?"

"Yes," Sarah said, slightly defiantly, "they're two and six years old, very well-behaved. They wouldn't…"

But the woman interrupted her, "That might work out well. My friend's a single mom with an eight-year-old son. She's looking for someone to share her house. She's a very fine painter."

"Where does she live?"

"About a ten minute walk from here. If you like, I can give you her phone number."

"That would be great, but first I think I'd like some lunch."

"Of course. I'll bring you a menu."

Sarah ordered a sandwich and a cup of coffee. The girl with the recorder had disappeared. When the woman brought the food over, she handed Sarah a piece of paper. "Her name is Emily Madison and here's her phone number. I'm sure Richard will let you use the store phone. My name is Sage — tell her I gave you the number."

Following the directions Emily had given her over the phone, Sarah walked up Kinderhook Street. The sidewalks were tree-lined and the street was narrow. The few cars drove slowly and carefully, avoiding boys playing stickball and two mothers with baby carriages walking in the road to avoid a hopscotch game on the sidewalk. Three girls and a boy on bikes and scooters swerved in and out from the road to the sidewalk using the driveway entrances as transitions.

Sarah thought of Sam and how he would enjoy being able to play with other children on the street without having to wait for her and Kari to be out with him.

The house she was looking for turned out to be a three-story Victorian, painted white with blue trim. On the wrap-around porch a woman and a boy were sitting together on a swing seat, enjoying a tickling match. The woman had red hair and a round face like a Renoir girl grown into woman-hood. She wore a long sky-blue skirt and a pale orange blouse that enhanced the similarity. The boy wore faded jeans and a blue T-shirt. He was thin and wiry and looked a little frail.

Sarah called up to them, "Hello, Emily? I'm Sarah. I called you on the phone."

The woman quickly stood up, "Hi, yes, I'm Emily, and this is Paul." She held her son to her side. "We've been looking out for you. Come on in. I've made us some hot chocolate. But you can have coffee if you prefer."

"I'd love some hot chocolate," Sarah said, not adding that she hadn't had it since she was a child.

"Good, come on in."

Emily led her directly into the kitchen, which was painted yellow and white. It was filled with sunlight from large windows and there were pots of geraniums every-where. Paul joined them at the kitchen table where Emily poured out hot chocolate and nudged a plate of oatmeal rai-sin cookies toward Sarah. As they sipped and munched, Emily said, "You said on the phone you had two young children. We were hoping they were coming with you."

"Oh," Sarah said, "I should have explained. They're in the city with my mother while I look for a place for us. Sam is six, and Kari is two."

"Well, Paul is eight." She turned to him, "What do you think, sweetie, would it be fun to have a six-year-old to play with? You could show him the ropes. Introduce him to the school and stuff."

"Does he like trains?" Paul asked Sarah.

"I don't think he knows much about them," Sarah said.

"Paul has a huge set of train tracks up in the attic," Emily said. "We'll show you if you like."

"I'd like that very much," Sarah said.

Emily turned to Paul, "Since the children aren't here, do you want to go play with Davie like you planned?"

"Yeah, I guess so," though he sounded uncertain. "Don't forget to show her my trains. I laid all the tracks myself," he said to Sarah. "You can tell your kids that I'll show them how they all work." Then he took a cookie for the road. "See you later," he said to his mother, and he was gone.

"He's feeling a little bereft," Emily said. "We've been living here with my parents ever since he was born. Last summer my mother decided that she could not face another winter here, so she convinced Dad to rent a place in South Carolina. Now they've found a house they want to buy and they plan to live there year round. I'm glad for them, but it means I'll need help paying the mortgage and heating bills. That's why I'm looking for housemates. Also Paul spent a lot of time with Mom when I was painting or working, so I was interested to hear that you have children because I thought we might take turns with child care. Shall I show you around?"

"Sure," Sarah said, glad that Emily hadn't wanted to talk about their common single-parent status. The living room had a wood stove and doors that disappeared into the walls, 'pocket doors' Emily called them. When the doors were open, the room was large with a bay window that brought in lots of light. When the doors were closed, the two small rooms they created were cozy. The smaller one, without the bay window, had an upright piano. Emily told her that Paul was learning to play the piano and preferred the doors closed when he practiced.

Upstairs Emily showed her the three empty rooms for rent. Each one had a big window looking out on the street. These had been Emily's parents' bedrooms and her mother's sewing room. They were small, but Sarah had the feeling they'd all be spending a lot of time downstairs in the kitchen and living room.

Emily then showed Sarah her own bedroom and Paul's, and then they went upstairs to the attic, that had been converted into a huge studio lit by skylights. Paul also had an area in the attic for his trains, which were set up on a large piece of plywood lifted off the floor by red bricks. Emily's canvasses were turned toward the wall, except for one on an easel. It was a portrait of Paul. Sarah was astounded by how vibrant and childlike he appeared.

Emily took Sarah back to the kitchen where they discussed the rent, which turned out to be one tenth of what Sarah was paying for the loft. Sarah agreed to it immediately and asked if she could move in during Christmas vacation. "Of course," Emily answered. "Do you want to come before Christmas itself? I'd be happy to make a Christmas Eve dinner for all of us."

Sarah turned away to hide her tears; Christmas without Joe—it didn't seem possible. Perhaps he would come back for Christmas. What if he came looking for them in the city? "Thank you," she said, not looking at Emily, "After Christmas, I think, but thank you." She turned back towards Emily, having wiped her eye with her sleeve.

Chapter Thirty

DR. APPLETON SEEMED pleased as he poked and prodded Joe's abdomen, and listened to his heart. "Is there any cancer in your immediate family?"

"Yes, my mother died of liver cancer. That's why…that's why I came…I just couldn't have my family watch…" instead of finishing his sentence Joe shook his head, like a dog coming out of a pond. He sat up and swung his feet over the edge of the examining table. He was not going to have this conversation lying down.

"Does your family know you're here?" the doctor asked gently.

"No, nobody knows," Joe responded, looking at the floor. "It's better that way. They'll be fine without me. I would have been a terrible burden."

He looked up then at Dr. Appleton's face, hoping or dreading, he wasn't sure which, that the doctor would try to contradict him. But the doctor only said, "You may want to get in touch with them when you're feeling better.

Meanwhile," he continued before Joe could deny this possibility, "I want you to meet Señora Garcia. She is our art therapist and will be working with you on painting."

Señora Garcia turned out to be an American as well. She was beautifully dressed, Joe thought, in a long bright red skirt of some silky material and a white tunic embroidered around the neckline with yellow, red and blue birds in green palm trees. She looked to be in her seventies with short white hair swept back off her face. Her studio looked out on the courtyard and had lots of easels leaning against the wall, but that morning there was only one easel out and on it was a square flat board with a large piece of paper taped to it.

"We will begin with making a color circle using water colors," Señora Garcia said. She showed him where to put a patch of yellow at the top of the paper and a patch of red down two thirds of the way on the left side and a patch of blue two thirds of the way down on the right side. "Now the idea is to create a circle blending these colors but with no breaks in between. For example, as you bring the yellow down into the red, you'll have darker yellow and then orange before you get to the red, but I want you to try to do it in a way that one can never say where the yellow ends and the orange begins or where the orange turns into red. Do you see what I mean?"

Joe thought he understood, except it seemed too easy a task so he might be missing something. So he nodded, "Yes, I think so."

"Good," Señora Garcia said. "Then why don't you begin."

It turned out to be much more difficult than Joe had imagined. In fact as he worked, he decided that it might be a scientific impossibility to make the colors blend without showing when one began and the other ended. Perhaps this was a fool's errand. Señora Garcia stood near him as he worked. She made suggestions about his brush strokes, telling him to breathe out with each stroke, to imagine himself painting the sky, to use his whole arm and not just his wrist. "Trailing clouds of glory, that's what you want to be doing." Joe was annoyed; the exercise was difficult, if not impossible, and was being made more so by his not being allowed to do it in his own way. But after a while, he found that the brush strokes made with his whole arm while he was breathing out were helping him to blend the colors more seamlessly. He worked for two hours while Señora Garcia stood behind him encouraging and suggesting. When it was time to stop, the circle still looked blotchy. "We will go on with it next time," she said. "I will see you in two weeks. You have done very well."

Joe felt exhausted as he sat on the bench outside the clinic to wait for a ride back into Mérida. But as he looked around him at the rather stark landscape, almost flat, dry and sandy with mountains in the distance, he realized he was seeing more color in the sand, in the mountains, in the walls of the clinic than he had seen before. This continued to be true as they drove to the pension. Mérida had always seemed grey with diesel fumes or overwhelmingly yellow with the baking sun, but nothing in between. Now Joe noticed the colors of the painted doorways, and the clothes people wore and even the fruit that the children in the street sold from small trays.

When Joe went back in two weeks, Dr. Appleton listened to his heart, massaged his abdomen and asked, "How are you feeling?"

"Well," Joe answered, "I'm sure not enjoying the food you've got me on, but I don't seem so exhausted all the time."

"That's a good beginning," Dr. Appleton said. "Señora Garcia says you did well and that you're ready for intensive art therapy. That would mean coming in every day. Do you think you could swing that with your job at the Pension?"

"Sure, if it's during the day. But what about the cost?"

"Feel free to contribute when you can. There's a box for contributions in the front hall. But, meanwhile, you're part of my research project into liver cancer. Does that sound okay?"

"It sounds very good, and I'm exceedingly grateful."

"Good. Now, I'd like to give you an intravenous injection. It will take about twenty minutes and then you'll need to lie still for another half hour."

"What sort of medicine is it?"

"It's made from a plant that grows a little south of here. It's experimental, of course, but we've had some good results. Just wait in the waiting room will you? The nurse will set you up. Then when you're done with her, it'll be time for painting therapy—this time you'll be part of a group. I'll see you in a couple of weeks."

Chapter Thirty-One

THE FOUR OTHER patients in painting therapy greeted Joe with smiles. There were two young French girls. One was bald and gaunt with a large stomach, as though she were pregnant. The other had long dark hair in a thin braid down her back and walked with a cane. They stayed very close together and whispered to each other in French all through the session. There was an older Hispanic man in a wheelchair, elegantly dressed in a suit and tie, who spoke only Spanish, and an American woman from Alaska who looked to be in her fifties, very thin, very friendly, with an obvious wig of blond curls. She told Joe that her brain tumor made it impossible for her to read and write, but she could still talk. She watched the French girls for a moment and said, "I wish I'd done better in school. All we studied were conjugations." She was going to say more, but Señora Garcia came up and said to Joe, "Mr. Wilson, I'd like you to work over here," and led him to a far corner. Joe noticed that she put the American woman's easel next to the man in the wheel chair who was working at a table.

That morning, Señora Garcia did not stand over him but came over to see his progress and make suggestions every once in a while. Near the end of the session, Señora Garcia lined up all their paintings together so they could look at each other's work. They had all begun with the color circle that Joe was working on, but some of them had gone further. One of the French girls had turned hers into a lush land-scape. The American woman had tried to turn hers into "a rainbow or a sunset, I'm not sure which." The Spanish-speaking man was still working on the circle itself, just as Joe was, but his colors were much more vibrant and joyous than Joe's. "Esto es magnífico," Joe said pointing to it and smiling. The man gravely nodded his thanks.

The other French girl, the one without hair, had turned her color circle into an impressionistic portrait of a woman with long flowing dark hair and a voluptuous body. "Now, isn't that nice," the American woman said, pointing to it, and smiling at the girl, who had tears in her eyes.

During Dr. Appleton's next examination of Joe, he asked, "So how's it going with painting therapy?"

"I'm enjoying it."

"Good. Señora Garcia is pleased with your progress. And how did it go with the intravenous drip?"

"It went well, I guess. I fell asleep almost immediately. Is that what it's supposed to do?"

"It's supposed to help your body work on the tumor. I'd like to continue with those once a month. We're going to keep you busy. I'll see you in two weeks. You're doing well, most gratifying."

Painting therapy continued for two more months. Joe found he enjoyed it more and more and was beginning to allow his colors to brighten. He also felt connected, although in an oddly impersonal way, with the other patients in his group. He knew nothing about their lives, but he knew a good deal about their struggles with color and form. He was sad when Señora Garcia announced one morning that this would be their last class.

That day they did something completely new. The six of them sat on stools and stared at an easel with a large empty canvas. Beside the easel was a table with paint brushes and little jars of colored paints. "Today you're going to paint a picture together. You'll take turns, and each person will try to add and enhance what has been done already. The idea is not to try to make the picture your own, but to become as aware as possible of what the people before you were trying to do, and then to enhance their vision. We'll do this without talking at all. The only conversation will be between the colors themselves." She repeated her instructions in Spanish and French, and then a hush fell over them.

They worked for two hours. Not a word was said. They took turns approaching the canvas, making a few brush strokes with one color and then sitting back on the stools and staring, until someone else felt ready to contribute with perhaps another color. The most important part of the experience, Joe felt, were the times in between, when they all silently stared at the painting, asking it what new color or form it wanted.

When the painting was finished, they got off their stools and hugged and kissed each other, which they'd never done before, and left the painting studio still silent, flying high on the experience.

The next therapy Dr. Appleton suggested was "movement therapy." It was taught by Señor Trejo. Señor Trejo was a Mexican man in his twenties. His body was slim, flexible and strong. He had been part of the Mexico City Ballet Company until he broke his knee and the operation to repair it was botched. As with Señora Garcia, Joe's first session with Señor Trejo was on his own. "Make like me," Señor Trejo said, and they were off. First they both lay on their backs on the floor and lifted legs and arms in unison. Then they turned onto their stomachs and lifted both arms and legs at once as high as possible, which was inches for Joe. Then they got onto their hands and knees and kicked one leg out at a time as though they were horses being shod. Finally they scrambled, or in Senor Trejo's case, jumped, to their feet. There they played 'mirror,' Señor Trejo standing opposite Joe, and Joe following his movements as exactly as possible as though he were Señor Trejo's reflection in a mirror. After about 45 minutes, Joe was exhausted. Señor Trejo looked closely at him and said, "Good." He shook Joe's hand. The session was over.

The next week Dr. Appleton said, "I think we're going to make some changes in what you eat. Señor Trejo says he thinks you have some calcification in your shoulders and hips and left foot."

"So what should I do?" Joe asked aloud, and silently to himself he wondered, "What could it possible matter? How much longer do I have?"

"Just follow Señor Trejo's exercises," Dr. Appleton answered, "and give these instructions to that wonderful cook of yours." He handed Joe a sheet of paper. Joe noticed that this time the instructions were in Spanish. "How are you feeling?"

"Okay, a little stiff but okay."

"How's your digestion?"

"Okay, I'm getting somewhat used to the stuff. It sometimes feels as though there's a ferocious battle going on in my abdomen, but every once in a while they call a truce."

"Good, that's the spirit. Have a good time with Señor Trejo," and Dr. Appleton stood up to shake hands. The appointment was over.

Movement Therapy had three other men in it, as well as an older woman at the piano. Two of the men seemed older than Joe. They were both bald; even their eyebrows were gone. They stood very erect but took small steps and seemed afraid of falling. They spoke German to each other. The third man, when Joe got closer to him, seemed to be in his late teens. He was small and thin. He said nothing the entire time. Señor Trejo did not introduce his patients to each other. He simply said, "Make like me." The pianist started playing something that sounded like wind in the trees and Señor Trejo was off, taking large strides around the room. His patients followed his example as best they could. Then he walked on his toes, and then on his heels, sometimes with his arms above his head, sometimes with his arms stretched out at his side. Finally he got down on his hands and knees and crawled like a child. The pianist kept up with all his different movements and began playing nursery rhymes. His patients attempted to imitate everything, the German men talking to each other all the way. Up they got again onto their legs and Señor Trejo ran for a moment while his patients stumbled behind him. Suddenly he stopped. He said, "We play statues." He then tapped the boy on the shoulder and the boy froze in space. The other patients began to move as quickly as possible away from Señor Trejo but soon he had tapped each one of them and everyone was standing motionless. Finally, he clapped his hands and said, "Good. Free." The session was over.

As the weeks went by, Joe found that he was becoming more flexible. Señor Trejo began to create obstacle courses for them, a long narrow plank to practice balancing, a rope held low by two people that they took turns getting under without touching. The German men no longer chatted through the session. They were competitive when it came to games and focused on outdoing each other. Finally Señor Trejo created an intricate climbing wall against the outside of the building. He put a belt around a patient's waist and then attached it to a rope that ran through a pulley on the roof of the building. Then all the other patients, and Señor Trejo himself, grabbed on to the other end of the rope while the patient careful worked himself up the climbing wall a few feet, going higher each session. Each time a patient reached the top of the wall, Señor Trejo took a photograph of him waving from the wall's summit. The day that every one of them got to the top of the wall, Señor Trejo celebrated by enlarging the photographs dramatically and exhibiting them in the reception area of the clinic.

Chapter Thirty-Two

AFTER TWO AND a half months of movement therapy, Dr. Appleton decided that Joe was ready for 'Music Therapy.' "Also," he said, "I think we'll cut back on the intravenous drip. We'll see if you need it again later, but for now, just music therapy and a slightly modified diet. Here are the instructions. Some of this may taste a little better than what you've been having. I think you'll be pleased. See you in a couple of weeks."

The music therapist turned out to be Sally Appleton, the doctor's daughter. She was tall and large-boned and wore her blond hair in a long braid down her back. She wore blue jeans and a faded blue tee shirt and looked very much as though she had just come in from the barn on a Midwestern farm.

During their first session together Sally played the piano and asked Joe to sing scales with her. Then she brought out a variety of instruments including a lyre, bongo drums, and bamboo flutes, "Do you want to take one of these home to get used to it, perhaps practice a bit? Tomorrow you'll be part of our orchestra and you may want to get the feel of the instrument first."

"Sure, perhaps the drums. I do play the oboe. Would you like that as part of the orchestra?"

"That's right! You're a musician. Dad told me, but I'd forgotten. I wondered how you managed to have such good pitch. Yes, of course, bring your oboe. I'm not sure in what ways we'll use it. It might drown out the other instruments, but bring it. Meanwhile, why don't you take the bongo drums home with you overnight to get the feel of them."

The next day Joe joined the music therapy class. There were four other patients. They sat in a semicircle with their instruments in their laps. There was a teenage girl holding a lyre and wearing what looked to be her father's fedora on her bald head, the two German men who Joe had met in movement therapy had wooden recorders of different sizes and the American woman from Alaska who smiled when she saw Joe and patted the empty chair next to her had a large drum on the floor between her legs. When Joe sat down beside her, he asked, "How're you doing?" But instead of answering, she just smiled and smiled. He realized she could no longer find words.

Sally drew her chair in front of the semicircle facing them. "Well, my friends, let's get started." Then she spoke in German to the two men and in Spanish to the teenager. She continued in English, "We're going to begin by introducing our instruments to each other. When I gesture to you, please play three or four notes very slowly on your instrument. The most important thing at this time is to listen to the silences between your notes. See if you can make the silences between your notes sing."

Each patient then played one note after another with long pauses in between while they all listened to the silences.

Then Sally asked Catalina, the teenager, to change places with her. Catalina faced the others and Sally took her place and picked up her lyre. Catalina gestured to each musician not in turn but in the order she chose, and each musician played until Catalina would make a sign for them to stop and gesture to the next. Sometimes she had more than one musician playing at once. They tried hard to enhance each other's notes rather than drowning each other out. Then it was the American woman's turn. She grinned broadly and gestured a little wildly, and the music she conducted was filled with enthusiasm. Each of the musicians took their turns as conductor, and their turns with different instruments. When it was Joe's turn to conduct, he found he had tears in his eyes as he watched their careful but joyous playing.

After the next day's session, Sally asked, "Did you bring your oboe?"

"Sure did."

"Would you like to play some duets? I'm free till tea time."

"I'd like that a lot, but I don't have any sheet music with me."

"I have heaps. What about a little Mozart?" And they were off. After that, they played each day after music therapy class. Sally played the piano well, but her favorite instrument was the clarinet. Sometimes they played trios with Señora Martinez, the pianist for the movement therapy sessions. Sometimes Joe played piano as accompanist to Sally's clarinet. Sometimes they just played wind instruments. Sometimes an elderly patient would join them who could do amazing things on the harmonica.

One day Sally confided to Joe that she wanted to go back to California. "There's a man there I'm crazy about."

"Why don't you go then?"

"This place means so much to Dad. He's asked me to stay on until he can find another music therapist. I said I would, but that was ages ago. I've really got to get back there before Steve gets tired of waiting. What I was wondering is if you'd be willing to pinch hit for me till Dad finds someone."

"I don't know anything about therapy." Besides I'm dying, he added to himself.

"I could train you. I wouldn't leave until Dad said you were ready."

"But I'm dying." This time he said it aloud.

"Dad says you're doing well," she answered. "At least," she amended quickly, "that's what I understood." She looked a little abashed and then went on, "We're not supposed to talk about medical stuff. It just slipped out. I'm sorry."

Joe blushed with confusion. If he wasn't dying, what the hell was he doing there?

After waiting a minute, Sally said, "Well, please think about it."

Joe grunted, picked up his oboe case and headed outside for the ride back to Mérida.

Chapter Thirty-Three

SARAH HAD ASKED Joan to stay on for a few days in New York City while she looked for a place to live in Carleton. Once she'd found that, she'd asked her mother to stay on till she could find a job. Joan enjoyed her time in the city. She explored the museums, visiting paintings and statues that were like old friends she hadn't seen in a while. She and the children bought pastry extravaganzas in Little Italy, and mysterious looking vegetables in China Town, and smoked fish and bagels on the Lower East Side. On cold, wet days they stayed home. The children played board games and petted Bruce while Joan sorted and packed books, the children's summer clothes, dishes, toys, and all the odds and ends found in desk drawers. Sarah was busy teaching at the acting school, finding a new renter for the loft, and traveling back and forth to Carleton for follow-up interviews for the job at the theater.

After three interviews, the theater said they wanted to hire her, but they couldn't give her a full time job until April.

"We're pretty much dead in the water right through the winter, but we'd sure like to have you on board when we get busy."

Sarah asked at the bookstore if they needed help, or if they had ideas about job possibilities. Sage closed the café for ten minutes and walked with Sarah next door to the bakery because the counter girl was planning to leave after the Christmas rush to have a baby. Edward, the baker, was a friend of Sage's and supplied all the baked goods for the café.

So, although Sarah had no experience, Edward said he would give her a try, "If you don't mind sweeping floors and cleaning pans. In fact," he added, "it would be really helpful if you could start tomorrow. That way Julia could show you the ropes before she leaves to have her baby."

"Can I let you know in an hour?"

"That would be fine."

Sarah walked back to Emily's. "Of course you can move in now," Emily said, "with or without the children."

Then Sarah called her mother.

"We'll be fine, dear," Joan said. "Will you be here for Christmas?"

"Yes, Edward said we'd be closed Christmas and New Year's."

"Well, that's good. So I'll finish packing up, and when you're here we'll figure out how to make the actual move. Do you want me to price moving vans?"

"No thanks, Mom. I think I'll ask around here. You're sure you're okay with this?"

"Absolutely. Do you want to talk with the kids?" Sarah explained her plans to the children, who seemed perfectly at peace with being left with their grandmother. Then she walked back to the bakery, and she and Edward shook on the deal.

Joan and the children were busy in the city, buying and making Christmas presents, finding and decorating the perfect Christmas tree, walking along Fifth Avenue to look at store windows, and stopping at Rockefeller Center to watch the men put up the largest Christmas tree they'd ever seen.

Sarah came home late Christmas Eve. The children were up and excited and proud as she told them how beautiful their tree was, especially with the hand-made decorations. They all went to St. Patrick's Cathedral for midnight Mass. Kari slept during Mass, but Sam said he liked the music. The day after Christmas, they packed everything into a rent-a-van, and Joan's car, and headed up to Carleton.

Joan liked the house immediately. It was filled with winter sunlight from its large windows. The children chose their rooms and left the largest one for Sarah. "You'll need room for Dad," Sam whispered to her in explanation. Emily and Paul greeted Joan, the children, and Bruce, warmly. Paul was shy, but he enjoyed showing the kids around the house and telling Sam about their neighbors. Emily insisted that Joan stay for supper, and for dessert they had a cake from Sarah's bakery that said, 'Welcome Home.'

After supper, Joan put Bruce back in his carrying case and took off, even though everyone asked her to stay. Sam even offered to sleep on the floor in Kari's room so she could have his bed. Joan was surprised by how eager she was to get away. She was glad that Sarah had found such a wonderful place — Emily seemed to really enjoy having them there — but, she felt not unwanted so much, as unneeded. So she and Bruce took off. They spent the night on the way home at a dreary motel. Joan wondered about her bad mood as she shifted channels on the television and then turned the light out.

It was very quiet back in Ipswich. Joan felt at loose ends. The weather was grey and cold. She spent most of her days at the animal shelter, but a high school student came in now most afternoons and seemed to have a way with the dogs, even those who might bite. He did most of the exercising while Joan was left with cleaning the cat boxes, sweeping the floors and doing some of the paper work. Joan knew that she should be happy that this boy was taking such an interest in the shelter, but instead she felt jealous and ashamed of the feeling. Her work there no longer seemed important. She was frightened by how lonely she felt. She thought that Sarah and the children were now in such a lovely place that they'd have no reason to come to Ipswich. She called Angelica, who was still at the Danvers State Hospital. Joan wondered how long she should go on paying Angelica's rent at the loft, but she didn't want to acknowledge, even to herself, that Angelica might never be able to get out.

Angelica seemed to sense Joan's worry, for she said, "Hey, Mother, you're talking to a professor of painting. They've got me teaching the young kids who land in here after overdosing on their drug of choice."

"Good for you, dearest." Joan had no idea whether to believe her or not. "Does that mean you'll be coming home soon?"

"No, you ridiculous woman, it means they're going to keep me here longer, now that I'm finally useful to them."

"Shall I come visit you?"

"No, mother, please don't."

"I don't see why…"

"I know you don't. How can I make it clearer? Please do not visit me. I may be teaching, but I'm still in the loony bin and a visit from you…well, there's no telling what might happen. Are you paying my rent?"

"Of course. Do you want me to air the loft out, wash the curtains and so forth?"

"No, mother, please do not visit the loft either. How the fuck do you have a key?"

"Well, your friend…"

"Listen, Mother, stay out of my loft. Stay away from Danvers. Just give me some room to breathe. Okay? Just for now, please give me some breathing room. Okay?"

"Okay, dear. Do you think I should talk to your doctor?"

"He's in Asia. Leave him alone. Hey, Mother, I'll tell you what you can do."

"What's that?"

"You can send me five Camel Hair paint brushes. Pick five different sizes. And don't get conned by anything other than Camel Hair, okay?"

"Yes, I'll do that." Joan realized she was grateful for the task. It made her feel a little less useless.

Chapter Thirty-Four

ON THE LAST day of February, Joan received a call from Angelica's friend, Jessica. "I'm sorry to disturb you, and I'm sure Angelica will be angry, but I don't know what else to do."

"What's the matter, Jessica? What's happened?"

"Well, I called Angie this morning. Sometimes she comes to the phone and sometimes she doesn't, but today they told me that she'd signed herself out last night. So I went to the loft. She's not there! She didn't answer when I knocked. I called and called. Finally, I went on in. I had taken her key with me. She wasn't there. It was really cold. I don't think she's been there. I don't know what to do, Mrs. Fitzpatrick. I know Angie will never forgive me for calling you. She made me promise that I wouldn't. But I just don't know what to do." Jessica began to sob.

Joan was silent. She was furious at the hospital for not calling her and she was cold with fear about Angelica. As far as she knew, Jessica was her only friend. Finally she pulled herself together to say, "Thank you, Jessica. Do you know if she has other friends she might be visiting?"

"Not that I know of. She would have said something if..."

"You're right," Joan interrupted her. "I'll call the hospital now. If you hear from her, please let me know right away." She hung up before Jessica could respond.

Without stopping to let herself imagine where Angelica could be, Joan called the hospital. Because the receptionist was on the other line, a volunteer forwarded Joan's call to the nursing station on Angelica's floor. Gisela answered. Angelica had told Joan about Gisela. She was a heavy-set nurse in her sixties, completely relaxed around the patients, able to laugh with them, tease them and console them better than anyone else on the floor, including the doctors. When Joan asked what had happened, Gisela told her. "Last week, Angelica announced that she had tried to kill herself. I wasn't on duty so I don't know exactly what happened, but I was told that she managed to break the window with a piece of pipe that she detached from her bed. Then she told the resident that she had swallowed shards of glass. He didn't believe her, but he had her moved to the fifth floor."

Joan knew about the fifth floor. Angelica had been there briefly before and had told her about it. Some patients sat on the floor and rocked back and forth, humming to themselves, for hours on end. Some patients lay on the floor of their rooms with a mummy suit tied in the back so they couldn't move their arms or legs. Many of the patients were eerily silent; others never stopped moaning.

Most of the nurses on the fifth floor were strong men, although they were as gentle as possible with the patients. "You might have to go to the fifth floor," was often all a doctor needed to say to calm a patient on another floor who was having hysterics.

"While she was up there," Gisela continued, "Angelica acted like Florence Nightingale, helping the patients who could talk by listening to their stories, and flirting with the cleaning man until he began whistling while he mopped the floor.

"She was sent back to the third floor in three days, and I can't tell you how glad I was.

"Then last night, she ups and tells me she's very grateful for all our help but she'll be leaving now, and would I please arrange for the papers to be filled out. I asked her where she was going to go, and she said Boston. 'I have lots of friends there,' she said. Then the resident came, and after a talk in his office, she left, taking nothing. In fact before the resident got here, Angelica went from room to room giving her belongings away."

"Why didn't the resident call me? How could he let her go like that? Why didn't you call me?"

"I'm so sorry, dear. I assumed the resident had discussed it with you."

"Gisela, what should I do?"

"You could notify the police that she's missing. You could also call the other hospitals to see if she signed herself in somewhere else. And you could call the shelters. If none of that works, then I would let it rest, dear, I really would. She's in God's hands. You know that."

"You're right, Gisela. I know you're right. Thank you."

"I'll keep you both in my prayers, you hear?"

"Thank you."

"God bless."

Joan lit a cigarette. She kept a pack of them in the back of her desk drawer for emergencies. She puffed on it wildly and breathed in deeply creating a crescendo of coughing. Then she poured herself a glass of cooking sherry and called Sarah.

"Oh, Mom, I'm so sorry. What can I do to help?"

"You can get your butt up here fast!" was what she wanted to say. Instead, she said, "Is there any chance that you and the children could come for the weekend? I can't leave here in case she calls, but I would very much appreciate your company while I wait for the phone to ring. I'll make the calls Gisela suggested and if I find out anything tonight, I'll let you know. Otherwise, think about coming here."

"The trouble is, my new job and Sam has… Oh hell, of course we'll come. We'll leave tonight. Edward will understand. I'll give Paul a note to take to the kids' teachers tomorrow."

By the time they arrived, the kids were fast asleep. Sarah and Joan carried them into their room and tucked them in.

Then they went into the kitchen and closed the door.

"Who have you called?" Sarah asked.

"Nobody." Joan answered. "I just couldn't, except Angelica's friend Jessica. I called her a few times tonight but she has no news. I've been wracking my brains for other names, but I can't think of any. Do you know any of her friends?"

"I don't think she had friends besides Jessica. I'm going to call the police."

"Are you sure? What if she's visiting someone?"

"She should've told the hospital where she'd be. I'm going to call them. You can blame me if she gets mad."

Joan sat back, breathing deeply, grateful for her daughter's self-assurance. She heard Sarah describing Angelica on the phone, "She's thirty-two, tall, thin, long dirty-blond hair, turning grey. She usually wears it in braids. No, I don't know what she was wearing when she left the hospital, but usually she wears jeans and high heels with no stockings. My mother's phone number is… Yes, that's right. Thank you, that would be helpful." Then there was silence as Sarah wrote things on a piece of paper, and finally Sarah said, "Yes I'll do that. Thank you," and she hung up.

"They put her right on the missing persons list because she signed herself out of a hospital. They gave me some phone numbers for local hospitals and homeless shelters. I'll call them Mom. Why don't you go to bed? I'll come in if I find out anything."

"Will you wake me up?"

"Of course, if I hear anything, I'll wake you up."

Feeling both annoyed and relieved, like a tired child being sent early to bed, Joan said, "Thank you, dear. I think I will." As she passed a bookshelf in the living room, she pulled out "Sense and Sensibility" to be her companion for the night.

Chapter Thirty-Five

JOAN WAS GETTING dressed when the phone rang the next morning. The children were still asleep, but Sarah was in the kitchen and Joan heard her pick up and say, "Yes this is Sarah Wilson." Joan slipped into her shoes and almost ran into the kitchen. Sarah stared at her but said nothing, either to her or into the phone. Time passed as the two women stood staring at each other. Finally, Sarah said into the phone, "Yes, I'll come. Where is it? I mean where do I come?" Then she wrote something down and finally said, "Thank you," and put down the receiver.

Sarah was white and didn't speak. Joan began to tremble and carefully sat down. Still there was silence.

Finally Joan whispered, "Is she, is she dead?"

Sarah looked at her mother as the tears flowed down her cheeks.

"They think so. I mean, they think the person they've found is Angie. She was in a doorway in downtown Boston. There was an empty pill bottle beside her. The police took her to the ER, but she was pronounced dead on arrival. They want me to come down to the morgue to identify her. If it is her. Of course, it may not be."

Then Sarah drew her chair next to Joan's and they held hands for a while and said nothing at all. Joan was crying so hard she couldn't see Sarah, despite how close she was, just sheets and sheets of tears in front of her eyes. She remembered when she was a kid and had followed a friend into a cave behind a waterfall. It was a magical place. The rocks behind her and the rushing water in front and all the sunlit world seen as shimmer through the rushing water. For a few minutes she was in that place again.

After a while, Joan heard Sarah's voice, "Let's drive to Boston together; you can take the children somewhere and I'll go to the police. If it is Angie, we'll tell the children then."

Her words made Joan's tears dry up. She heard herself say, "I think I'll go alone, dear. I'll take the train. In fact, I think I'll go now before the children get up."

"But Mom…"

"Where am I to go?"

"Are you sure?"

"Yes, dear, I am. Where should I go?"

"Here, it's a police station." She handed Joan the paper.

"Thank you. I'll call you from there, and if it is her, I'd be grateful if you'd tell the children before I get back."

"But…"

"Listen, dearest, you'll have to trust me. I know my way around Boston much better than you do. I need to do this and I need to do it alone. I will call you as soon as I know anything. And I'll call you again from Back Bay so you'll know what time my train gets in."

"I love you, Mom"

"And I love you, and I am so grateful you came out here to go through this with me."

"That's why…"

"Part of going through this with me will be for you to be here when I come home. I need to do this alone. But it is a thousand times easier, knowing that you, Kari and Sam will be here for me when I get home." Joan reached into the closet for her coat and pocket book. She then grabbed her keys and fled without looking back at Sarah's tear-stained face.

At the police station, she was met by a woman police officer who led her to the morgue. "Do you want me to go in with you?"

"Yes, if you would." Joan said, realizing she was a little dizzy.

"Please take my arm," the police woman said. "We won't stay there any longer than you want to."

Joan saw immediately that there was no question. Angelica's hair was spread over her shoulders. Her face was beautiful, at peace, at rest. Everything about her was beautiful in its peace and harmony after so much pain and anguish. Joan stepped away from the police officer and asked her, "Could I have a chair please?"

"Of course. I'll be right back."

Joan pulled the chair close to Angelica. After the officer had slipped out again, Joan took Angelica's hand. It was stiff as well as cold, but she held on. She could feel Angelica raining blessings down on her. She wished for a minute that she had let Sarah come so she could experience the blessings too. "No need to pray," she told herself. "Just sit here with her."

Angelica was out of harm's way. Nothing could hurt her now. She'd been struggling for so long against an insidious illness, but now she was free. Joan thought of Charlie. "She will comfort him now, and he her." Joan sat very still.

"All is well. All is well." The air seemed filled with that proclamation. Joan sat on, crying with gladness, sadness, it didn't matter which.

When she heard a knock at the door, Joan let go of Angelica's hand slowly, reluctantly, "Come in."

"Mrs. Fitzpatrick, the sergeant said you might not realize how cold it is in here. You may want to come out and rest awhile and warm up. He also has some questions for you if you feel ready to talk with him. Shall I tell him you're ready?"

"Yes," Joan said still staring at Angelica. "I'm ready." As the door closed again, she said aloud to Angelica, "I feel we're both ready now. Ready for anything."

Chapter Thirty-Six

JOAN WAS GRATEFUL that Father Sullivan of St. Mary's in Ipswich never questioned how Angelica had died. He would be pleased to do the Funeral Mass, he said, although he had never set eyes on Angelica.

"Would you like to choose some hymns? Were there some she was especially fond of? How about the Psalm?"

As Joan told him her own favorites, she thought, "I hope these will please you. Perhaps we'll be closer now?" And she heard Angelica answer, "Especially if you stop trying to please me."

Emily and Paul drove to Ipswich for the funeral and then Emily took the three children back to Carleton so Sarah could stay on with Joan for a few days. But they weren't much help to each other. They found themselves repeating again and again. "You were wonderful to her. You did everything possible. Nothing that happened was your fault." They couldn't stop saying it, and it was almost a relief to Joan when Sarah left two days later.

But being alone was difficult as well. Sometimes, as Joan walked up to the big house, in spite of the exercise and the fresh air, she was overtaken by a tidal wave of pain and guilt that would make her stop in her tracks and gasp for air. It seemed to happen whenever she became conscious of enjoying herself—reading the New York Times, taking a walk, luxuriating in a hot bath. It was like being tumbled over and over by a wave coming hard against the shore. For a while she called Sarah three or four times a day, just to hear her voice and or talk with the children.

Sometimes she walked up the drive to the big house at night, despite the dark and the cold. Angelica used to say, "February is my favorite month, all bleak and cold with no Christmas tinsel to redeem it." All sorts of memories flooded in at odd moments: Angelica as a sunny toddler, running toward her father's outstretched arms; Angelica teaching Sarah how to walk by walking backwards herself and urging Sarah to catch up with her; Angelica comforting Sarah when their father died.

There was no forgiveness in the night sky with its stars and moon floating in and out of view as she passed under the trees. "There is no forgiveness for such a failure," Joan said aloud into the cold night air. "Especially," she thought before she could stop herself, "because besides the guilt and pain there is, for seconds at least—relief."

March showed no signs of spring. It was grey and over-cast and cold. Joan continued working at the shelter because she couldn't imagine how she would get through her days if she didn't have a place to go to. She spent her evenings with Bruce on her lap, reading Jane Austen, Charles Dickens—books she knew almost by heart. She wanted no surprises.

By the end of March, Joan wondered if she had sunk into a depression too deep to climb out of without help. So, she called Sarah and asked if it would be okay if she came and visited for a few days.

"Of course, Mom. You know you're always welcome, always. But if you come this weekend or for the next week, really, it would mean sleeping on the sofa."

"Why on the sofa? I thought you said you had a cot that you could put in Kari's room for me."

"Yes, but right now some friends of Emily's mother are staying with us. I moved Sam in with Kari and gave them Sam's room."

"Who are they?" Joan persevered, trying not to sound desperate.

"Well, they're a couple from New Mexico. Their son was killed in Nicaragua."

"Oh, how awful!" Joan dutifully responded, though she couldn't see why their losing a son in far-away Nicaragua should mean that she couldn't sleep with her own grand-daughter.

"Yes," Sarah went on, "the Contras killed him. He was helping to build something in a village. For that, the Contras killed him. The Contras, Mom, paid for by our taxes. It's outrageous!"

"It sounds awful. I'm so sorry. But, how come his parents are at your house?"

"Their son's death has fired them up and they're speaking all over the country about what's happening in Nicaragua. Their last talk was in Boston and now they're going to New York, but I think they won't try to stay there. Some people get very angry at them, saying that they are supporting the Communists. Anyway, they feel comfortable and safe here, so we said we'd drive them down for their talk and they could stay here until they're ready to move on. Emily's mother was a friend of Melinda's and she suggested they look us up. I think you'd like them."

"Oh dear," Joan finally acknowledged the truth, "Perhaps it's a bad time for me to come. I don't know if I'm ready…"

"Please come. These people are also grieving. I really think you'll like them, and I know they'll like you. And I could use your help. I'm not used to cooking for so many, and Emily is 'in the thralls of a painting' as she puts it, working day and night. We hardly ever see her. There's no one like you for making guests feel happy and well fed. Please say you'll come."

After a moment, Joan decided to pretend to believe her, "Of course, if I can be helpful, I'd love to come."

"Great. You'll make things much easier. I'm sorry I didn't call you earlier. I just didn't know how you'd feel about seeing other people so soon and sleeping on the couch. Oh, gotta go, someone's at the door. I love you. See you tomorrow," and she hung up.

Joan took Bruce with her. Sam and Kari loved to play with him and he would keep her company on the sofa. She arrived the next afternoon, bringing two apple pies and a pan of brownies that she'd baked early that morning. When she got there, Sarah and the Lancasters were sitting around the big kitchen table drinking tea, and Joan was glad she could immediately share her brownies. The children rushed into the kitchen when they heard her voice. Kari climbed up onto Joan's lap; Sam let Bruce out of his carrier; and then he and Paul stood on either side of her chair, munching brownies. Joan sighed with relief at being with them again and drank some tea.

Melinda and John Lancaster talked about their son, Bill. He had been part of a team sent down by his church to build a school and a health clinic in a village in Nicaragua. He had been killed by the Contras, with arms given to them by the American government.

That evening Melinda offered to help Joan make supper. Joan's response was quick—after all she had come down to help, "Oh no, I'm happy to do it; I don't need…"

But Melinda interrupted her, "Please let me. Being away from home can be disorienting, especially trying to give these talks about Bill. If I don't keep my feet on the ground with what I'm used to doing, I feel I could go off the deep end." Her eyes filled with tears.

"I know exactly what you mean," Joan said. "If you'll make the salad, I'll get started on the soup." And as they washed and chopped and stirred, Joan told Melinda about Angelica.

"Let's sit down a minute," Melinda said. "I think we need a glass of sherry. We brought some with us." She poured them each a glass. When their glasses were empty, Melinda took both of Joan's hands in her own. Joan began to cry and then she saw that Melinda was crying as well. After a bit, they smiled at each other through their tears, and Melinda got up to bring back a couple of napkins to dry their eyes.

By the time Paul and Sam were sent into the kitchen to get plates and silverware to set the table, Joan and Melinda were laughing over their third glass of sherry.

Chapter Thirty-Seven

BEFORE DAWN ON Sunday morning, Joan drove John and Melinda into New York City so that they could give a talk at St. Mark's Church on the Bowery. The congregation turned out to be a mix of the homeless seeking shelter, middle-aged men and women in business suits, and young hippies in torn jeans, some of them carrying babies in colorful home-made knapsacks.

At Communion, everyone made a big circle around the altar where a loaf of bread was passed around and each person tore off a small chunk. After the service, there was a discussion group in the common room, where coffee and doughnuts were served. That was where John and Melinda gave their presentation. They showed large photographs of the village in Nicaragua where Bill had been working, as well as photographs of the small healthcare clinic he had helped to build. The clinic had a long line of mothers and children waiting in front of it. There were also pictures of

Bill and other volunteers building a school with lots of children in front smiling at the photographer.

John and Melinda took turns talking about Nicaragua and the revolution that had overthrown a dictator. They talked about how educated people, mostly from the cities, had gone out to the countryside to teach the farmers how to read and write, and how groups of volunteers were building schools and healthcare clinics in the villages, as well as getting electricity and water to people's houses. Then they told how the American government had declared the new Nicaraguan government "Communist" and was sending weapons and money to help the Contras overthrow and destroy everything the people had achieved.

"They say our son was a Communist, that it was his own fault that he was killed. 'He shouldn't have been there in the first place.' That's what they say." Melinda's voice was loud and clear, although her eyes were filled with tears.

"We want you to know what is actually happening there," John said. "We believe that if enough people know the truth, we can stop our government from invading Nicaragua." Joan stared at the photographs as they were passed around: small cement-block houses along dirt streets; laughing children; proud mothers holding their babies. In some strange way, the village and its people looked like home to her.

As Joan drove them back to Sarah's, Melinda sat beside her. John was dozing in the back seat. After they were out of the city and Joan could relax a bit, she asked Melinda, "Have you ever been there?"

"Yes." Melinda said, "We went to the funeral. Two volunteers from Spain were also killed in the explosion. Daniel Ortega was there and gave a short speech. The whole village was out in the street—we paraded with the three coffins around the village and then to the graveyard. I knew Bill would want to be buried there rather than be brought home. People were so kind, Joan. All sorts of people came up to us and kissed us, some of them weeping. I had no idea what they were saying, but they were weeping with us. And the children, Joan—the children were so thin, and all in rags. I hope to go back there some day. But I'm not ready yet."

As she lay in bed that night, Joan remembered Melinda's words, "Some day I hope to go back, but I'm not ready yet." Then she thought, "Maybe I should go. Maybe I could be helpful there? I could cook. I could knit sweaters for the children. What am I doing here? Sarah's managing so well. Angelica has made her peace... Maybe I should go to Nicaragua."

The next morning she offered to drive her new friends to the airport for their flight to Chicago.

"Oh, Joan, that's very nice of you," Melinda said quickly, "But we have plenty of time. We're planning to take the train into the city and then the bus to the airport. You don't have to worry about us."

"We can't thank you enough, all of you," John added. "You've made this part of our journey very enjoyable indeed." Melinda became a little teary and John patted her arm.

"Actually, I'd like to drive you; that way you won't have to carry your luggage," Joan persisted. "If you're willing, I'd like to ask you more questions about Nicaragua. Of course, I won't if it's too painful."

"No, Joan, it's never too painful to talk about Bill or Nicaragua," Melinda said. "It's our way of... Well it's our way. We'd be very grateful for your ride and glad to answer any questions."

"Good," Joan said, feeling rather excited.

The drive took about four hours, because Joan got distracted by the conversation and took a wrong turn. After that, John drove, and Joan concentrated on asking Melinda questions about Nicaragua—"What were the cities like? Who did you stay with? How did you get from the airport to the village where Bill died? What was the food like? Did anyone there speak English?" Melinda answered the best she could, and every answer led to another question. When they arrived at the airport, Joan admitted, "I really put you through it. And I thank you. And thank you for driving," she added, turning toward John.

John smiled warmly as he responded, "Whatever your plans are, we're right behind you."

"Yes, please keep in touch," Melinda added.

From the airport, Joan drove downtown to the Lower East Side and the school where she had taught before Sam was born. She asked the receptionist if Robert Golightly would be free to see her. He was now the principal of the school, but for many years he had worked in Columbia, setting up schools for the street children. Just as the receptionist said she wasn't sure, Robert himself appeared, coming down the stairs. As she watched him descend, he said, "Joan, dear, how lovely to see you. I meant to write you. I was so sorry to hear… I am so sorry."

"Thank you. You were very kind and helpful to me during some of those bad patches. I don't think there's anything more I could have done. It seems it was a disease, like any other, and the fact that she couldn't conquer it was nobody's fault."

"Of course you're right. Of course you are," he said as he shook her hand. Then he looked at her closely and went on. "Could I take you to lunch? I'm half-starved. If you've had lunch, could you come have a drink with me while I eat, so we can talk?"

"Thank you, I'd love to have lunch with you."

"Terrific." He turned to the receptionist. "I'll be back in an hour, Susie. Thanks." As they left the building and went down the brownstone stairs, he said, "Do you like Italian? There's a good place near here. It's in a basement, and doesn't look like anything, but the food is terrific. That sound okay?"

"It sounds wonderful," Joan said and then felt surprise, because it did. She couldn't remember anything sounding or seeming wonderful since Angelica's death, but, in fact, this did. "I love Italian," she added.

Over spaghetti with clam sauce, she told Robert about Bill and his parents and her desire to go to Nicaragua.

"I know just the thing for you," he responded eagerly. "You could go with Witness for Peace."

"What's that?" she asked, feeling both foolish and excited.

"It's an organization that is trying to stop our invasion of Nicaragua. They're doing it by taking trips there with delegations, who, when they come back here, tell everyone in their local churches and schools about the situation in Nicaragua. The idea is that if enough people know the truth about what's going on there, we won't let our government invade."

"I think I could do that," Joan said musingly. "Would you invite me to talk at the school?"

"Of course I would. Do you know Spanish?" Robert asked after a short pause. When she shook her head, he continued a little soberly, "That's a difficulty. Anything you found out would be hearsay. You'd have to trust interpreters who might have an agenda of their own. I think the best thing would be to study Spanish for a few months, and then go in the fall."

"I don't know," Joan demurred. "I live out in the sticks. I'm not sure I could find classes in Spanish."

"I can lend you the books I learned from. They're written specially for community organizers; they give you the vocabulary you need for interviewing, for finding your way around, and for asking the way to the nearest clinic if someone gets into difficulty. And I'll give you the address for Witness for Peace in Boston. I have a friend there, so be sure to use my name."

Joan felt both excited and a little frightened as they walked back to the school together so that he could get the books out of his office closet for her. That afternoon, she drove back to Sarah's to pick up Bruce and then, even though it was late, she kept going to Ipswich. She didn't want to hang around with the family, because she had the feeling that if she blurted out her plans, Sarah and Emily might try to talk her out of it. As she and Bruce drove back to Ipswich, Joan told him about her new schedule: get up at 6:00 and study Spanish for an hour before breakfast; then for two more hours, from 7:00 to 9:00 every evening. She figured that three hours a day should be sufficient. "By then, I'll have memorized the books Robert gave me," she told Bruce, who was asleep in his box on the floor beside her. As she drove on, she sang to him all the songs she used to sing with the girls, until she could almost hear Angelica singing with her, which brought on tears. She had to pull off to the side of the road and wait for the tears to run their course, before she could drive again.

Chapter Thirty-Eight

THE NEXT MORNING, Joan got up early and writing out the verb "to be" in Spanish on an index card, she recited it, over and over, as she walked to the big house and back. That evening, after coming home from the animal shelter, she spread her books out on the kitchen table and read aloud to Bruce, the days of the week, the months of the year, and the numbers from one to twenty.

At the beginning of May, when the beauty of the spring made her feel ready for any adventure, Joan went to Boston to the offices of Witness for Peace. They told her that there was an opening in a delegation leaving for Nicaragua after Labor Day. They asked about her knowledge of Spanish. "It's getting better and better," she replied quickly. "I hope by then I'll be almost fluent."

"That's wonderful!" one of the ladies responded. "You're just the kind of person we need, experienced in life,

but at the same time adventurous, and most especially—
bilingual." On the train back to Ipswich with one of her
Spanish textbooks on her lap, Joan wondered if she had lied.
How could she know if she were fluent when she had no
one to talk with? She vowed she would work harder, taking
her textbook to the shelter and studying during her lunch
break.

One night, towards the end of May, Sarah surprised Joan
by asking if she wanted to come down to Carleton for a
party. "It's a going away party for Emily. She's going to
Florence. She got a grant to study there."

"What about Paul?"

"Paul's going to stay with us."

"With you? How long will Emily be gone?"

"The grant is for three months. But she's hoping to be
able to teach there and stay on longer."

"I don't understand; what about Paul?"

"Mom, this is something Emily's wanted to do for years
and years. This was the third time she applied for the grant.
Paul has been given a choice between joining his grandparents in South Carolina, or staying here with us. He wants to
stay here, which I'm glad about. He's wonderful with Kari
and a great playmate for Sam. They're already a lot like siblings."

"How will you manage economically?"

"Oh, that's been taken care of. Emily's parents are
sending money for Paul's upkeep. Actually they're sending
more than I'll need, so it will be a help all around. So, can
you come a few days early and help me organize the party?

And please bring Bruce—talk about being one of the family."

"I'd love to come. But, how can Emily leave Paul for so long? I don't understand. He's only nine. Anyway, I'm happy to help out. Give my love to everyone, including Emily of course."

"I will, Mom. It will be lovely to see you."

The afternoon before the party, Sam and Paul helped Joan make batches of brownies for the next day. There was a Star Wars movie playing in town and Joan said she'd be happy to stay home with Kari, if the others wanted to go. To her surprise, Paul announced, "I think I'll stay home and help Gran put Kari to bed. I know the songs she likes."

Joan was about to protest that she and Kari would do just fine on their own. She wasn't sure she liked being called Gran by Paul. But the thought of Paul's mother deserting him in a few days made her say, "That would be lovely, Paul."

He gave her a grateful smile, and the others went off.

It turned out that Paul was making a surprise going away present for his mother. Sarah had given him the money to buy a picture album. He was filling it with old photographs of his mother and his grandparents, and himself as a baby, and also recent drawings that he'd made.

After Kari was asleep, Joan sat with Paul in the kitchen drinking a cup of tea while he worked on the album. "How will it be for you," she asked, "to have your mom so far away?" She wondered if anyone else had asked him.

"It'll be okay, I guess. Can Bruce sleep on my bed?"

"Sure," Joan said.

"Should I put this one in?" He pointed to a picture of himself as a baby in Emily's arms on the edge of an ocean.

"Yes, it's beautiful. She'll definitely want that one."

"Uh oh, I hear them. Don't let them come up for a few minutes, okay?"

"Okay."

He quickly gathered everything and rushed upstairs.

Emily focused her going away party on Paul by having his favorite foods: hot dogs cooked on the grill and baked macaroni and cheese. She invited his friends from the neighborhood and Margo, who had been his favorite babysitter before Sarah moved in. She also invited Margo's parents, Sage and Richard, who had sold one of her paintings in the bookstore café. She was wary of inviting other adult friends who might question her decision to leave her son for such a long time.

She was very grateful that Paul hadn't made a fuss. "I know I'm asking a lot," she'd said to Sarah. "I'm asking him to be remarkably brave about my going, and I'm asking you to take care of him."

"I think we'll be okay," Sarah had answered. "The kids get on so well."

"Oh, absolutely! They're like siblings. Otherwise I'd never have asked you to take him on." After a pause Emily continued, "You don't mind, really truly, do you? You know you can always send him to my parents if things become too difficult."

"But he said he didn't want to go to South Carolina. Wouldn't you rather come back if things become too difficult?"

"No. I can't explain it, but I need to do this, not only to paint better, but to be a better person. I need some space around me where I can stretch out in new ways. Otherwise, I'm not sure what will become of me. I promise I'll do the same for you when I get back. I can't tell you how grateful I am."

"Don't worry about it. Paul is wonderful. I think we'll all be fine."

The late afternoon was warm, and everyone was happy to be outside. Richard took charge of grilling the hotdogs. He wore one of Emily's painting aprons and Sage worried that the paint splotches on it might catch fire. Paul carefully carried paper plates of hot-dogs and macaroni and cheese to his guests, who were gathered around the grill. Sam followed him with a pan of sauerkraut in one hand and a bottle of mustard in the other.

Everyone knew that this was Paul's party. Margo had even brought Paul a present. It was a kitten that she had found on the edge of the road, starving with one paw crushed. She had nursed it back to health and brought it to Paul in her bike basket. He looked first at his mother and then at Sarah to ask "May I keep it?" His mother looked at Sarah who said, "Of course."

After the party, the children biked, scootered, and roller-skated to their respective homes. Sage and Richard gave Emily big hugs and then walked home holding hands. Margo biked home ahead of them.

Paul and Sam took the kitten into the kitchen to get milk, and then they made a litter box from a shoe box and some dirt from the empty lot across the street. They decided to call the kitten Puddle, because she had the coloring of a puddle after the rain. Then they introduced Puddle to Bruce who immediately set about washing her from head to toe. After that, Puddle followed Bruce to a low easy chair and they curled up together and went to sleep. Kari and Joan sprawled on the living room sofa as Joan read aloud from Winnie the Pooh. Sarah and Emily did the dishes in the kitchen, singing songs from the Beatles.

Monday morning, Sarah and Paul waved goodbye to Emily at Hartford International Airport. Joan was home with Kari, and Sam was in school. On the drive home, with Paul in the front passenger seat, Sarah could see that his face was white and his hands were clenched in his lap. She asked him if he wanted to be dropped off at school or if he wanted to go home. "School, I guess," he answered listlessly. They didn't talk after that. Sarah knew he was trying not to cry, so she let him be.

Late that evening Sarah came into Joan's bedroom. Joan was reading a Spanish text book. Sarah sat down on the edge of the bed and said, "Mom, do you think you could stay on a little longer? I'm concerned about Paul. If you could stay on, just a bit, until we get into a rhythm, it would be a great help."

"If you think it would be a help, of course I'll stay." Joan felt the familiar relief of being needed, but this time she also felt a little impatient. She hoped this wasn't going slow down her Spanish studies. "I'd love to," she added, hoping to convince them both.

Chapter Thirty-Nine

JOAN WAS STILL there when school got out in June. She was concerned about Sarah, who seemed very lonely. Joan realized, to her chagrin, how much more fun Sarah had with Emily than she could have with her mother. Joan also worried about Paul. At times, he seemed bewildered, as though he didn't belong in his own house; other times, he seemed to feel that Sarah and her children were intruders holding him hostage. But when his mother's letters started coming, describing her adventures, and also commenting on things that Sarah had written to her about him, Paul began to relax and to enjoy school again, especially his art classes with Sage. Sage took her students to a hill behind the school from where they could look down on the campus. They made quick sketches and then went back to school to paint the scenes. Paul's paintings were much praised by Sage, and then by Joan and Sarah when he brought them home. One day he asked Joan, "Do you think I'm good at painting because of my mother?"

"I don't know," she said, "but it's possible. Perhaps you learned by watching her paint and living with her paintings." Paul began to make sketches — of his room, the swing seat on the porch, even a rather difficult one of Sarah cooking supper. He sent these to his mother.

Emily's letters were filled with enthusiasm for these gifts. "It's as though your wonderful paintings, which I have put up on all four of my walls, are hugging me with their beauty and with your courage and goodness. You're my hero!"

Back in February, Sarah had decided that she could combine her baking job with acting in summer stock. She'd auditioned at The Globe and won parts in two of their summer productions. At that time, she'd been counting on Emily to take care of the kids in the evenings. Now, with Emily gone, Sarah realized that she was really stuck. She couldn't leave the kids alone at night. "The thing is, Mom," she said late one night, "I signed a contract. They're counting on me. The shows are fully cast. I simply can't back out now. I don't know what to do!" This last had been said with a bit of a wail. Sarah sounded to Joan as she had as a ten-year-old begging her mother to let her stay home from school because she hadn't done her homework.

"Well, dear," Joan said, after a moment's pause, "I think when they get out of school, I should take the children back to Ipswich with me."

"Oh, would you? That would be wonderful. They love it up there. But, of course," she added, "I wouldn't be able to help you. I couldn't come up on weekends." After a pause Sarah went on, "Maybe you should just stay here? We're getting on pretty well aren't we? Maybe you could live here with us for the summer."

Joan had been missing the beach, her walks up to the big house, the horses in the nearby field. "If it's possible," she said wistfully, "I'd much rather be back in Ipswich. The children love the beach, and so do I," she added with a slight emphasis.

"Let's let the children make the decision." Sarah said, ignoring the emphasis. "I think I might be lonely if you all go."

"Ok," Joan answered unhappily. After all, she told herself, it would be no fun having the children with her in Ipswich if they really preferred staying in Carleton.

The next afternoon, Sarah explained to the children how she was going to be in two plays that summer, and so would be rehearsing and acting most afternoons and evenings. She said that Gran had offered to stay in Carleton with them, but that she had also offered to take the children with her to Ipswich. Paul was very quiet, not sure whether he was included in the invitation. Joan saw this and was about to say something, when Sam turned to Paul and exclaimed, "You'll love it there. The beach is huge and the waves are big enough to dive through. I'll teach you how. And Gran likes to paint at the beach, so you can too. When can we go Mom, the day after school?"

"What about you, Kari?" Sarah asked.

"Can we bring Puddle?"

"Of course," Joan said, with a sigh of relief.

And so it was decided.

The summer turned out well. It was Kari who followed her grandmother's example and did crayon drawings of the waves and the sand dunes and the brightly colored bathing suits of the waders on the edge of the water. Paul sometimes joined in—using the pastels his mother had sent him from Florence to create large abstractions on newsprint that Joan bought for the purpose. But often Paul joined Sam in a game of keep-away with some boys down the beach. Joan painted and studied Spanish at the beach.

In the evenings she cooked simple meals, and the boys washed and dried the dishes while she put Kari to bed. Then she and the boys played Scrabble or she read aloud to them until their bedtime.

Sarah came to Ipswich toward the end of August. Her plays were over and she was eager to bring the children and Puddle back to Carleton. "Why don't we take Bruce with us also, since you're leaving from Boston. That way you won't have to make a special trip to drop him off."

Joan watched them go. She would miss them all hugely. But now, she told herself, she would study Spanish non-stop until her Labor Day departure.

Chapter Forty

MANAGUA WAS A surprise, both good and bad. Joan was delighted by the strange new spiky-shaped plants, especially the palm trees. The sun was blinding hot and she was grateful for the splotches of shadow the palm trees made. The streets were dirty and the grimy buildings were mostly one-story cinder-block shacks. Many of them had little stores in the front selling Pepsi, that the vendor poured into a plastic bag and poked a straw into, or slices of cut melon and papaya that Joan was warned to be wary of because of the flies that settled on them.

Maria, the local representative of Witness for Peace, met them at the airport. She was young, perhaps seventeen or eighteen, and very pregnant. She wore a tight red dress that pulled at her belly so that the front of the dress was somewhat higher than the back. She held a hand printed Witness for Peace sign, and eight men and women, most of them grey-haired, obediently came to stand beside and behind her as they got off the plane. She then shepherded this elderly flock out into the street and pointed to five teenage boys wearing torn shorts and dirty T-shirts. When the boys saw the tourists, they stood up and pulled handfuls of money out of their pockets, flipping through them as though they were playing cards. They called out something to the tourists. Joan stepped back, and felt automatically for the small but bulky pack she wore round her waist that held her money, passport and return ticket. She wore a man's shirt, borrowed from Sarah that came down over her hips in order to hide her pack. Maria gestured toward the boys and said authoritatively to her flock, "Give dollars; take pesetas." Joan stared at her, incredulous that one could expect anything from these boys besides robbery. Then she saw, one by one, the docile elderly delegates go up to a boy and hand him money and be given some in return.

"Can't we change money in the airport?" Joan asked.

"No, give dollars; take pesetas," Maria reiterated.

Joan finally imitated the others and handed a young man $50; he quickly counted out loud as he handed her pesetas of various colors. She thought she knew the numbers in Spanish, but realized she was never going to keep up with his counting and really she had no choice but to trust him.

Later that day, she counted it all out and marveled at the fact that the boy had given her exactly the exchange he had quoted.

When they all had some local money in their pockets, Maria announced, "One night in hotel. Come." Her flock followed her across a few streets and into a one-story building, a little larger than most of the others. At the desk, Maria introduced them to the thin grey-haired man who wore a dark suit, shiny with wear, and a black tie. He smiled at them and said, "You are welcome here." Then he handed Maria a piece of paper that he'd pulled from a drawer in the desk. Maria looked at it for a minute and then laid it on the counter. "List of beds," she said. "Find room number."

When it was Joan's turn to look for her name on the list, she saw she had been given two roommates. She sent up a quick prayer that she wouldn't have to share a bed with one of them.

The hotel had little rooms, each with two or three cots, surrounding a swimming pool. One of Joan's roommates was already there. She had her back to Joan and, facing the suitcase that was open on one of the beds, she seemed to be counting something. "Hello," Joan said from the doorway. She didn't want to surprise her roommate if she was doing something personal.

The woman straightened her back and turned around. She was tall and thin. Her short brown hair framed a gaunt and lined face that became almost beautiful when she smiled at Joan. "Hi, are you Lorna?"

"No, I'm Joan," she admitted, feeling that she had somehow failed a test.

"Oh, I'm sorry. I was just guessing. I'm Barbara. I'm so glad to meet you. I don't remember seeing you on the plane. I was sitting near the back, which turned out to be a good thing because one of my seatmates felt faint at take-off—I'm a doctor, you see. She was afraid she might be having a heart attack, but it was just anxiety. Anyway, I'm very happy to meet you." She gave Joan a strong handshake, almost pulling her into the room. "I'm looking over the medicines I brought. I just realized that I wasn't careful enough to check expiration dates on the things people donated. I heard about the free clinics established since the revolution and I figured they could use some supplies. I'm really interested in dengue fever. Have you heard there's almost an epidemic here?"

"No," Joan answered, trying not to become frightened. "What's dengue fever?"

"Well, it's spread by mosquitoes just like this critter," Barbara replied as she slapped a mosquito on her thigh. "It can be pretty awful—high fever, nausea, the inability to eat. A lot of people die of it, especially here where they don't have enough antibiotics."

"Do antibiotics take care of it?"

"Usually, if it's caught in time. But since they don't have enough antibiotics here, they're trying to find an alternative medicine. So far it's not working out, but it's still interesting."

Joan didn't know what to say to Barbara, but she told herself, that if she had any signs of the fever, she would fly home immediately. She was sure there were plenty of antibiotics in Boston. Then their third roommate came in. She looked to be in her eighties and somewhat frail, but she had bright eyes, high coloring and quick smile.

"How nice that this room is so large! We'll be fine indeed here. My name is Lorna. I'm so happy to meet you both. This is all very lovely. My son gave me this trip. He's a travel escort. Right now he lives in China. I always visit him wherever he's living, but I've already been to China twice, so he gave me this trip as a present for my eighty-fifth birthday.

Won't it be exciting to find out what's really happening here? I'm very interested in how this government works. I want to compare it to China and Russia. I've been studying Spanish with tapes for about six months, a present from my neighbor, who would have liked to come with us, but she's ninety and didn't feel quite up to it. Shall we speak Spanish together to warm ourselves up or shall we stick with English as a way of relaxing?"

"English please," Joan answered. "Because," she quickly added, "I want to hear all about your travels, and I want to be sure I'm understanding you."

"I agree," Barbara added, "We'll have lots of time to speak Spanish. I'm okay when it comes to talking about diseases and symptoms, but otherwise my Spanish is somewhat stilted. I went to Russia to volunteer after the nuclear plant exploded. What a beautiful country. What parts did you visit?"

And they were off. Joan sat on Barbara's bed, leaned her back against the wall, and sighed under her breath. How nice it was to have such interesting roommates, and how dull it made her life seem.

After a bit Lorna asked Joan, "What about you? What brought you here?"

"Well I met some friends whose son was killed here. You see my daughter had died; her name was Angelica. She'd been sick for so long so I couldn't really… Anyway, now I have time, so I decided to come here. No special reason…" she trailed off.

"Well, it sure is a pleasure to be here with you both," Lorna said, a little too quickly.

The next morning Maria hired a minivan that took the group to the city of León for a meeting with Witness for Peace organizers. They were welcomed and told about the Witness for Peace mission and about the history of Nicaragua, including the recent battles between the Contras and the local armies. "Of course there is some danger, but most of the fighting is being done in the mountains, so please stay in the villages where we've arranged for you to live and only visit the farms you can walk to. Please do not agree with anyone to travel up to the mountains." This advice was repeated three or four times during the afternoon's meeting.

Chapter Forty-One

AFTER THE MEETING, Maria drove Barbara, Lorna and Joan in an old Studebaker to Malpaisillo, a small village about twenty-five miles outside of León. They drove through a thunderstorm. Joan, sitting in the front seat with Maria, flinched each time she saw lightning. The dirt roads were now extremely slippery with long muddy ruts. Maria drove slowly, steering carefully around large potholes, and avoiding the deeper ruts when possible. She stared intently at the road, or what she could see of it through the rain.

Joan wanted to ask, "How far is it? Will we make it?" but she knew that would sound childish and pathetic. She was exhausted and depressed. It seemed ridiculous to be here in this wet dreary place sliding around on the muddy road, in a country where nobody spoke English. What had she been thinking? What if they had an accident? What if they did make it to Malpaisillo and then she got dengue fever? What if Maria made her live with a family by herself without Lorna and Barbara? She longed for Ipswich. She longed for the quiet and beautiful green path along the gravel driveway to the big house, with the horses in the pasture beside it. She longed for a cup of tea in her own kitchen with a corn muffin covered with butter and Bruce weaving himself around her legs until he finally jumped up onto her lap. She felt tears coming with her homesickness. Worst of all, there was no one to blame for her predicament. She had thought that this adventure was what she longed for. She was clearly an idiot—too stupid to live.

Suddenly, her thoughts were interrupted by the realization that the rain had stopped. The sun came out almost at the horizon and she saw a double rainbow. She had never seen one before. Maria pulled the car over to the side of the road. The four women got out of the car and stood together staring—nobody said a word.

When the rainbows had completely disappeared, everyone got back into the car and Maria started up again. Joan was still in the front seat, but without the pounding rain, she could hear Barbara and Lorna chatting in English and she felt less lonely. She got up her courage to ask Maria where she lived and the rest of the trip went by listening to Maria talk about her family and her work with Witness for Peace.

Finally, they reached Malpaisillo. When Maria turned off the headlights, Joan saw that there were no lights in any of the buildings on either side of the street. When they emerged from the car, people they could hardly see rushed up to them, shaking their hands and kissing Maria. A woman brought a candle to a table in a cafe on the street. She called to Maria who gestured to the others to follow her, and they all sat down at the table. Soon the woman reappeared with plates of rice and beans. As the four women ate, children stood near them, watching.

Lorna laughed a little nervously, "Do you think they might be hungry?"

"They interested. They want be friends," Maria explained.

"Do you want some?" Lorna said to the closest little girl. The girl looked at Maria for a translation and then shook her head. Lorna then turned the other way and this time she said in broken Spanish, "Quieres un poco?" But that child also declined, though all the children seemed delighted that Lorna could speak Spanish.

Then Maria stood up. "If you no want more food, we bring in supplies. We keep here." So the four women lugged from the car the suitcases of donations of medicine, school supplies etc. as well as gallon jugs of water. "Now," Maria said, "Is time find beds."

"What do you mean? Haven't all those arrangements been made?" Joan asked, trying not to sound querulous or panicky.

"Sí, sí, we find good house," Maria answered.

"Will we all be together?" Barbara asked.

"Of course," Joan said eagerly, just as Maria was responding.

"No house have three beds. Three houses, we find three houses. You happy. You sleep happy." They got back into Maria's car and headed away from the main street. Suddenly the windows in many of the houses lit up. They did have electricity!

Joan was the first to be let out of the car. Maria knocked on the door of one of the cinderblock houses that looked like all the rest. When a man came to the door Maria spoke with him for a minute or two. Then she came back to the car.

"This good house for you Joan. Good bed." She took Joan's hand and led her to the door and said to the man, "Quiero presentarte a Juana."

The man was about as tall as Joan, dressed in a dark suit. He smiled, a bit formally, said something that Joan didn't understand, and held out his hand. Joan shook it but couldn't remember any words having to do with meeting someone. Then he said pointing to himself, "Me llamo Oscar Estrada."

Joan pointed to herself and repeated as best she could, "Me llamo Joan, I mean Juana." At that, Oscar opened the door wider and stepped back. "Pásale" he said gesturing for Joan to enter.

Maria called over her shoulder as she got back into the car, "We meet tomorrow café in center."

"What time?" Joan called, trying not to wail.

"Seven is good time." She got back into the car and drove off.

When Joan looked back into her new home, Oscar stood there with three teenagers, two girls and a boy, whom he gravely introduced. Joan didn't catch any of their names but had no idea how to ask to have them repeated.

Then one of the girls gestured for Joan to follow her into the room off of the living room. It was just large enough for a narrow bed, a chair and a bureau drawer. The walls were cement block. The floor was tile and the windows were spaces between the cement bricks up under the eves. The girl pointed to herself and told Joan her name again. This time Joan listened carefully and repeated it a few times until the girl nodded—it was Eloina. She was a little shorter than her father and seemed to be the eldest of the teenagers. Her expression was sad when she wasn't smiling. She carried herself slightly hunched as though she was burdened with responsibilities. Her black hair was pulled back from her face with a green ribbon. She wore a dark grey skirt and a short-sleeved white blouse.

As Joan watched, Eloina took the blanket off the bed, exposing the mattress. She opened a drawer of the bureau for a sheet (clearly only used for special occasions), but Joan silently pulled the two sheets that she had been advised to bring out of her knapsack and then they made up the bed together. The bed sagged in the middle like a trough for feeding animals. Joan wondered about her back.

When the bed was made, Eloina handed Joan a plastic dish with a candle stuck into it. She led her outside through the back door. The moon was almost full and Joan was able to see pretty well as they walked through a dirt patio past a car and a sow with her piglets, some chickens, and the family dog, to the outhouse. While Joan used it, Eloina waited. They returned together, stepping around the animals to the other side of the car where there was a large stone sink. Inside the sink was a bucket of water and beside the bucket was a shallow plastic bowl. Eloina showed Joan how to dip the bowl into the bucket and then wash her hands with the water, not letting it fall back into the bucket which was their drinking water.

What Joan wanted more than anything else was to lie in a hot tub until some of the dust from the journey could soak out of her pores. Next choice would be to be left alone or at least with people who spoke English. She was exhausted from trying to understand this girl and she had only been there twenty minutes! She smiled and said "gracias" for the millionth time and then went back to her room, which she later learned was actually Eloina's. Along the way she said "Gracias" to every one she saw. And then she shut her door, Eloina's door. As she unpacked her nightgown, she thought for a minute about brushing her teeth, but then couldn't face it. She took off her clothes and got into bed. The bed was a lumpy trough, and as soon as she had closed the bedroom door, the television had been turned on in the living room. She heard every word, every sigh, every advertisement, and understood nothing. She knew that she would never be able to sleep in the noise. But she was wrong.

Chapter Forty-Two

THE NEXT MORNING, Joan was awakened by people talking and laughing in the patio. She looked at her watch. It was five o'clock. She pulled on her clothes and headed out to the outhouse, carrying her roll of toilet paper as unobtrusively as possible. But before she got to the outhouse, she was introduced to a large group of people, four of them in business suits, who were standing around Oscar's car. She had to put the roll of toilet paper in her left hand so she could shake hands with everyone, including one of Oscar's daughters whom she didn't recognize from the night before.

Then the people in business suits got into Oscar's car and he slowly backed out of the patio, giving the dog, the pigs and the chickens time to get out from behind him. The family and friends of the commuters waved goodbye, and then Joan went to the outhouse. When she was done, she considered leaving her roll of toilet paper there—the family used torn newspaper that they discarded in a box by the toilet so that it wouldn't fill up the pit. But she didn't know how fast the roll would be used up. What if she got Montezuma's revenge? She didn't want to have to resort to newspaper, so she took the roll back with her to her bedroom.

When she reemerged from the bedroom, Eloina showed her how the shower worked. The shower stall was a cylinder of corrugated iron standing upright with one piece cut out to form the door. Once inside the cylinder, you moved the extra piece to cover the opening. Within the cylinder was a bucket of water, and in the bucket was a small plastic bowl. Eloina pantomimed dipping the bowl in the bucket and pouring the tiny amount of water in it over her head. Joan had a feeling that this one bucket of water might contain "showers" for the whole family. She realized she would never be able to wash her hair with the shampoo she had brought, because there would be no way to rinse it.

She thanked Eloina and said "Mañana" which she hoped meant tomorrow. She couldn't picture getting undressed again for such a measly amount of water.

It was now about 5:30. She was to meet the others at 7:00, but she had to find her way back to the café. She decided to head out and look for it. If she couldn't find it, she was hopeful that Maria would come looking for her. She went back to the precious privacy of the bedroom, hers, at least for the present. She carefully made the bed and put everything she had back in the suitcase on the tile floor. She hid her money and passport in a money belt that she wore around her waist though it made her cotton blouse look very bulky. She put on her straw hat and the sunglasses she had been told to bring, grabbed her water bottle and stepped back into the living room. Eloina asked in pantomime whether she wanted to eat something. Joan had been told under no circumstances to eat anything that had been cooked in local water. That was why they had been told to use the one café where Maria had left a supply of water brought especially for them. When Lorna demurred, saying that it seemed very elitist, one of the leaders in León explained that it was because they were not used to the water. Barbara added that it would be a pity to spend their short time here being sick. Joan said nothing. She'd been told in Boston that the water of this village was not drinkable, that the children and old people were dying from the bacteria, it contained.

So clutching her private water bottle, Joan smiled an apology. She had no idea how to say "I'm going to meet my friends for breakfast," but she did remember the word "amigos" and, repeated it once or twice as she left.

When she was outside, she looked down the street and realized that she should keep track of how many blocks she walked and the turns she made, because the houses along these dirt streets looked almost exactly alike. They were all one story, made of cement brick, with open spaces up near the roofs. There were no numbers or street signs of any kind. After about fifteen minutes of carefully counting blocks and turns, she came to an open square from which she could see the main street where the café was. Then she turned around and headed back toward the Estrada's house to make sure that she could find her way back. Once she could see their house, she turned around again and made for the square, feeling a little silly but also a little less worried, because she now had two places she knew how to get to.

The square had no benches or trees for shade. It was much too early to go to the café. Joan felt sweaty and at a loss as to what to do next. She didn't think she could face Eloina's questions if she went back to the Estrada's house. She walked down a dirt street in a different direction and saw a dormant volcano in the distance. She decided to walk straight toward it. She noticed men, standing in the door-ways staring at her, neither friendly nor hostile, just staring. She tried smiling at them, but their response was derisive laughter. Perhaps she was being rude just looking at their houses, but there was nothing else to look at except the distant volcano.

When the road ended abruptly, Joan decided she couldn't turn around and walk back in front of those men, so she made a left turn with the hope of finding a parallel street back to the square. But after walking a while she realized there wasn't one, and she began to feel a little panicky. She told herself that the town wasn't all that big and the square was probably at its center and she was going more or less in the right direction if she kept the volcano behind her.

Finally she came to a church. The front had huge wooden doors that were closed, so she went around to a path between the church and the rectory. There she found a normal-sized door that, she thanked heaven, was not locked. Once inside, she sighed with relief. She was out of the sun; there was nobody looking at her; and there were benches. She sat down heavily and looked around.

It was very spare, with high blank walls of concrete block. The windows, as in all the houses she'd seen, were simply open spaces under the eves. The pews were wooden benches, the kneelers bare wood as well. Against the front wall was a wooden crucifix. The altar was a table covered with a white cloth. To the right of the altar was a large almost life-size brightly painted wooden statue of Christ carrying his cross. The statue rested on two crossbars before and behind.

Joan knelt down to pray, but the wooden kneeler dug into her knees so painfully that she immediately got back up onto the bench. "Angelica, please forgive me for all my mistakes. Now you and your father can laugh at me together." The thought of this made Joan smile. So many times she had longed for Charlie to be alive to help her take care of Angelica. Now they were together and perhaps were doing what they could to help her out in this adventure.

Then she prayed for Joe. "Please take care of him wherever he is. Please help him come home. Please help Sarah and the children be joyful despite missing him so terribly. And me too, please help me be joyful in all the strangeness of life."

She sat for a while, musing, until her surroundings slowly reminded her of why she had come to Nicaragua. "Please help the people here. Please help me learn more about them so I can talk to people back home. Please show me how to be helpful. That is what I long for! Our Father, who art in Heaven…"

When she opened her eyes again, she felt calmer. She sat for a while longer. Then she prayed one more prayer — to be able to find the café before her new friends had given up on her. After that, she headed out into the brilliant, but now more friendly, sunlight. She continued in the same direction and before long she was back in the central square.

Across the way she could see the café.

Chapter Forty-Three

BARBARA WAS ALREADY there with a woman in a nurse's uniform. As Joan approached, she could hear them talking excitedly as they looked over papers together. Barbara had told Joan that she'd learned her Spanish at the Worcester Hospital. Diseases were something she could talk about especially with a lot of charts and statistics in front of her. Joan envied how comfortable she looked. But, as Joan climbed the step from the street into the café, Barbara looked very relieved and with a quick "Pardóneme" to her new friend, rushed toward her. Taking Joan's arm, Barbara brought her over to their table. "Mi amiga Juana," she said to the woman, who stood up and smiled and, a little to Joan's embarrassment, kissed her on both sweaty cheeks.

"Mucho gusto," she said to Joan.

Joan repeated "Mucho gusto" back to her, assuming it was a friendly greeting.

Then the nurse started gathering her papers. "Nos hablaremos más tarde," she said to Barbara.

"Sí," Barbara answered.

"Váyate con Dios," the woman said as she smiled warmly.

Barbara answered "Sí" again, but Joan had the feeling that Barbara wasn't sure what she was saying yes to. Then the woman left, and Barbara almost pulled Joan down onto the seat the woman had occupied. "I'm so glad you're here," she said. Then she took a deep breath, "To tell you the truth, I'm getting a little spooked."

"Why, what happened?" Joan asked.

"Nothing, but I'm homesick in a big way. I know I'll get over it, but I wanted to tell you the truth before Maria arrived, and I wanted to say it in my own goddamn language."

"Me too," Joan quickly concurred as Maria and Lorna climbed the step into the café, followed by a group of children.

"Well, gentle ladies," Maria beamed, "I find good houses?"

"Yes, thank you," they said, almost in unison.

"Good," Maria said, and with one of the older children's help, she quickly moved three tables together to form a long boardroom-like table. Then she straightened up and saw a group of women approaching the café. She announced, "Now I present you the mothers and wives of war martyrs. They tell to you what they live."

They seemed to Joan to be a dour group as they trouped in and took chairs around the table. All but one had gray hair and their faces looked battered and sad and somewhat angry as they faced the Americans. The one younger woman spoke first and Maria translated.

"We desire give greetings to you and your families. We lose our families, our sons, our daughters, our husbands in this war against the Contras. They use your weapons. We no angry at you. We angry at government. Please tell people this…"

"Thank you," Lorna interrupted. "We are grateful that you do not blame us. And I, I mean we, cannot express to you how sorry we are, how desperately sorry, for what our government is doing." Maria translated for her.

One of the older women with a very lined face that had looked sour before but now looked only intense, began to speak slowly and distinctly, looking directly into Lorna's eyes. "Before this, young people come to villages and mountains to teach us alphabet. They live with us, some far into mountains. Finally we read. We read!"

A third woman, desperately thin, with a narrow face and bony arms crossed over her stomach continued the story, "Then more people come, doctors, nurses and now we have clinics in much villages."

A fourth added triumphantly, "In our village we have water in our houses and electricity."

Then the younger woman spoke again. "The Contras use planes, bombs and guns of your government. They attack us. They kill doctors and teachers. They kill American who shows us to have electricity. They take our cattle. They kill my husband who protects his family. Please tell your people. Please tell your government to give no weapons to Contras. We ask you this."

There was a long silence. The women, including Maria, stared at the Americans.

Joan looked at Lorna who was crying, and then at Barbara who frowned and shook her head as she continued to take notes even in the silence. "What are we doing here?" Joan thought. "What am I doing here? What did I think I was going to accomplish? These people have opened their hearts to me and I have nothing to say." Joan looked down at the floor and waited for someone to save the situation.

Then Barbara put down her pen and notebook and began to speak. "We want to thank you for telling us what you have said. I am a doctor, and I know about the war and the history a little, but it is important for us to hear it from you and we thank you. We know it must be hard to talk about it," and here she looked at Maria, who was doing the translating, "especially with us, because we are Americans. It is important that you know that we are ashamed of our government's actions. We heard a little of what you have told us before we came, but it is not being reported in our newspapers and our television news. Most of the people of the United States do not realize what the Contras are doing to your country. We promise that when we return to the United States, we will tell the people what you have told us. We will tell it in churches and synagogues and town halls. It is essential that as many people as possible know what you have told us. We thank you for meeting here with us to tell us this. And we thank you for understanding that it is the government that is sending the money and arms to the Contras, not the people of the United States. You have given us important information and my friends and I will be sure that many people hear it. I have taken many notes from what you have said and I will write a report from these notes which I will send you, through Maria, so that you can correct anything I have misunderstood."

Maria added in English and then in Spanish, "I am happy. I translate into Spanish. I give to each woman."

The women, at last, smiled broadly. And Joan sighed inwardly as she saw how beautiful these women were, each in her way. She also saw her companions differently. She was with women who knew what they were doing and why. Joan felt herself at a loss and overwhelmed, but Barbara and Lorna were truly here on solid footing. She'd be okay if she stuck close to them.

Chapter Forty-Four

THAT AFTERNOON, AFTER lunching on rice and beans and fried plátanos at the same café, they went to visit the medical clinic.

Here Maria let Barbara do the translating, filling in only when Barbara missed an important point. Maria told them that they were going to be on their own from now on, so she was getting Barbara ready to take over the translating job. The beginning of the meeting seemed to Joan much easier than with the mothers and widows. Barbara presented to the clinic, on behalf of the Worcester Hospital, three suitcases filled with medicine that she identified in Spanish with the help of a list she had brought with her. She also explained their purposes. But for the most part, the two doctors and three nurses seemed knowledgeable about them and were grateful. A nurse opened their medicine cabinet and showed the Americans their almost empty shelves. It wasn't until the nurse turned to face the Americans, that Joan realized that she was Eloina. Joan gave a little wave, and Eloina beamed back at her.

Then Isobel, the head nurse, made a little speech that Barbara translated. "We give thanks to you and to your families for these medicines, and for your visit. May God pay you, (is that right Maria?)" she interjected. Maria nodded and smiled. Isobel continued, and Barbara rushed to catch up with her, "We thank you for these medicines. We will use them right away. But what we need more than any medicine is new water. In our…"

Barbara interrupted her, touching Isobel's arm, "Perdóneme. I'm sorry. I just got lost." She turned to Maria and smiled a little pleadingly.

Maria nodded and then said, "In our water-holding tank" and then she nodded to Isobel to continue, "there are cracks. Poisons enter. We have much dysentery. Children die. We have kidney stones. Old people die. We need new well. New well costs much money we no have. Our government fights Contras. We have no money for well. Please tell your people we need well and holding tank for water."

The Americans looked at each other in dismay. After a long silence, Lorna stepped forward, looked at Maria, who nodded, and Lorna said as Maria translated, "My name is Lorna. I want to thank you, Isobel. We will certainly tell the people back home about your need for a well and a holding tank. We will do all we can to explain to them how urgent this need is. We have enjoyed very much meeting you all and I hope we can have further conversation in the future. I would like to take a photograph of you for my children and also for when I talk about your situation when I'm back home. If you wouldn't mind, I'd like to take the picture outside where it is a little lighter."

When Maria finished the translation, everyone smiled. Then some one began to clap and then everyone was clapping, the doctors and nurses, Maria, the children hanging out in the doorway, and the Americans, laughing and clapping. The doctors and nurses kissed each of the Americans on the cheek before they all wandered out into the street so that Lorna could take a picture.

That evening, as they ate supper in the cafe, Lorna looked tired and worn down for the first time. The women had very little to say to each other, but, Joan thought, "At least we're able to say it in English."

While they ate supper, Barbara read aloud from the itinerary that Maria had given them for the next day. After breakfast, there would be a meeting of the teachers' union at the café. Maria would not be there. Joan would present the pencils, crayons and paper that she had bought in bulk from a school supplier, and Barbara would translate. In the afternoon, another Witness for Peace volunteer would pick them up and take them into the city of León to a weaving co-op. Barbara looked up from her reading and said, "I think they may be hoping we'll buy some of their weavings to sell in shops back in the States."

"I guess they don't realize that we don't have that kind of money," Lorna said. Joan sighed; this was yet another way that she was not able to help the people of Nicaragua.

Chapter Forty-Five

WHEN JOAN RETURNED to the Estrada's house, she was exhausted. Oscar immediately turned off the sound of the television at her arrival, and pointed her to one of the two rocking chairs that one of the teenagers quickly vacated. Oscar asked Joan a question that she couldn't understand. She pretended an interest in the television. Oscar shook his head regretfully. Joan could tell that he wanted to learn more about his visitor and her life in the north, and what she thought of his country, and the reason she had come to visit. But, there was no way that she could really understand his questions, much less respond to them. When she pretended interest in the television, he sighed quietly, but turned up the sound again, to the relief of his children.

Joan listened carefully as Oscar talked to his children and this time she memorized their names. Eloina's she already knew. Yeni looked to be about fifteen. She had a friendly smile but seemed shy of attempting to talk with Joan. The boy was Juan. He looked to be about seventeen and had a resigned expression, as though he had been hoping for more excitement in his life.

After about twenty minutes or so of watching some sort of soap opera without understanding a single word, Joan slunk off, first to the outhouse and then to her room which was so close to the television that, even with the door closed, she could still hear every incomprehensible word.

She sat on the broken-down mattress. She felt angry at herself for being there. She'd thought she'd learned Spanish, but she hadn't really. The way they spoke in Nicaragua didn't sound at all like the language tapes she'd listened to in the privacy of her kitchen. She wondered why she hadn't thought of spending time in the Boston parks where the Latinos played soccer. There she could have listened to real Spanish. She felt like a fraud. When she got home, whatever she said about Malpaisillo would be second hand, filtered through interpreters. Robert Golightly had told her that she could not really know what was happening and therefore could not be a helpful advocate until she could speak the language. She could no more help the people of Malpaisillo than she could help Angelica. She was, in a word, useless.

"I hate it here. I want to go home," she announced to herself. Then she lay down on the remarkably uncomfortable mattress, pulled the sheet up over head to try to drown out the sound of the television, and fell asleep.

The next morning she waited until she heard Oscar pull out with his commuters before getting up and going to the outhouse. Having admitted that she hated being there and that she was worse than a fool to think she could help these people in any way, she felt better. First of all, she enjoyed the shower—dripping a small bowl full of cold water over one's body in the stifling heat, with the sun shining down and the family chitchatting out of sight, but nearby, was lovely. The preciousness of the water made it poignant as well. She used very little. Barbara had explained to her that each family only got two buckets of water. The spigot was turned on for people in the Estrada's part of town in the middle of the night and someone in the household needed to stay awake to move the first bucket so they could put the second under the spigot.

By the time Joan pushed back the corrugated-iron door to the shower, Eloina had left. Yeni was working on a sewing machine and Juan was sweeping the tile floor of the living room, collecting the dirt that had blown in through the doors and window openings. He carefully stopped sweeping as Joan walked past him. She collected her sunglasses, bottle of water and hat and headed out the door, calling back to them "Adios" and "Gracias." On the street, she looked both ways to see if people were staring at her. She didn't see any and started out for the café.

As they ate breakfast, Joan considered telling Barbara and Lorna how useless she felt, but she didn't feel up to talking about it. There was nothing they could say or do that would help in any case.

The day began with a meeting with the teachers' union at the café. Joan presented a suitcase full of paper, crayons and colored pencils. The teachers were politely grateful, but this gift was clearly nothing in comparison with their need. Although this had also been true of the medicines Barbara had brought, Joan took it as yet another sign that she was not up to snuff.

Then they were taken to the city of León to visit a cooperative weaving studio. Joan sat with Lorna in the back of the pickup truck. They didn't talk because of the noise of the truck and the dust off the road. Joan stared out at the scenery, dry and desolate with a few run-down houses and skinny cows. She began to cry. Why had she thought she could do any good here? She wanted so much to be home where she could actually make a difference… Suddenly, she felt a cold sweat. There was no one to help at home. Sarah was doing well and her children were thriving. Angelica and Marianne were gone. She couldn't help in Nicaragua because she'd been too lazy or too dumb to learn Spanish, and now there no one at home who needed her. She put her dark glasses on, pulled her floppy straw hat lower over her face and let the tears flow. She figured if Lorna asked, she'd say dust had gotten into her eyes. But Lorna didn't ask. Joan sat with her arms around her knees, bumping along the rough roads and shivering under the hot sun.

The rest of the day was like traveling through a fog. She followed the group through the crowded streets of León, jostling between strangers to keep from getting left behind. The weaving studio was impressive. It employed about fifty women who learned how to weave and then became co-owners of the organization. An American had amassed the funding for the looms and the studio space. He had also found stores in Chicago, New York and Washington ready to sell the brightly-colored shawls, table-runners and place-mats the studio produced. Joan wandered among the thirty huge wooden looms with their colorful weavings, comparing her own uselessness to this enterprising American, who knew just what to do to help people.

On the way back to Malpaisillo, Joan was offered a seat in the front of the truck, but she refused it. She preferred being bounced around in the back in the open air where nobody would expect her to talk. Back in Mallpaisillo, they met with the Sandinista party leaders. There weren't enough chairs, so Joan sat on the floor with her back against a wall, not even listening to the English translation that Barbara struggled with for her benefit and Lorna's. While Barbara talked, Joan wondered if she could possibly get a plane home early. What could she use for an excuse?

That evening, when Oscar asked Joan something that she assumed was, "How did your day go?" she admitted for the first time that she did not understand the question and had no words for an answer. "No puedo hablar, (I can't speak)" she said with an exaggerated shrug of her shoulders. She didn't care if he thought it was because her tongue wasn't working, or that she was too tired, or if he understood that she had only been pretending to understand him before. He smiled, nodded a little wistfully, and settled her in the rocking chair that Yeni had gotten out of. Yeni sat on the sewing machine stool and the television volume was turned back up.

Oscar pulled his chair beside Joan's, and every now and then he made a comment. Joan turned and smiled at him, hoping he wasn't expecting a reply. She noticed, after perhaps their third exchange of this kind, that Oscar had a beautiful smile and that his eyes shone with friendliness. He didn't seem annoyed by her inability to talk. He seemed happy to have her sitting beside him, despite her silence. She wanted to tell him what a fraud she felt for pretending she knew Spanish. She wanted to ask him what had happened to his wife and how long he had been raising his children by himself? She wanted to tell him about Angelica's death, and Joe's disappearance. But she had no words.

Chapter Forty-Six

ONE AFTERNOON IN August, after Joe and Sally had played duets for the patients and the staff to celebrate the tenth anniversary of the clinic's opening, Sally, with her father at her side, announced that she was leaving in a few days to return to San Francisco. She was engaged to be married. After the celebration, Dr. Appleton asked Joe to come into his office. "I think Sally told you a while ago that she was considering this move. She had planned to wait until we found another therapist, but her fiancé grew impatient. Understandable, I guess; it has been a couple of years. She suggested that I ask you to consider filling in for her, until I can find another therapist. You're a fine musician, and you know many of the patients already. It would involve making music with them, one on one and in groups, in a way that makes them feel excited by the potential of the sounds they create to bring harmony out of dissonance. With a trained therapist it's much more complicated, of course, but that's what we'd be asking you to do. We could give you a stipend and room and board. What do you think?"

Joe stared at the ground for a moment. Then he looked up and said very softly, "Dr. Appleton, perhaps I'm not supposed to ask this, but how much time do you think I have?"

"I'm awfully sorry, Joe, I couldn't tell you."

"You have no idea?"

"Not really. I know there are a lot of music therapists out there, but I don't know if they'll want to move here, and we can't pay them very much…"

"But that's not what I meant," Joe persevered. "How much time do I have? How much time before I die?"

"Before you die?"

"Yes, before I die."

"I've no idea. None of us know how long we have on earth, Joe."

"Isn't there a time frame you can give me for people with liver cancer?"

"Joe, you've come to the wrong place if that's what you want. We don't get involved with statistics. We try to meet the patients at the level of their soul and help the soul heal the body. Sometimes the body is healed by the work of the soul and sometimes it isn't. But in either case the soul work has changed the person's life. Sometimes we fail and we're not able to reach the level of the soul in a patient. That patient may be cured of the cancer or succumb to it, but we know we have failed in either case."

Joe stared at Dr. Appleton without saying a word.

"I will tell you this, Joe," Dr. Appleton finally went on, "I think if you went back to your doctor in Boston, he'd be pleased by how well you're doing. And so am I, come to that."

Joe still couldn't speak. Finally, Dr. Appleton put out his hand as he said, "Well, if you're not sure, could you let me know in a day or two? I will be looking for a therapist in any case, but it would mean a whole lot of switching around of the schedules if we're not going to offer music therapy while I look."

Joe shook hands with Dr. Appleton, still speechless. Dr. Appleton didn't let go immediately which made Joe look into his face. He saw that the doctor was smiling broadly.

During the ride back into Mérida, supper in the kitchen, and playing music for the guests until almost dawn, Joe had no idea what he was saying or doing. His mind ricocheted from, "I'm going to live! I have life ahead of me!" to "Do Sarah and the children think I'm dead?" to "Has she married again?" And then, worst of all, to "Would I destroy their lives by returning?"

When the restaurant closed for the night, Joe sat on his bed with paper and pen. He wanted to write Sarah immediately, to tell her all that had happened, to ask her if she would take him back, if she would forgive him, if she would let him see her and the children in order to explain everything. He found, though, that he couldn't keep his eyes open, so he leaned back against the wall for a minute to rest his eyes, and fell asleep with his clothes on.

The next morning, when he woke up, with all his joints aching, writing a letter Sarah seemed an impossible task. He felt sure that she wouldn't want to hear from him, that she'd married someone new who would never abandon her and the children just because he thought he was dying. He had no right to interfere. He had created an impossible situation for her and the children, and now he was about to ruin whatever life she had built up for them.

Chapter Forty-Seven

INSTEAD OF WAITING in front of the pension for the minivan that came by each morning to take him up to the clinic, Joe started walking the streets of Mérida. After a while he found himself in front of the large imposing and ornate Cathedral. He went in. He was hot and sweaty from his walk, and he looked forward to sitting in the cool of the church. He sat down on a bench near the confessional. Men and women stood in a quiet line a short distance from the confessional cubicle. Behind the heavy curtains of the confessional Joe could hear only a murmur of voices. The line moved slowly. After four or five minutes in the cubicle, each penitent came out, found a bench, and knelt down to say penance. "If only it were that easy," Joe thought. "If only a few Hail Mary's could help in any way."

After a while, he decided to join the line. "What the hell," he thought. "It can't make things worse." As he slowly shuffled closer to the confessional, he realized he had no idea what the word for "sin" was in Spanish. How was he going to say, "Forgive me, Father, for I have sinned." He also wasn't sure about "forgive." Finally he worked out the Spanish for, "Pardon me, Father, for I have done wrong."

When it was his turn, he sat down on the warmed bench in the stuffy cubicle and said his carefully practiced opening sentence. To Joe's surprise and delight, the priest answered in American English. "How long has it been since your last confession?"

"You're an American!" Joe exclaimed.

"Yes, I am. How long has it been since your last confession?"

"A long time. Forgive me, Father, I beg you, for I have sinned against my wife and children."

"Well, my son, if you have sinned against your wife and children, then you have sinned against God as well."

"Yes," Joe said, "against God as well."

"Are your wife and children living with you?"

"No, they're in the States. It's been almost a year since I've seen them or spoken to them. They don't know where I am or if I'm alive."

"Tell me, my son, what has happened."

Then Joe told the priest his story and his dilemma.

At the end of Joe's story, the priest said, "God has forgiven you. God is mercy. As for your family, the only way to receive their forgiveness is to ask for it."

"But…"

"I pray that God will teach you how to forgive yourself and write to your family. It is essential, my son, that they know you are alive. They may need you now or sometime in the future. If your wife wants to marry another man, surely you want to make it possible for her to do so legitimately."

Joe wanted to argue, to explain again how he didn't want to hurt them, but the priest continued, "Meanwhile, I suggest you pray to our Blessed Mother, thanking her for your new-found health and asking her for help as you go forward into your life. I absolve you of all your sins, in the name of the Father, the Son, and the Holy Ghost, Amen," and Joe knew he was being dismissed.

"Thank you, Father," he mumbled as he pulled back the curtain and left the stuffy cubicle, suddenly realizing that he'd held up the line for a long time

What he wanted was to get out into the air, but instead he sat down on a nearby bench and then dropped to his knees and prayed the rosary, using his fingers to keep count of the prayers.

He wrote Sarah that night. Wanting to make sure the news of his survival would not give more pain to her or the children, he added, "I know it's possible that you don't want to see me or even to have the children know about me. I can imagine what you and they have been through, and you may have created a new life that I can't be part of. Therefore, I'm writing simply to tell you that I'm alive, and to ask what you want me to do now. Shall I come home? Or should I stay away and perhaps send money to support the children? Please let me know. Here are the phone numbers where you can reach me. I love you and the children with all my heart, and your happiness is all that I long for."

He wrote the same letter twice, sending one copy to his New York City address and another in care of Joan to

Ipswich. The letter to New York was tossed in the dead letter bin—Sarah had been gone too long to have it forwarded. The letter to Ipswich arrived the day after Labor Day, and Joan was on her way to Nicaragua.

Chapter Forty-Eight

THE NEXT DAY Joe told Dr. Appleton that he would be glad to be an interim music therapist for a little while. "I'm hoping for news from home which may mean I'll have to leave quickly."

"That's fine. We'll plan our schedule week by week."

Joe was glad to be so busy—giving what passed for music therapy during the day, and continuing to play at the restaurant in the evenings. He had decided to continue to live in the Pension while he waited to hear from Sarah. But after four weeks without a call, Joe resigned himself to the knowledge that she no longer wanted him involved in her or her children's lives. He couldn't blame her, but he felt in a state of shock realizing that no matter how long he lived now, he might never see his family again.

One evening as the restaurant was closing, Joe picked up a newspaper left on a table by one of the tourists. It was a New York Times, dated months before, probably having been used as wrapping material. Joe sat down at the table to read it. Old news was still interesting to him—especially when written in English. He read about a talk given by the parents of an American engineer, Bill Lancaster, who'd been killed by the Contras while trying to build a health clinic in Nicaragua.

Joe took the newspaper up to his room to finish the article. He read about a group of Americans who had traveled to Nicaragua hoping that by putting themselves in harm's way, they could discourage the United States from bombing the country to support the Contras.

The next morning, he went back to the Cathedral. Confessions weren't being heard, but he asked a very pregnant young woman who was sweeping the floor if he could speak with the American priest. She nodded and disappeared. Joe knelt in the front pew for a quick prayer, then sat back in the pew to wait. In a few minutes the young woman returned with an elderly dark-skinned man dressed in a brown robe who held her arm with one hand and a white cane with the other.

Joe got up to meet them, thinking that the woman had misunderstood him. He was ready to apologize to this priest for having disturbed him. But before Joe could speak, the priest spoke, looking straight ahead. "Maria says you were asking for me," he said. "Is there anything I can do for you?" It was the same confessor.

It took a minute for Joe to gather his thoughts. He had imagined such a different person from the sound of his confessor's voice. Then he said, "Father, I am sorry to disturb you. I came to you about a month ago for confession and I was wondering if I could speak with you again."

"Of course," the priest responded, looking more directly toward Joe now. "Would you want to continue the sacrament of confession, or would you like to speak with me in my office?"

"In your office, I think, if that would be okay."

"Kindly give me your arm, and I will endeavor to lead us there." He turned to the woman and said softly, "Muchas gracias, Maria, este hombre me ayudará."

"Muy bien, Padre," she said, and let go of his arm. She went over to the wall to retrieve her broom and began to sweep again with long careful strokes on the stone floor. Joe stepped forward and offered a bent elbow to the priest. When the priest didn't move, Joe took his hand and placed it in the crook of his arm. Then, they both turned and went back the way the priest had come.

The priest's office was a whitewashed room, just large enough for a cot, a table and two chairs. When they sat down Joe said, "I don't know if you remember me, Father. I'm the person who walked out on his wife and children because I thought I was dying."

"I remember you well, my son. Have you written to your wife?"

"Yes, I wrote that very evening."

"Good for you, my son, and how did she respond?"

"Her response has been silence. I think she is too angry or too hurt even to write or call."

"Well, be that as it may, my son, you've taken the first step. I think in the future, when you have forgiven yourself for what you've done, you will need to return home, to meet with your wife face to face, and discuss together the best way for you both to go forward. What are you planning to do now?"

"I found an article in the New York Times. I never see the paper, you know, but this piece of the Times was left where I couldn't miss it. I wonder if it's a sign that I'm supposed to go to Nicaragua."

"What did the article say?"

"I have it here. Would you let me read it to you? It's very short."

"I am eager to hear."

When Joe finished reading, the priest asked, "Are you a builder, an engineer?"

"No," Joe said. "I'm not, but..."

"What sort of skills could you take to Nicaragua? What would you be able to contribute, besides being cannon fodder, which I gather is your plan."

"I was thinking more about being a 'human shield' rather than cannon fodder," Joe said.

"But as you see in that article," the priest responded, "the Contras we support don't care whom they kill, including Americans. No, I don't think you can ask the Nicaraguans to put you up, or even put up with you, just because you don't mind dying."

Joe was silent for a moment.

"What was your profession before you got sick?" the priest asked.

"I played the oboe, I still do—that's how I'm living here."

"Classical or popular?" asked the priest.

"Both," Joe said.

"Are you good?"

"Good enough to make a living, but not as good as I hope to become."

"Well then," the priest smiled, "perhaps you could be useful. Music is always important. I suggest you write to Father Rafael Gonzales, a priest with connections in the Nicaraguan government. You can write to him in English. Tell him you're ready to sing, or rather play, for your board and keep. In fact," he continued, "We have our own method of postal service. Why don't you write your letter here and now, and I'll pass it along."

And so Joe did just that, sitting at the bare table in the priest's office.

When he was done, the priest asked Joe to read aloud from other articles in the New York Times.

"Thank you," he said when he had heard them all. "I don't hear much news from the north. If you come back in a couple of weeks, I may have an answer for you from Father Gonzales."

That afternoon, Joe hitchhiked out to the clinic and told Dr. Appleton that he was hoping to go to Nicaragua, perhaps within the month.

"That sounds like a good idea—a rough place right now, but all the more important to have music. We'll have you finish up here in two weeks, but we'll pay you for the month, a little bonus to help you get started there."

"I can't tell you how grateful I am for all you've done for me."

"You've done a lot for us as well. We've learned a lot about liver cancer from your stay here. And I thank you for pitching in with the music. You might consider therapy training one day. Your patients were delighted by your work with them."

"Thank you again," Joe said, and this time, uncharacteristically, he gave Dr. Appleton a hug, which Dr. Appleton returned, surprised but pleased.

Chapter Forty-Nine

JOE WENT TO the Cathedral every day before catching a ride to the clinic. He prayed for Sarah, and the children. "Let them be happy. Let them be healed from the pain I have caused them. Let them be filled with joy." And, he prayed for himself, "Please, Lord, show me the path I should take, and give me the courage to stay on it." These prayers became his mantra, repeated silently while working with patients at the clinic and entertaining the guests at the Pension.

One morning, Joe arrived at the Cathedral in time for early Mass. There were two priests at the altar. One was young and looked to be Mexican; the other was the American priest. After Mass, coffee was served in a reception room. Joe followed the other parishioners in. After accepting a cup of coffee, he went up to the American priest, who had taken off his robe and wore black pants and shirt, both shiny with age. He had not used a white cane during Mass, but now he leaned on one as he talked in fluent

Spanish to a teenage mother with a toddler clinging to her skirt and an infant in her arms. When the teenager turned away, Joe introduced himself to the priest and asked if perhaps he had heard from Nicaragua. "I have indeed, my son. I have a letter for you from Father Gonzales. He writes in Spanish, so perhaps you would like my help in translating it. In any case, with your permission, I am very curious about what he says."

"I'll definitely need your help in translating it, Father," Joe said with a smile, "both in what he says and in what I should read between the lines."

"Well, then, bring a coffee for both of us, why don't you, and let's go into my office." Joe stuck his oboe case under his arm and went to ask for another cup of coffee.

In the office Joe placed the coffee cups on the table and remembered to reach for the priest's hand to show him where the cup was. "Thank you. That's helpful," the priest said. "And here is your letter." He pulled out a small draw and handed Joe an envelope with a rubber band around it. It was addressed to "Padre Paul Brown, Cathedral, Mérida, Mexico" and had no stamp.

"It's addressed to you," Joe said. "May I open it?"

"Of course, of course. It's for you. And if it isn't, we'll soon find out. Please read it aloud."

So Joe did, in halting Spanish. It was handwritten but the letters were carefully formed—the writer knew that Father Brown would need to ask someone to read it aloud to him. From what Joe could understand, the letter said that there was a patriotic band that traveled around Nicaragua, and an oboe would be a good addition to the group. Father

Gonzalez cautioned that the band's work was dangerous because it traveled in and out of the war zone. Joe might also consider the National Orchestra that played in Managua. Father Gonzalez thought an oboe would be wanted there as well. He added that the government had no money, but if Joe played well enough, they could feed him and find him lodging.

When Joe was finished reading, Father Brown said, "Your Spanish is pretty good. Did you understand everything you read?"

"Yes, I think so, Father."

"And do either of these proposals interest you?"

"Yes, I think the patriotic band that travels around Nicaragua would be the best. That way I could see the country…"

"And you might get yourself killed," Father Brown interrupted. "I believe you're still thinking that might be a way out. But, be that as it may," he continued, "that is in God's hands. Meanwhile, before I help you send your reply back to Father Gonzales, I would very much like to hear you play the oboe."

"I could play for you now, Father, if that is convenient."

"That would be very convenient. Let's go back into the hall. There may be people still there who would like to hear you as well."

In the hall, the young priest and some nuns sat and talked around one table as three other women gathered the used coffee cups to take to the kitchen. Standing in the doorway, Father Brown announced, loudly enough for the women washing dishes in the kitchen to come out wiping their hands, "Mi amigo, José, va a tocar para nosotros. Vamos a darle un poco de quieto. Maria, ayúdeme por favor a una silla." Maria came over and took Father Brown's hand to lead him to a chair. Soon everyone was seated, and staring at Joe.

Joe took his oboe out of its case and began to play the Mexican songs that his friends at the Pension had taught him. The nuns began singing, soon joined by the other women and the priests. Then Father Brown called out, "That was great. How about some classical?" So, Joe played an arrangement for oboe of a Bach cantata that had been his audition piece at Tanglewood.

When he was done, the priests, nuns and women helpers all stood as they applauded. Then they gathered round to shake his hand and thank him. Joe went to Father Brown, who had also stood to applaud. They shook hands as Father Brown said, "Thank you, my son. That was very fine."

"Thank you, Father, for giving me the opportunity."

"I'll write to Father Gonzales today. But mind, I suggest this only for a few months. I'm hoping that by then you'll find the courage to go home and face the music. Galloping 'into the shadow of death' will not bring peace to your situation."

"It's the best I can do at this time," Joe admitted. "But I will bear in mind what you've said."

"Please do," Father Brown said. He reached up and touched Joe on the shoulder, then turned and began walking, with the help of his cane and Maria's gentle guidance, toward his office.

Joe watched him go, and then cleaned and packed up his oboe, before going out into the blinding sunlight.

As he walked toward the corner where the minivan for the clinic would pick him up, Joe smiled at the thought of the standing ovation. Suddenly, he stopped walking. He had just realized that for the Patriotic Band he would need to learn how to play while marching! Would he be dodging bullets as well? It sounded both frightening and exciting. Just thinking about it gave him relief for a few minutes from his worries about Sarah and the children.

Two weeks later, Joe's gig at the Pension was interrupted by a long distance phone call. It was Father Gonzales himself speaking in English.

"How soon you join us, Mr. Joe?"

Joe thought a minute. He had finished his time at the clinic, and Señor Gomez could find one of the many local musicians to take over at the restaurant. "I could leave here tomorrow, Father," he said. "Or whenever it is convenient for you," he added, realizing that they might not want him right away.

"Good. Come to Managua tomorrow and we arrange where you join the band."

Joe took down the address and then went back to the restaurant to finish his gig. When the guests left, he told Señor Gomez of his plans.

"That is sad for us," Señor Gomez said. And as Joe began to explain and apologize for the short notice, Señor Gomez slapped him on the back. "You have been good to us. We wish you happiness. Go with God." Then he took Joe into the kitchen to announce that he was leaving.

"Pero quien va a cocinar para ti?" the cook asked.

Joe realized he hadn't thought of his special diet; it had become so habitual now that he followed it without thinking. After a moment or two he said to the cook in Spanish, "I think you have made me well, my friend, and I thank you from the bottom of my heart." The cook kissed him on both cheeks and Mr. Gomez added money from his own pocket to the basket marked "por la música" before handing its contents to Joe. Joe thanked them, wondering why he'd been so eager to leave, and went up to his room to pack.

Chapter Fifty

THE NEXT MORNING as Joan stretched and yawned, listening to Oscar leave with the commuters, she decided that from now on she was going to be honest about how little she understood. She would carry her dictionary around with her and if anyone spoke to her and seemed to expect an answer, she would simply hand them the dictionary. If she had fooled herself into thinking she could be helpful, that was bad enough; at least she would stop trying to fool other people. Before leaving for breakfast, she pulled up a chair next to Yeni who was working at her sewing machine. Joan began pointing to things and asking "Qué es esto?" Yeni replied with the Spanish word. Joan repeated it four or five times and then told Yeni the word in English. Yeni was eager to learn and quickly memorized "sewing machine" "table" "chair" "window" and "dictionary."

Then gathering her sunglasses, straw hat, camera and water bottle, Joan left to find the others at the café for breakfast.

The plan for that day was to interview people about their lives under the present conditions. Joan announced to her colleagues that her Spanish wasn't good enough to be interviewing on her own. For a moment, they pretended surprise and attempted to reassure her, but soon Lorna said she'd love to have Joan join her. Lorna was so friendly and determined to understand and be understood, that her Spanish was rapidly improving. She had brought a tape machine that made her fearless, she said, because whatever she didn't understand could be translated later. She asked Joan to take pictures so that they would have a record of the people they'd interviewed. They decided to meet up with Barbara at the café for lunch to compare experiences.

It was a nice morning. Lorna and Joan headed down one of the back streets knocking on doors. Lorna enjoyed the people so immensely that they simply understood her and they happily talked into the tape recorder that Joan showed them, waiting for her to change the tapes when necessary. Lorna had made a list of questions that seemed to be good choices because the people talked and talked. And they all seemed to enjoy having their pictures taken, posing as though for a family portrait, even though they never asked if they would be able to see the pictures once they were developed.

At lunch, the three decided it was too hot to work that afternoon. Joan went back to the Estrada's. She was glad not to see anyone in the living room. She went into her little room, closed the door, dug "Pride and Prejudice" out of her knapsack, took off her shoes and sat on the far edge of the moat of a mattress. She leaned against the wall and managed to let go of the present and disappear into eighteenth century England.

It would have been cooler on the patio in the shade, but Joan didn't want anyone to ask her anything in Spanish. Her body was too hot to try to think. As she read, despite the heat, despite the lumpiness of the mattress and the grit and sand from the road that blew in through the window opening, she began to feel better.

Later that afternoon, Yeni knocked on her door and then opened it saying something about "amiga." Joan looked up and there was Lorna.

"Joanie," she said, "Please come with me. I've found the public library. It's not far, and it's filled with children and good books by people we've heard of, like Pablo Neruda."

"In English?" Joan asked.

"Not that I saw, but who knows, maybe there are some in English. Do come." Lorna came into the room and looked around for a place to sit.

Joan, afraid that Lorna was going to join her on the bed which would probably make it collapse, stood up somewhat stiffly and said, "Ok, if it's not far." After all, she said to herself, she might as well be a tourist if nothing else. So together they walked back toward the center of town.

The library, like all the other buildings, was made of concrete bricks. It had a large door opening onto the street. There were lots of children there, some looking at books, others talking. Most of the girls of eight or older were carrying smaller children, or holding their hands, while they talked with each other or looked at books. Lorna introduced Joan to the librarian, whose name was Martha. Then she and

Martha began to talk about the supplies the library needed. Lorna wrote down everything that Martha said, planning to translate the words she didn't know later. She told Joan that she might be able to obtain a good many of these things from the women's guild of her church.

Joan sat down on the stoop in front of the library with a children's book that had lots of pictures. She was surrounded immediately by a group of children, so without thinking about it, she began to read aloud. She knew how to pronounce the words, even when she couldn't understand them. One child crawled under her arms and into her lap; some stood behind her and leaned against her shoulders to see the pictures. Others sat snuggled beside her on the stoop. When she finished the book, a child behind her immediately handed her another one, and Joan began again. She had loved reading to the children when she was a kindergarten teacher, but this was even more joyful because there was no need to teach or discipline the children. They were all simply enjoying themselves. When Joan mispronounced a word, the children laughed uproariously. After a while, they began to point to the drawings and ask if she could name the animal or activity being shown. When she couldn't, they happily told her what it was, made her repeat it until she got it right, and then clapped with delight at her success. As a child handed her a fourth book, Joan felt contentment fill her to the brim.

After supper with Lorna and Barbara at the café, Joan returned to the Estrada's house. As she walked toward their house, she hoped they would all be watching television so she could simply sit with them and not have to talk. To her chagrin, when she arrived she found the television was off. Oscar was reading a newspaper and the children were in the patio washing the dishes. After using the outhouse, Joan walked toward the sink to wash her hands and heard Juan teaching his sisters "I Want to Hold your Hand" from the Beatles. As she got closer, she joined in, singing the words that to Juan were only sounds. The girls asked her repeat line after line until they too had memorized all the sounds if not the words. They all went into the house together. Juan brought in his guitar and, smiling at his father, began to play what Joan realized was a hymn. At first, Oscar sang alone with Juan's accompaniment. Joan was amazed by the richness of his voice. He sounded almost operatic, and at the same time filled with feeling for what he was singing. On the second verse the girls and Juan joined in. They sang in four-part harmony. Joan leaned back in her rocking chair smiling at the beauty of it and humming along with the melody on the refrain.

After a few hymns, they asked Joan if she would sing one. When put on the spot, she could only think of Christmas Carols, so she began "Silent Night". They smiled as she sang, and then, when she couldn't remember the words of the second verse, they sang it in Spanish.

"Por favor, teach me it in español" Joan begged. And so they did. Oscar led off, singing a phrase which Joan imitated. Then Oscar sang it again and listened to Joan, and then again until Joan could pronounce the phrase and even remember the words. It all took quite a while, but in the end the entire family, including Joan, sang three verses straight through. Joan was thrilled by her accomplishment. She gave each of the beaming family a kiss on the cheek. Then she went to her room to get her bottle of water, her toothbrush and toothpaste and the roll of toilet paper before heading to the outhouse. She came back almost empty handed, having left the roll of toilet paper in the outhouse where it belonged and her bottle of water on the edge of the sink because the water bucket was completely empty.

Chapter Fifty-One

ON FRIDAY, MARIA joined Barbara, Lorna and Joan for lunch. They gave her their notes from their interviews. "Thank you, gentle ladies," Maria said. "I type these and give you back copies. This afternoon there is procession for Lent. You go."

"I'm actually going to the beach this afternoon," Lorna said quickly. "My family has invited me on this lovely outing. Barbara was with me at the time and so they invited her as well. I'm sure," she continued, looking at Joan, "since we're going in a truck there'd be plenty of room for you as well."

"No, thank you," Joan said. It was difficult enough, she thought, knowing how to be friendly in Spanish with people she knew; she wasn't ready to try it with a new family who hadn't even invited her. "I'd forgotten that it was Lent," she said to Maria. "Please tell me more about the procession. Where does it begin and what time?"

"You know Catholic church, yes? Around three o'clock you go to Church and you see. I no come with you. I return to León. You like. You see."

"Thank you," Joan said. Soon after that, everyone said goodbye and Joan began to walk up the dusty dirt road toward the church.

As she walked, to her growing surprise, people emerged from almost every cement block house along the road, each carrying a small bucket of water. They dipped a bowl in the bucket, and sprinkled water on the dry, sandy, gritty road. With water so scarce, this seemed very strange. Also strange was that every once in a while a family came out of their house carrying a table which they set up outside their front door. Then a neighbor came over with a white cloth and carefully covered the table.

The church was empty when Joan arrived. She figured she had misunderstood Maria, but she enjoyed being there. It was shadowy and cool with benches and solitude. What could be better? She sat toward the front, staring at the color-fully-painted life-sized wooden Jesus carrying his cross, and at the plain altar. There was nothing else to stare at. Then she looked up at the sun streaming in the high-set window openings and realized that although she felt vulnerable, almost helpless, in this country, she also felt happy and relaxed, at least for the moment. She closed her eyes and prayed the rosary, using her fingers instead of beads.

She opened her eyes again when she heard a noise, and looked around. Two elderly women were sweeping the packed-earth floor raising clouds of dust. Then they too brought out a bucket of water and a little bowl, and were sprinkling water over the floor. After that, people began to come in and fill up the pews, including two young men with guitars who sat in the front. Then the priest and the altar boys processed in, and Mass began.

At the end of Mass everyone continued to kneel on the exceedingly uncomfortable wooden kneelers. The pain from the kneeler protruding into Joan's knees now began to radiate down her legs and up into her back. She looked around to see if other people had settled back on the benches but no, old and young alike were kneeling tall on the kneelers and looked ready to go on doing so for ever.

Finally, the priest told them to rise, and he and the choir with the two guitar players led the way to the back of the church, followed by the statue of Jesus and his cross with the crossbars in front and in back resting on four men's shoulders. The congregation and Joan followed behind them. As they walked, everyone sang a hymn. Joan found that she understood the chorus "O Señor ten piedad a tu pueblo (Oh Lord have mercy on your people)." Singing all the way, they circled the church once and then began to walk down the road toward the center of town.

Outside the first house that had a table in the street, the four men carefully set the heavy statue down on the table. The priest read a piece from the Bible. The congregation prayed the Lord's Prayer. Then everyone began to sing again, asking for mercy as four different men hoisted the statue onto their shoulders.

The procession continued. At each table they stopped and the priest read from the Bible. Then four new men undertook to balance the statue, heavy and awkward, onto their shoulders, while everyone sang asking for mercy. After a while Joan realized they were doing the stations of the cross. The street was filled with parishioners. Old and young helped each other to keep up with the group. Children weaved in and out of the procession, sometimes running along the edge. And all along the sidelines, people stood watching as though it were a parade. Everyone sang. It felt to Joan as though she were inside the heart of the people as well as in her own heart, begging for mercy.

Hours later, they arrived back at the church. It had become dark. Someone lit a candle so that the priest could read the Bible at the last stop. Then the entire procession entered the church again, knelt and prayed. When the priest dismissed them, everyone dispersed and Joan went back to the Estrada's house.

The family was just sitting down for supper. They quickly pulled another chair up to the table for her. Joan smiled, but shook her head, and went out into the patio to use the outhouse. She planned to head back into town to the café where she would probably meet her colleagues. But, if not, she would eat there by herself because that was where the safe water was that had been brought from León for their use. They had been warned not even to brush their teeth with local water because it was so toxic. As she went back toward the house through the starlit patio, careful not to step on the sow or her piglets or the chickens with their heads curled under their wings, she looked up and saw Orion, very bright, rising above her.

Suddenly, she felt mortified to be refusing to drink the water that everyone else had to drink, toxic or not. She went into her room and gathered up the three mangos she'd been given that morning by a family they'd interviewed. When she came out into the big room, she placed the mangos on the center of the table. Oscar asked if she would be so kind as to do the family the honor of joining them for their simple meal of rice and beans. She hoped she'd understood the gist of what he'd said, and she answered, "Sí, gracias." and sat down with them.

From then on, Joan almost always had supper "at home" and never once got sick. Each day she shopped in the market trying to find something festive to bring home as her contribution. Sometimes Yeni and Eloina shook their heads at her gifts, expensive foods that they had no idea how to prepare, and that led to the even greater pleasure for Joan of cooking with them over the charcoal stove in the outside cooking area on the edge of the patio.

One evening Oscar invited Joan to go for a walk with him after supper. They didn't talk as they walked along the dark streets under the stars—they needed to see each other's gestures and facial expressions to converse. They simply walked, enjoying the coolness of the evening, the patches of light and shadow as clouds went across the face of the moon, and, Joan thought, in some mysterious way, each other.

The next Friday Oscar announced to Joan that 'her family' would like the pleasure of taking her to the beach on Sunday after church if she were free.

Joan understood the word for "beach" and "Sunday" and smiled happily as she said "Sí, Sí, muchas gracias," which was as close as she could get to, "Yes, thank you, I'd love to." Yeni and Juan were surprised and delighted at the plan. Joan had the feeling that they hadn't been to the beach in a long while. Saturday morning, Eloina and Joan shopped together for the picnic. Then they made tamales. The girls showed Joan how to grind the corn into meal, then to mix it with water and press it into thin layers. On the charcoal stove, they cooked up some meat and onions and jalapeno peppers. When this mixture had cooled, they flattened out a corn husk, put a layer of corn meal on top, then put some of the meat mixture in the center of it and carefully rolled the corn husk up and placed it in a pan. As they worked, the girls taught Joan a song about Nicaragua. "Nicaraguita" they called it. Joan learned much of it by heart simply by singing it again and again. Then Joan taught them "Tea for Two" with broad gestures to get some of the meaning across. When Oscar returned from work, Eloina and Yeni sang it to him, gestures and all, which had him chuckling all through supper.

On Sunday afternoon, the trip to the beach was glorious. Most of what Joan had seen of Nicaragua had been cinder block houses along dusty dirt roads with volcanoes in the distance. Now, after a long bumpy ride in Oscar's car, they came out onto a beautiful sandy beach. They immediately shed their outer clothes and headed into the ocean. The water was wonderfully cold. Juan and Eloina raced each other doing strong crawl strokes parallel to the beach. Yeni dove again and again looking for beautiful stones or shells. Oscar and Joan swam slowly and sometimes floated on their backs. Once, their hands touched by chance as they floated. Oscar took hold of Joan's hand without a word, and they floated together like two pieces of seaweed, cool under the hot sun.

Later, they gathered bits of driftwood and lit a fire. They put a little seawater in the pot of tamales and put the pot on to boil. Joan laughed with pleasure as she ate a tamale, stared out to sea, and scrunched her toes into the sand. Oscar sat beside her, also laughing, perhaps at something Yeni had just said. Then he reached over to Joan and tucked behind her ear a lock of wet hair that was about to get mixed up with her tamale. She turned to smile at him, but he stood up and offered her his hand. She took her last bite of tamale and allowed him to pull her to her feet. He said something to the children, and then, still holding Joan's hand, he led her to the water's edge so they could explore the long length of the beach while walking ankle deep in the incoming waves.

Chapter Fifty-Two

A PARTY WAS planned for the delegation and their host families on their last night in Nicaragua. Oscar's Evangelical church did not think people should dance or drink, so Joan wasn't surprised when he refused her invitation, but she was disappointed. This was to be her last night in Malpaisillo. She really wanted to spend it with Oscar; but since everyone, including he, assumed she would go to the party, she didn't know how to explain to Oscar that she'd rather, much rather actually, stay 'home.' He walked her to the house where the party was being held, and gave her a quick kiss on the cheek before leaving her. The cinder block house was a small one-story rectangle right on the street. The door was open and the music was blaring. It had been decades since Joan had been to a party where dancing was the main idea. She went to the corner of the room where Lorna was talking with a young man in a combination of English and Spanish. Lorna introduced her, and Joan stood next to them for a while, trying to look as though she were interested. She was tired and confused and very ambivalent about leaving the next day. She didn't have the energy to talk in Spanish.

The music came from the tape deck Barbara had brought for transcribing interviews. Someone had managed to rig it up to speakers. It was going full blast—a somewhat blurred loudness with an extra heavy beat. Little children danced around in circles or chased each other in amongst the dancers. Most of the teenagers danced in one corner as a group, arms in the air, hips gyrating. There was a girl standing near Joan, watching the teenagers while cuddling a sleeping baby in her arms. Joan reached for the baby, and the girl immediately gave him to her and went off to join her friends.

With the baby in her arms, Joan left Lorna, and swinging her hips more or less to the beat, strolled toward the center of the room surrounded by dancers. Despite the beat of the music and the rocking and butting and sashaying bodies all around them, the baby slept on. So, holding the baby against her shoulder, Joan rocked and swayed and felt like one of the crowd. No need to talk, the music said it all.

Much too soon, the teenager left her friends and took the baby out of Joan's arms. Joan, now feeling foolish, quickly retreated to the edge of the room. From there she pretended to watch the dancers, but in fact, she was having the exact same feelings of humiliation that she had had on the sidelines of high school dances.

As she enviously stared at the dancers, she noticed a large, gray-haired—woman, who looked American or European, dancing the light fantastic with a very thin dark

Nicaraguan man. The woman was obese but at the same time wonderfully flexible and sensuous in her movements. The man was skinny and fast and acrobatic in his dancing. They were an astounding couple.

After a while, the man turned his back on his partner, and began dancing with someone else. The woman turned and smiled at Joan and headed towards her with her arms outstretched. Joan found herself dancing towards the woman with all the joy and abandon she'd had as a teenager, giving herself up completely to the music. Joan and her new partner smiled into each other's eyes as though they had just crossed half the world to find each other, until, suddenly, her partner turned her back on Joan and started dancing with the tall skinny guy again.

Feeling self-conscious and vulnerable, Joan made her way through the dancers and headed for the door. It was time to get out of this horribly noisy, airless, overcrowded room. As she was about to step outside, Martha, the librarian, came dancing toward her with arms outstretched. As they danced, Joan felt that they were celebrating their friendship, and that this was goodbye, because they'd probably never see each other again. After Martha, came other women, some Joan recognized as having seen before, some not. All seemed thrilled to be dancing with her and with each other, everyone beaming with pleasure. Soon Joan no longer cared if she had a partner or not. Everyone was her partner, and the looks of love that passed among the women inspired Joan to more and more unselfconscious movement as she let the frenetic music have its way with her.

Then the music changed, becoming slow and romantic. This couldn't be danced to alone. One needed at least a baby asleep on one's shoulder. Joan looked around and realized that most of the men had gone home. Barbara and Lorna were sitting on the front stoop talking. There were a few teenage boys entwined around their dancing partners, and there was the host, a little formal but also very romantic, with his wife; their children did their own circle dance in one corner. The rest of the dancers, many of the couples were women, held each other close and danced slowly and romantically. Joan knew from the interviews that many of these women's husbands had left them and their children to take up with another woman, often in the same town. So, despite the dearth of jobs, these women somehow managed to make enough money to feed, clothe and house their children and at the same time take care of the young ones who couldn't be left alone. As Joan watched them dance in couples, it seemed to her that they were celebrating the knowledge that men may come and go, but women stand by each other through thick and thin.

And then Carmen, a thin young woman, younger than Joan's daughters, came toward Joan, took her into her arms, and held her close; they danced for a while cheek to cheek and then holding both hands they continued dancing as though they were branches of a single tree being blown by the wind.

When the music ended, the party did as well. Carmen said she and Martha would walk Joan back to Oscar's house.

They walked through the streets, wonderfully quiet after the blaring music, and cool after the hot dusty day. Joan sighed with happiness. These women had accepted her. They seemed to know that her life, too, had been hard. They had taken her in as one of them. Joan was close to tears.

Then Carmen broke the silence. She spoke slowly and carefully. Joan didn't understand everything that was said, but what she did make out showed her how wildly she had underestimated these women and their struggles. Carmen told her that she and Martha and some of the other women at the fiesta had been part of a women's battalion during the revolution. "We fought in the mountains. Some of us died, but we won. Now we have clinics and schools. Now we can vote. The Contras want to destroy us. We will fight again. Please tell your people…"

"Yes I will," Joan promised with tears blurring her vision. The tears were for the women, and for her foolishness in thinking that she had understood. She kissed Carmen and Martha and held them close. Then, not looking back, she opened the gate onto Oscar's patio.

Oscar was waiting up for her. He had brought the two rocking chairs out onto the patio. He stood when she arrived, gave her a peck on the cheek, and gestured toward one of the chairs. He sat beside her, and, for a while, they rocked back and forth in silence. The house was completely dark and the stars and moon were very bright. Oscar reached for her hand. Joan felt his energy rush into her as they both stared into the moonlit sky.

Then Oscar asked in careful slow Spanish, "You are happy to go home?"

Joan began to cry as she answered in her slow, botched Spanish, "In the north I have a daughter and grandchildren. But here I am home." After she'd said it, she wondered what she'd meant and what he'd think she'd meant. She had no words to explain, even to herself, how she felt.

They were silent again for a long time.

Then Oscar said, "Yes, you are home here."

Joan didn't reply, and they rocked in silent unison.

After a while, Oscar repeated solemnly, "Yes, you are home here." Then he let go of her hand, sat up, turned toward Joan, and said in a low voice but as clearly as possible, separating each word carefully, "My children and I, we are happy if you remain here."

Joan looked at his face in the moonlight. She wasn't sure she'd understood him. Was he inviting her to stay a few more days? She smiled vaguely at him, and to her astonishment, he leaned toward her and kissed her gently on the mouth. Then he settled back in the rocking chair. He reached over and took her hand again and waited.

Joan was silent, listening to the energy that was coursing between them through their hands and their arms that touched from the elbows down. Her face felt as though it had become part of the starlight. She thought of Sarah baking cookies, of Kari cuddling Bruce in her arms, of Sam playing catch with Paul. They all seemed to be saying, "Yes, say yes!"

"Don't you need me?" she silently asked them.

"Don't be a fool," they seemed to reply in unison. And then one of them added, "How much longer do you think you're going to live?"

And she realized they were right.

"Okay," she said, "Sí."

Oscar let go of her hand and reached out to hold the back of her neck. Then all ambivalence fell away. Her life became simple. She wanted to fuse herself with this man who held her neck. It felt as though he held her entire body, in fact her entire life, in his hand. He stood up, still holding her, and pulled her to her feet by the nape of her neck. And then, as she stood in front of him, he kissed her roughly. There was nothing gentle or courteous about him now. Still holding her by the nape of her neck, he held her face to his as long as he pleased. She gloried in the pressure of his mouth against hers, rough, hard, knowing. His right hand held her neck and his left hand reached for her breast. Then, hearing something in the street, Oscar held her head away from him for a minute, stared at her, chuckled, and then put his arm around her shoulder. Letting his hand rest securely on her breast, he pushed her in front of him, into the house, and then into his bedroom.

Chapter Fifty-Three

TOWARD DAWN, JOAN woke up with Oscar's arms around her. He was snoring softly into her hair. She felt at peace with the universe. The night before, as Oscar pulled her dress over her shoulders, she'd thought of Charlie and of what he must be thinking. But then the Charlie in her head had said, "I'm happy for you." After that, she'd been nothing but happy throughout every part of her body. The world seemed to have opened itself up like a rose to enfold Oscar and her in its extravagant, fragrant beauty.

She turned over on her back, stretched, and stared up into the darkness, chuckling at her memories. When the window grew a little lighter, she realized she needed to look at the immediate future. She got up without waking Oscar and went into her room carrying her clothes. There, she put on the dress she had left out of the backpack for the trip home. She went to the outhouse, sprinkled some water on her face at the communal sink and sat down at the table in the still-dusky patio to think. The stars were beginning to fade, but dawn had not yet come. Very soon, Oscar's children would be wide awake and ready with their goodbye wishes. And then Maria and Barbara and Lorna would be there to pick her up and head out for Managua and the airport.

Oscar had not spoken of any of this. Joan thought that perhaps she should wake him up so they could decide together what to do, but at that moment he appeared, stretching and yawning in his shorts. He kissed her briefly on his way to the outhouse. When he came back, he sat down at the table with her. "I tell children, okay?"

"Yes," Joan answered grateful for his decisiveness. "Okay."

And then he shouted, loud enough to wake the neighbors, and the children came running, Juan in his shorts, Yeni and Eloina pulling dresses over their heads as they came. They stood in front of the table where Oscar and Joan sat holding hands.

Then Oscar pulled Joan to her feet and holding her hand high in the air roared an official announcement that Joan understood only one word of, "madrastra" stepmother. The children, smiling broadly, crowded closer, and hugged and kissed first Joan and then their father.

"Now you stay here," Yeni declared.

"Sí," Joan responded, wishing she could tell these children how blessed their welcome made her feel.

At that moment there was a sharp knock at the door. Joan headed for the door and Eloina went with her, putting her arm onto Joan's shoulder. Barbara was at the door. Maria and Lorna were in the car and the engine was running.

"Hi," Barbara said. "We're running a little late. Are you all set? Can I help you with your bag?"

"No, thank you," Joan said a little slowly as though trying to think what her next words would be. "I've decided to stay here. I'm not coming with you."

"You've decided to stay here, in Malpaisillo?"

"Yes, right here in this house. We've become good friends and…"

"I know it's heartbreaking to leave," Barbara interrupted. "I know just what you mean. But Joan, it's not safe here. There's a war going on and your Spanish isn't so great, and Maria won't be here to help. Joan, come back with us and then we can plan another trip in the future."

"No, I'm going to stay here. I'm hoping I can learn the language the way you have. But meanwhile, I'll muddle along."

"But, what will you do?"

"Have a good time, learn Spanish, and be happy."

At this point Oscar came to the door, having put on his pants and shirt, and stood beside Joan and took her hand. He beamed at Barbara as he greeted her with "Buenos Dias."

"Buenos Dias," Barbara replied a little mechanically. Then she looked at him again and at Joan. "You don't mean…"

"Yes, I do," Joan said quickly.

"But you've only known each other a few weeks! Joan, don't you want to come back to the States and think about this first. What will your family think? How long do you plan on staying?"

They were interrupted by Maria honking the horn. Then she got out of the car and joined them at the door. She asked Oscar something and when he answered, she said, "We must go now to arrive at plane. I desire for you happiness, Juana. Maybe we see each other later."

"Look," Barbara said quickly, "I'm going to give you my phone number. You call me at any time, you hear? If you need money for the trip home, you just call me and I'll wire it to the bank in León. Okay? You promise?" As she spoke, she wrote on a piece of paper that she tore off from her ticket envelope and handed it to Joan.

"I promise. And thank you. You've been wonderful all through this adventure."

"I put my address there too. Please write and tell me how you're doing. What about your plane ticket?"

"Shall I give it to you? Do you think someone could use it?"

"No, no, keep it. Maybe they'll let you use it later."

"We go now, Barbara," Maria insisted, taking her by the arm and heading back to the car.

Joan followed them to the car. "Thank you for every-thing," she whispered into Barbara's ear. She waved to Lorna in the back seat. Lorna didn't see her. She was con-centrating on reading a letter through a blur of tears. Maria honked goodbye as they drove off.

Chapter Fifty-Four

JOAN WENT BACK into the house and found Oscar moving things around in his bedroom. When he saw her in the doorway, he gave her a hug and said into her ear, "We give Eloina room, okay?"

"Okay," she said and went into what had been her bedroom to get her carefully packed backpack which she brought into Oscar's room.

Then Oscar's car pool folk arrived. When Oscar told them Joan was coming to León as well, the two people in the front seat quickly doubled up, a young woman sitting on the lap of an older one, so Joan could squeeze in. They hadn't discussed her coming to León, and Joan thought maybe Oscar just wanted her company, but when he had let the other passengers out, he turned to her and said, "You send telegram your child?" and Joan realized that of course he was right. Sarah would be worried.

Oscar drove her to the telegraph office, which was in the middle of town. They both got out of the car, and, standing in front of the telegraph office, Oscar pointed up the hill to the Cathedral and down the hill to a building he called the biblioteca and said, "Books, English books. I see you in la biblioteca five." He pointed to five o'clock on his watch. Joan nodded. "You have money telegram? You have money eat?" Joan realized they'd had no breakfast and she wouldn't see him until the afternoon. She nodded and showed him her wallet. She figured she'd find a café. She felt ready for any adventure Nicaragua could offer. As Oscar turned to get back into his car, she wanted to hug and kiss him and show the world what had happened to them, but he quickly pecked her on the cheek and pointed to his watch again, then to the library and drove off.

Joan went into the telegraph office. The clerk spoke some English. He gave her the form to fill out. Joan took it over to another counter to compose her message, and then realized she didn't know what to say. What would Sarah think of what she was doing? What about the children? Suddenly they seemed very close, confused and even hurt by her. She realized she'd have to write a long letter and that the telegram was just to make Sarah not worry.

"Staying longer. Very Happy. Will write. Love, Mom" That would have to do for the present. Joan left the telegraph office and headed uphill toward the Cathedral. The day was hot and she was sweaty. It had been a long commute in a crowded car. She'd forgotten her hat. The sun beat down on her as she trudged uphill. When she reached the Cathedral, she was almost panting. Once in the shadowy darkness, she went forward to sit in a front pew as far as possible from the large doors open to the sun.

She closed her eyes. Her breathing slowed to its normal pace. Her skin seemed to drink in the cool duskiness as though it were rain after a drought. She looked down at the bare wooden kneelers and decided to pray where she sat. First for Charlie, who seemed close and caring and happy for her. Then for Angelica and Marianne. Then she prayed for Sarah and the children and for Joe—let him be okay where ever he is. Then she prayed her thanks for Oscar and his children and the amazing experience of being in love. Then she prayed for her new country, "Please don't let the U.S. invade Nicaragua."

"At least I can pray for these people," she thought, "if I can't do anything else." But then, as she sat in the magnificent Cathedral, filled with hundreds of years of prayers, she remembered having heard that praying for people was worse than futile without actively helping them as well. Her sweat turned cold. It was as though she'd been skating over a beautiful lake in the mountains, and had suddenly heard a loud cracking sound. "Who the hell do I think I am?" she wondered, "Being so happy, making love all night. Maybe Sarah needs me. Or maybe Joe has tried to get in touch. He won't know where to find them if I'm not in Ipswich. How can I possibly stay here?" She quickly crossed herself, got up, left the pew, bobbing to a kneeling position beside it, and left the Cathedral.

She started walking; at first she was careful to keep track of each turn, but soon she realized that she could see the Cathedral from almost everywhere and she knew how to get to the library from the Cathedral, so she would not get lost.

But inwardly she felt completely lost. She missed Barbara and Lorna, and even Maria. She missed having an itinerary to fulfill, a mission to accomplish. She had no colleagues and no purpose.

She saw nothing as she walked. The people were moving objects to dodge, the stores and venders, obstacles to get past, the busy streets held no fear or interest as she crossed one after another. She refused to think. To think might mean having to tell Oscar she'd been wrong to stay. To think might mean knowing Joe was looking for his family first in New York City and then in Ipswich, and then giving up. Or, worst of all, to think might mean acknowledging that she was of no help to anyone either in the States or in Nicaragua.

After walking a long time, she felt too hot to go further. She went into the first café she saw and ordered a plate of beans and rice and a cup of coffee. She couldn't understand how much it cost, so she held out her hand filled with coins and let the waiter take what he would. After lunch and sitting a long time over a second cup of coffee, she walked back to the Cathedral, and from there to the telegraph office and from there to the library. They did have some books in English, mostly paperback detective stories and thrillers, probably left by tourists in hotel lobbies. She found a P.D. James that she hadn't read and settled down at one of the tables. She didn't look up again until Oscar touched her shoulder.

At the sight of him and the feel of his hand, all her loneliness and confusion dissipated. She sprang up, dropping the book, which he gravely picked up, and then followed him to the librarian's desk where he signed out the book.

Driving back to Malpaisillo, Joan was wedged between Oscar and two women, one sitting on the other's lap. Oscar chatted with the commuters but Joan didn't try to follow their conversation. Instead, she thought about her conversation years before with Father McGinley. He'd said she should be a role model for her daughters rather than always trying to help them. At the time she'd been angry with him, angry and confused. But now Angelica was dead, free at last, and Sarah was creating a good life for herself and her children. Perhaps it was time to consider being a role model. She could model the fact that love comes where and when it will. She reached up and touched Oscar on the cheek. A commuter in the back seat chuckled.

When Oscar drove slowly through the gates that closed off the patio, Joan saw that someone had brought the table outside and placed chairs around the edges of the patio which had been swept clean. She could see Eloina and Yeni cooking. As the commuters got out of the car, Oscar talked rapidly to them and they laughed happily as they headed home. Then he turned to Joan, "Tonight, my Juana, we have fiesta!"

Every guest brought something: food, drink, plates, cups, or chairs. They crowded throughout the patio, among the sow and her litter, the chickens, and the dog, all lit by the stars and the candles that Juan had stuck on the big sink and the outhouse roof. They did not dance, but they leaned against trees and posts and the sink and each other, and they sang. They sang hymns to God and songs in praise of Nicaragua. Some of the guests recited poetry. Yeni, Eloina and Joan sang, "I Want to Hold your Hand" and "Tea for

Two" with Juan creating an accompaniment on the guitar. At the end of the evening, Oscar, holding Joan's hand in the middle of his friends, made a speech.

After that, each guest went up to Joan, said something that sounded welcoming, and kissed her on the cheek. Then they picked up their plates or chairs or bowls or baskets and left. Joan could hear some of them singing as they walked toward their homes.

Everyone was tired. Juan and Yeni blew out the candles. Eloina put the bucket under the spigot in case water would come through that night. Joan and Oscar carried leftover food to the kitchen area and covered it with a cloth. Then Eloina went to bed in her own room and Joan went in with Oscar.

The next morning, after Oscar and Eloina left for work, and Juan and Yeni for school, Joan took paper and pen out to the patio where a small table was set up against the wall. She drew up a chair with the plan of writing to Sarah.

She put her pen down again. Sarah might not want to hear about her mother's falling in love, especially while they still had no news of Joe. At the same time, Joan didn't want Sarah to worry about her. After three botched beginnings, she finally wrote the following. She was unsatisfied with it, but gave a deep sigh of relief when it was over.

Dearest Sarah,

I hope all is well with you and the kids. I've decided to stay on here for a while. I've become good friends with the family I'm staying with, especially with Oscar, the widowed father of the three kids. It's amazing how close to them I feel, despite not being able to speak Spanish.

I'll come home for a visit in a month or so to collect clothes and stuff, and I'll tell you more.

I love you and the kids with all my heart, and I'll let you know when I can come and visit.

Love, Mom.

Chapter Fifty-Five

JOAN SLOWLY BECAME accustomed to living with very little water. At first she felt self-conscious—it was a rare treat when they had enough water left over at the end of the day to wash their clothes in. Her showers were very pleasurable but not all that effective, once she learned to leave enough water in the bucket for everyone else in the family. But each night Oscar made her feel beautiful. They laughed and wrestled, exploring curves and crevices. Joan felt remade in his image of her.

The days were also extraordinary. Oscar left around five-thirty in the morning. He now took Juan with him. Juan was attending computer classes in León so he could help his father in his office. Eloina left soon after for the clinic, and then Yeni left for school. Joan washed the breakfast dishes, using as little water as possible, then she swept out the house. The dust that poured in every day through the doors and windows was really grit from the road, black and grimy.

Then she took the marketing basket into town by way of the Catholic church, where she sat and prayed for a while. Sometimes there were other people praying as well, but usually she was on her own. In the market, she bought hand-made tortillas and fruit to add to their usual meals of rice and beans. She loved the morning walks, although some people continued to stare at her. At first she wondered what they were saying, and worried that she was ruining Oscar's reputation. But as the days passed, she stopped caring what they thought. She began to think her own thoughts.

She no longer focused on the political situation in Nicaragua; she thought about Oscar and the children. She thought about her struggle to learn Spanish. Sometimes as she walked, she reviewed in her head all the Spanish words she could remember. Oscar and the children all spoke very slowly with her and she found now that she could usually understand the gist of what they were saying and even respond in Spanish, with a lot of hand gesturing to make herself clearer. She had become so comfortable with the family that sometimes she spoke in English, forgetting that she was in a foreign country. Then one of them would say, "Mamacita, español por favor."

She couldn't understand anyone who spoke at normal speed, and so was still useless to Witness for Peace. But, she felt very happy as she swept the floor, went to the market, and cooked for her family.

After supper, Oscar and Joan often took a walk holding hands in the moonlight. Sometimes Juan would join them, and Oscar would rest his hand heavily on Juan's shoulder and they would talk about Juan's courses. Neither Oscar nor Joan knew enough about the language of computers to really understand what Juan was describing, but they enjoyed hearing about it all the same. It reminded Joan of when Angelica tried to explain color theory to her. Joan had soon stopped trying to understand, but at the same time she had reveled in Angelica's pleasure in being so knowledgeable. Here in Malpaisillo, Angelica's death seemed more distant, in time as well as in space. But Angelica herself, as a joyous child, as a loving older sister to Sarah, and as a painter immersed in the glories of color, seemed very close. Sarah, Kari and Sam, on the other hand, seemed far away, and difficult to communicate with.

Sarah had sent two telegrams in response to Joan's letter. The first one was: "Please don't make any decisions before we talk." The second telegram arrived the next day: "Please ignore last. I want only your happiness. Love, Sarah"

Two weeks later, a letter arrived.

Dear Mom,

I hope everything is still wonderful, but I'm enclosing some money (I hope it actually gets to you) in case you want to buy a ticket home. We miss you hugely. Sam is on the soccer team; Paul is painting oils now; and Kari takes Bruce everywhere she goes, except for school. She's rigged up a little halter for him with a leash and she "walks" him to the soccer field to watch Sam play or over to a friend's house. Bruce seems fine about it and now sleeps on Kari's bed, to Sam's annoyance.

I'm eager to hear more about your life there, and about Oscar and his children. Do you have a date yet for coming home? If you come into Albany, we'll pick you up and you can come here for a while. We'll all be thrilled to see you, including Bruce, who of course is no trouble at all, and has been doing a good job keeping the mice at bay.

All my love, Sarah

P.S. You'd let me know if anything were wrong wouldn't you Mom? I can fly down there at any time. I've already made arrangements with a neighbor about watching the children. They all send their love. Paul wants to be included. It's been a while since we've heard from Italy. I feel almost as though I've adopted Paul and I think he feels that way too. He is so dear with Kari. When they come home from school, Paul often plays board games with her. Sam usually prefers to play with some friends up the street. He's gotten into ping pong in a big way. Love from the four of us,

Sarah

A few weeks later, a second letter came.

Dear Mom,

I haven't heard from you yet. I hope the mail works down there. I'd love it if you could call me. Is there a phone where you're living? If not, could you send me another telegram? Oh dear, I see that this one came from León so I guess it's not so easy. Well, I want to tell you something, so I guess I'll just go ahead; then, if you call me, we can talk about it.

I've finally realized that Joe will never come back. I think he's died somewhere. Otherwise, I know he would have been in touch by now. Realizing this makes me feel less desperate. I'm getting ready to grow into a new life. The children are doing well, really well. I'm beginning to look at other men differently, and funnily enough, men seem to be looking at me in a new way as well. At one of Sam's soccer games a few weeks ago, his coach asked if I wanted to go out to dinner on Friday night. We went and had a nice time, low key, but nice—my first date in a very long while. Then the next week, our new neighbors, yes the house to the right of us was finally bought by a friendly family with five children, invited us to their open house. There was an architect there, divorced, with two teenage girls. We had a good talk and I think he might call me. I hope he does. I feel a little like a teenager myself.

Kari had a painting chosen for an all-schools show at the county fair this summer. Paul was amazingly not jealous. His paintings are getting really good. He did a wonderful painting of the hammock on the porch. He has sort of taken Kari on as his student, more like a disciple. He lets her go with him on his trips to paint different views in town. She sets up the easel you gave her next to his and works with her crayons absolutely silently beside him. Every once in a while, he'll look at her drawing and give some constructive criticism and then go back to his own work. I watched them

do this as they each painted a picture of the porch. Sam has become a real athlete. His soccer coach tells me he's a natural. He's already talking about Little League in the spring. And doing well in sports seems to be giving him giving more energy for school work. I heard him explaining to Paul about long division—what a pleasure to listen to Sam expound on something that used to have him baffled.
I love you Mom—we all do. Please write.

Love, Sarah

The afternoon after receiving the second letter, Joan sat on the patio with both letters in front of her and paper and pen and plenty of time to respond, but she did not write. For a while she pictured Sarah in the hammock in Paul's painting of their porch. She tried to bring her two lives together. The mother of Sarah and Angelica and grandmother of Sam and Kari and perhaps Paul, and the lover or even fiancé of Oscar and more or less stepmother to his children seemed to be two separate people and she felt amazed that they both somehow fit into her somewhat shapeless body. Later in the afternoon, when the girls came home and then when Oscar and Juan returned from León, the Nicaraguan aspect of her life intensified and the US aspect of her life receded. She hardly thought about it again until she had the house to herself the next afternoon.

A few weeks later, Sam wrote her,

Dear Gran,

I hope you come home soon. I made three goals today. I'm also good at ping pong. We play at my friend's house in his basement and I win a lot. Mom is reading aloud a book about The Hardy Boys. Bruce comes to me when I whistle. He sleeps with Kari now, which is good because she has nightmares and I don't. We had Thanksgiving upstairs at the bookstore with Margo. We had fun but I miss you.

Love, Sam

It was Sam's letter that brought Joan's northern family to the forefront of her thoughts. She decided to ask Oscar about the possibility of phoning Sarah. Maria had told them that there was a telephone in the Mayor's office that could be used for emergencies. But instead, as Oscar and Joan were taking a walk after supper, Joan heard herself say, "I need to go to the United States."

Oscar didn't ask her why. Instead, he asked very somberly, "You will remain in the States?"

"No," Joan said, eager to reassure him, "I will remain here in Malpaisillo with you. I will visit Sarah and I will return, soon."

Oscar drew Joan to him and kissed her long and hard in the middle of the street. Then they turned to go home.

The next day Oscar bought Joan's plane ticket for her while he was in León. It was for the following day. He'd arranged to have the day off so he could drive her into Managua.

Chapter Fifty-Six

A BAND, MADE up of old men and women, was playing songs from the revolution outside the airport. They had a couple of guitars, clarinets and oboes, a French horn, and a drum. Oscar and Joan held hands and listened. Joan was impressed by how well they played, despite how old and somewhat decrepit they looked. Close to the band was a group of businessmen holding briefcases. Oscar pointed to a man who wasn't carrying a briefcase and told Joan that he was the president of Nicaragua. An announcement was made over the loudspeaker. The band stopped playing, and the President said something to each of the musicians as he shook hands with them. Then he and his entourage went into the airport.

Oscar and Joan were about to follow them when she noticed one of the oboe players. He was squatting to clean his oboe and put it away in the case that lay on the ground. She was surprised that he could squat so comfortably at his age. She wished she could do that. She looked more closely at him. There was something about the way he moved, his gestures so efficient and at the same time flowing, almost like a dancer. He couldn't be as old as the other musicians, who were cleaning and packing up their instruments in ways that showed their difficulties in bending and lifting. There was something familiar about his hunched body. She could not look away, although Oscar had put his hand under her elbow and was giving a little tug. Then the oboist stood up and faced her.

He stood still, as though turned into stone, and stared at her. He was desperately thin. His eyes seemed to have retreated back into his face as though he was looking out from dark caves. His unkempt hair and scruffy beard were almost white. He wore, like all the band members, a black suit, shiny with wear and not very clean. It hung loosely around his body. His shoes were sneakers patched in places with black tape. But he wore the wide wedding ring that he and Sarah had picked out together.

This wedding ring, so familiar, the twin to Sarah's, gave Joan the courage to disengage her arm from Oscar's hand and walk tentatively toward the man whom she had prayed for every day since his disappearance. As she approached, Joe didn't move. His expression slowly changed from shock, to fear, to relief as she got closer. Finally, when they were close enough to touch, Joan put out her right hand, as if they were acquaintances, and said, "Oh, the joy of being able to speak in English."

Tears came to Joe's eyes as they silently shook hands and then continued to stare at each other. Finally, Joan gave a sob as she put her arms around his neck and hugged him long and hard.

When she leaned back again, Oscar was at her side. She pointed to Joe and said in her broken Spanish, "Joe, husband of Sarah." She looked at Joe's face and was relieved to see him beam as he shook Oscar's hand.

"Mucho gusto" they said to each other.

And then Joan added in English, "Oscar is my fiancé."

Joe looked back at Oscar, "Su novio?"

"Sí," replied Oscar, smiling broadly.

"Mucho gusto," Joe repeated as he shook Oscar's hand again. Then they began talking together in rapid Spanish. Joan, who had stopped trying to understand them, heard her flight being announced.

She reached out to touch Oscar's arm as the announcement was repeated. Then she stared wildly at Joe. Would he still be here when she came back? She couldn't bear it if he disappeared again. She reached into her wallet and pulled out the four hundred dollars Sarah had sent and that she had planned to give back when she saw her. She turned to Joe and showed him the money. "Please come with me. I am going to Sarah's. Please come — if only to see your children. I beg you to come with me!"

For a moment Joe said nothing. He seemed about to blurt out a reason that he could not come, but in fact he said not a word. Then suddenly he asked, "Are you sure?"

"Yes," she said and handed him the money. Her plane was being called for the third time.

Joe handed her his oboe and ran over to the band leader to explain. Then he ran toward the ticket counter, calling over his shoulder, "Kennedy?"

"Albany," Joan shouted, "via Miami."

Oscar and Joan headed toward the boarding gate. Joan felt terrible that she had no words to explain what was happening, so she grabbed his hand and held it tight and leaned toward his ear and whispered, "Te amo, mi amor" and "Regreso pronto." If it wouldn't have embarrassed Oscar, she would have grabbed him around the neck and kissed him hard until he couldn't breathe, but she knew he'd have hated that, so she just held tight to his hand.

Soon, Joe joined them and took his oboe back. Joan said a little plaintively, "please explain some of this to Oscar. I haven't the words." So Joe and Oscar talked rapidly back and forth and then Oscar gave Joe a bear hug and said, what Joan recognized was, "My house is your house."

Then came the final call for the flight. Joan quickly kissed Oscar on the mouth and not looking at his face to see if she'd embarrassed him, she headed out toward the waiting plane. Joe followed her with his oboe in one hand and her backpack in the other.

Chapter Fifty-Seven

THE PLANE WAS not crowded. The seat next to Joan's was empty, so Joe slid in beside her. During the takeoff, Joan stared out the window, hoping to see Oscar when they banked a curve and trying not to be frightened as the plane lumbered, with a lot of complaining noises, into the air. It wasn't until they were above the clouds and horizontal, that Joan looked at Joe. His face was grey, as though he might vomit.

She smiled at him and put her hand over his, which was clinging to the arm rest between them. She was about to sympathize about the awfulness of flying, when he asked, "Do the children think I'm dead?"

Joan realized to her surprise that she didn't know. "I'm pretty sure Sarah's never told them you'd died. I'm sure she would have told me if she had. They stopped asking questions a long while ago. They used to make up stories to tell friends where you were—adventures you were having. But I'm not sure what they really think."

"Do they have a stepfather? Has Sarah married again?"

"No, she hasn't married again. She's still married to you as far as I know." Joan paused, and then went on, "But she may have fallen in love. I've been away a while."

"Aren't you afraid I'll hurt her by reappearing? I hope we, I mean I, haven't made a terrible mistake."

It hadn't occurred to Joan that his reappearance might be hurtful to Sarah.

"I wrote to her, you know. She never replied."

"No, I didn't know that. Where did you write to?"

"To the apartment in New York, with a copy to you in Ipswich."

"But I never got the letter in Ipswich. When did you write?"

"Early September I think."

"Well, the letter's probably there waiting for me. Sarah and the children are in Carleton now. They'll be picking us up in Albany."

"I don't want to hurt anyone," Joe went on, "I mean more than I have already. If the children think I've died I don't know what will happen when they see me. And if Sarah has found someone else, and perhaps told him that I've died, I may be making trouble for her. I know it's a little late to be worrying about this. I should have thought of this before I bought the ticket. But it all had to be decided so quickly. Also," he said with a strained grin, "I was so grateful that you wanted me to come, that you thought they'd want to see me, that I really didn't think of anything else."

"Of course I wanted you to come," Joan said. "We've been looking for you for ages. But it did happen quickly," she continued, "too quickly to think through. I was afraid that you wouldn't be in Nicaragua when I got back, and I wouldn't know how to find you." She took his hand and held it with both of hers as though he still might take off. Then she continued more hesitantly, "I think it's important that the children know you're alive and that you'll be part of their lives in the future, no matter what..." she ended tentatively. "And as for Sarah, surely you both need to talk, so she can understand what happened, in order, well, you know what I mean..." Again she ended lamely, because she had no idea if Sarah could understand or forgive whatever he'd done.

"Shall I tell you news about the children?" Joan asked to change the subject.

"Yes, please. Yes, of course. But if they're fine, I want to tell you first why I left. It's not that I want you to tell Sarah. I'll tell her of course, but I want you to know now. You've been so good to me... Then I want to hear about everyone, including Oscar."

"All right, if you're sure." Joan said.

"To begin with, I don't know if you noticed, I never mentioned it to anyone, but toward the end of that summer I didn't feel well."

"Yes, well no, not really; I saw that you looked exhausted, but it was Angelica who said you weren't well. That's why I called the hospitals."

"You called the hospitals? Yes, of course you did. I didn't think of how you'd look for me. Well, in fact, I wasn't well at all. I had a lot of tests done in Boston. I didn't tell Sarah—I'm not sure why now. At the time, I thought I was protecting her from unnecessary worry. Well, the morning we were supposed to leave to go back to New York, I had an appointment with the doctor who had done the tests. He told me I had cancer of the liver."

"Oh, my God!" Joan said.

"Do you remember," he went on, "about my mother's death and how awful the whole experience was?"

"Of course I do," Joan answered.

"Well that was what she died of, cancer of the liver. It's thought to be 100% lethal. My doctor said he was very sorry but he didn't want to give me false hopes."

"Why didn't you come back and tell us what had happened? Or call and have Sarah meet you in town while I watched the children?"

"Looking back, I can't imagine why I didn't do just that. I could have walked with Sarah by the river and I could have offered to go away so she and the children wouldn't have to deal with my getting so sick before I died. I could have suggested that and then let her choose." He paused for a minute, breathing deeply as though keeping tears back. Then he went on, "But I didn't. I just couldn't bear the idea of Sarah and the children, especially the children, living through what I knew was coming. I'd been there, you see. I knew exactly what was coming. My mother had been my best friend. When she turned bitter toward me, never wanting me around, blaming me for how awful she felt, I wanted to die. I just couldn't put Sarah and the children through that. So I decided to disappear."

"Why?" Joan interrupted so loudly that the elderly man across the aisle stared at her worriedly and reached above his head toward the bell to summon someone. This gesture caught Joan's attention and she lowered her voice, "Why would it be better to disappear? How could that help us or you?"

"I'm not saying it was better," he answered so softly that she had to lean toward him to hear. "I'm not saying it was better. I'm just saying that was what I thought at the time."

"What do you think now?"

"I don't know. I expected to be dead within a few months of leaving."

"Are you very sick?" Joan asked, wondering how she could have missed that again.

"No. I'm in remission. My liver seems to have made an unusual comeback."

"Thank God. Were you being treated in Nicaragua?"

"No, in Mexico. 'I don't want to give you false hope' the doctor said, 'but there's a clinic outside of Mérida where some people who don't have a chance in hell go and once in a while get better.' So I decided to go there—a good place to disappear, I thought, a good place to die."

"Oh my dear," Joan said, but Joe went on.

"I drove straight to the airport. I had cashed my pay check at Tanglewood and still had some of it in my pocket. I put the keys in the glove compartment. I figured the police would return the car to Sarah."

"They never did," Joan said.

"Someone must have stolen it and changed the plates" he conjectured. "When the plane landed in Mérida, I found my way out to the clinic, but I hadn't thought that it would cost money. Well, clearly, I hadn't really thought about anything. So I ended up getting a gig at a pension in Mérida and made enough to become an outpatient. They put me on a strict diet regimen and did all sorts of therapies, and after a long while I began to feel better."

"When was this? Why didn't you just come home?"

"I'd burned my bridges Joan. You know that, both with Sarah and the children. There seemed to be no way home at all. Excuse me." Abruptly, he got up and headed toward the back of the plane.

Chapter Fifty-Eight

JOAN STARED OUT the window at the blue sky above a floor of clouds. When Joe came back, his face wan and glistening with water drops, Joan asked, "How did you come to Nicaragua?"

"I saw an article in the New York Times about an American volunteer who was killed by the Contras while trying to build a clinic in a small village in Nicaragua."

"Oh!" Joan said startled.

"What?"

"That's why… No, I'm sorry, go on. Please go on," she added when Joe hesitated.

"Well, I figured I'd take his place. Not as a builder, but as a musician. A priest in Mérida managed to get me a job in a traveling band. So I came. Managua was like another world—the earthquake devastation, the empty ruin at the center of town, the shacks people lived in. But the wonderful murals on the walls gave me a surge of joy that I hadn't felt since before the cancer.

"The band members were welcoming, kissing me on the cheek and banging me on the back. We began at once to rehearse so I could learn their music. There's no sheet music. We have about thirty pieces we play, but we improvise around them a bit and sometimes come up with new ones. Within three days we were back on the road. As you saw, everyone but me is either too old or too disabled to be in the army, but they manage the traveling and we have a great time together."

"Do you have a bus?" Joan asked.

"No, it's mostly hitchhiking."

"Hitchhiking?"

"Because of the war, the government put out a request for every car or truck to pick up as many hitchhikers as could safely fit into their vehicles. So often, getting a ride means clinging to the side of a swaying truck and trying not to be tossed back onto the road when the truck lurches over the potholes."

"You must have a difficult time keeping your oboe safe. How do you know where to go? Who's in charge of making your tour arrangements?"

"For the most part, we just go from village to village. When we arrive, we look up the local mayor, present ourselves and ask him if there's an event in his town that he wants us to help him celebrate. Usually these are funerals for people killed by the Contras, or an opening of a new school or health center, or a saying goodbye to young people who are heading off to join the army. If we are needed, they give us a meal of rice and beans and show us a place to sleep. Sometimes this is the floor of the new building we are celebrating, but usually they divide us up among local families who crowd their children four in a bed so that two of us can share another bed."

"It sounds dangerous if you're going into villages where people are getting killed."

"We've had some close calls. Sometimes the trucks we're traveling on get targeted, although we've never been hit straight on. The Contras probably think the trucks are carrying supplies. And once a clinic we'd been sleeping in was destroyed half an hour after we'd gotten out. I think the band members welcome the danger. It makes them feel part of the army."

"But you, Joe, you don't want to be part of the army do you?"

"The truth is, Joan, I've been welcoming the risk as well. I've been so afraid of hurting Sarah by showing up again, that being bombed in Nicaragua seemed like a better way out. I've been ready to die for so long that it feels almost strange, sometimes wonderful, sometimes horrible, that I'm still here."

"Oh my dear, I wish you'd called me. All through this time, if you didn't feel you could talk with Sarah, I wish you'd called me. Well," she continued, putting her hand on his arm, "thank God you're here safe, not bombed, not dead. You're awfully thin," she continued, "but you look well."

"I am well. There just hasn't been enough food to go around. The villagers share with us what they have, but especially in the mountains where the fighting is nearby, there's not enough food."

They sat in silence for a while; the image of widespread hunger making it hard to find words on any other topic. Then Joe leaned back in the seat, closed his eyes, and said, "I'm really grateful to you for getting me on this plane." After a minute, he continued, "even though I have no idea what's going to happen when we land." Then he opened his eyes, sat upright, and turned to Joan, as he said, "Please, tell me about you. How did you come to Nicaragua?"

"Well, I too have been on an adventure. But first of all I need to tell you that Angelica has died."

"Oh, no!" he made the sign of the cross, "Joan, I'm so sorry. Forgive me for rambling on like this. Can you tell me what happened?"

"Yes dear, it is, it was, awful. At first it seemed as though the sky had fallen. She killed herself."

Joe flinched and turned white. Then he took both of Joan's hands in his as he said very quietly, "She told me she hated life, 'I can't stand life itself,' was what she said. But I had no idea… I don't know what I could have done… Oh, Joan, I'm so sorry. I'll be quiet. Please tell me…" He couldn't finish the sentence.

"I don't think there was anything you, or any of us, could have done." Joan took her hands out from between Joe's and sat back as she said, "It took me a long while to come to that, but that's what I believe. I think she was afraid that she would get put into a state hospital that she wouldn't be able to sign herself out of—a prison. I think that's why she did it. Also, her doctor told me that the drugs he was hoping would help her had been forced off the market because of side effects. So there was nothing in the wings to hope for. She took her own way, signed herself out of the hospital and took an overdose of pills. I think it just felt as though she was going to sleep—no pain, or fear, or chance to change her mind." Joan wiped the tears from her cheeks with the back of her hand.

"Anyway," she went on, after blowing her nose, "after Angelica died, I met the parents of that American builder you were talking about. Their descriptions of Nicaragua convinced me to join a Witness for Peace delegation. I thought I could be helpful by spreading the truth about what was actually happening there. I told the organizers in Boston that I could speak Spanish. I'd been studying it for months and months and could talk back to those silly recordings. But when I arrived in Nicaragua, I realized that I couldn't understand or speak it at all. I'd been warned that if I wasn't fluent in Spanish I could be of no real help because everything I learned would be influenced by an interpreter. So, not knowing Spanish, I had failed Witness for Peace, and was helping nobody."

"You're always helping people. Look what you've done for me? How did you get to know Oscar? Are you really engaged?"

"Yes, we are." Joan paused for a minute, smiling to herself. "I was staying with him and his children. He's a widower. I was feeling so awful about failing the delegation after having failed Angelica, that I sort of hit rock bottom. Marianne and Angelica were gone, and Sarah and the children were doing fine without me. Well, you know what I mean," she interrupted herself, "as fine as they be could under the circumstances. Until then, I'd no idea how much I depended on being needed, being able to help someone. It was my reason to be alive." Joan paused and then sighed as though saying good bye to an old memory. "So there I was, of no use to anyone. It was like having to remove my mask, and show my face naked to anyone looking. But that led to my being able to see other people without my mask in between us. I was able to see Oscar and his children, and I fall in love. I haven't felt like this since my twenties when I first knew Sarah's dad."

Neither of them spoke for a few minutes. Then Joe said, "Congratulations, dear Joan! I think that's wonderful!"

Then they heard the captain announce that they were circling Miami.

They had a two hour layover. Once they got through customs and found the gate for their plane to Albany, Joe asked, "Shouldn't we call Sarah?"

"Of course we should," Joan answered as she sat down on a plastic chair.

"I think you should be the one to call her," Joe continued.

"You're right," Joan said. "Of course you're right," she repeated. She didn't move. Finally, Joe sat down next to her. "What'll we do?" she asked him, "What'll we do if she's so shocked that… I mean it's been so long… I don't know what she'll say."

"I know," he said, staring at the ground. "That's what I'm afraid of."

"What if we just show up?" Joan asked. "That way she could see you before she made up her mind, and the children could see you and you could see the children and…" by this time Joan was sort of babbling.

"Joan, I'd love that. You know I would. I'd love to see them; but, I think we should call first."

"Of course you're right," Joan repeated again. "Okay," she said getting up slowly to head for the phone booth. Joe didn't follow her.

The phone rang and rang, but there was nobody home. An hour later, at Joe's encouragement, Joan called again. Still nobody home. They made one more try when their plane was called. To Joan's great relief, Sarah still didn't answer.

Chapter Fifty-Nine

JOAN LED THE way out of the plane and through the accordion-shaped walkway to where she knew Sarah would be waiting. Joe was right behind her carrying her backpack and his oboe. As they approached the waiting crowd, Joan saw the children and Sarah look right past her to stare at Joe. Then suddenly, the children left their mother's side and raced toward their father. Even Paul ran toward them. As Sam and Kari banged into Joe's open arms, Paul gave Joan a glorious hug. Over Paul's shoulder, Joan looked at Sarah. She stood very still. She closed her eyes for half a minute and then opened them and continued to stare but not to move. When they all reached her, Joe put down the backpack and his oboe case. Sarah hugged Joan without speaking. She seemed about to put out her hand toward Joe but thought better of it. She put her hands out to Sam and Kari. They clung to their father tighter. Finally she said, "Hello," although Joan had never heard her voice so icy before.

Joe echoed her hello.

Then they both stood silent and the children were silent as well, waiting for their parents to speak. Joan wanted to blurt out all that Joe had told her. She hoped Sarah would listen before she condemned. Finally, she said, "I'm exhausted. Let's stop for coffee and ice cream."

"Hurray," Sam shouted and picked up his grandmother's backpack. Paul, wanting to do something, picked up Joe's oboe case, and Joan and the boys led the way down the corridor. Sarah and Joe followed, with Kari swinging from Joe's arm.

While they ate and drank, the children regaled their father with news of their new house, their school, their neighbors, and their friends; even Paul joined in and told about his mother's travels in Europe. Many sentences began with, "I can't wait to show you..." Finally there was a pause, as every plate and cup was empty. Joan paid the bill. Everyone thanked her, Sarah a little mechanically. Then, as they stood and gathered jackets, knapsack, and oboe, Sarah turned toward Joe, though not actually looking at him, "I suppose we can all fit in the Ford, if Kari sits on her father's lap. Why don't you come see the house, Joe, so they can show you the model railroad they've set up." Joan heard the emphasis on the word "see."

So did Joe, who replied a little cautiously, "Thank you, Sarah. I'd like that a great deal."

Sarah drove with Joan beside her. In the back seat, Joe had a boy on either side of him and a beaming Kari on his lap. Sarah and Joan were silent. The children talked happily about the train set.

They arrived home around four o'clock. The children rushed back and forth between their father, who was playing with their model railroad, and Joan, who unpacked the presents she'd brought for all of them. Then Joan went to look for Sarah to give her the hand-woven placemats she'd brought for her. She found Sarah in the kitchen, silently crying as she cut up cucumbers and tomatoes for a salad. Joan put her arms around her and she turned to cry on Joan's shoulder. "It's just the shock. I don't know what to do. Why doesn't he have a suitcase? Why didn't you tell me? I don't know what to do. I don't know how I feel." Then she pulled her head away and whispered furiously, "How could you not have told me?"

"I didn't know myself, dearest. I met him at the airport, just before I was boarding. I was afraid if he didn't come with me I might never see him again. He's with an army band. He could be killed at any time. I just thought it was essential that you..." at that point the children came bounding into the kitchen to show their mother their presents. Joe stayed in the living room looking at photographs and some of the children's artwork that was on the walls.

After an early supper, the children and Joe went across the street to the school soccer field to kick the ball around. Nothing had been said about where Joe would spend the night. Joan knew that the children assumed, almost aggressively, that he would stay with them. Sarah did not seem to want that, but couldn't talk about it with him in front of the children. So Joan said casually to Sarah as she dried the dishes, "I think I'll go for a stroll downtown and then go to a movie."

"Oh Mom, I hate your feeling that you have to get out of the way. We haven't said a word about you and everything that's happened."

"That's true and I have a lot to tell you. But right now, Joe's come home, I mean come back," Joan quickly amended, "and that's so huge that it needs focusing on. We'll talk about me and Oscar soon. You've been through a tremendous shock. Be easy on yourself, is my advice, and don't make any big decisions. But whatever you do, dearest, I'm behind you. Now," she put down the dishtowel, "I'm off. Say goodnight to the children for me." And she left quickly, grabbing a jacket, "Can I borrow this?" from the closet and closing the front door before Sarah could say yes or no.

The movie theater was a ten minute walk and Joan had given herself an hour and a half. She stopped on the way to watch Joe and the children play soccer. They had been joined by some neighbors and had divided up into teams. Joe was the goalie for both teams and they took turns trying to get the ball past him into the net. Joan watched as Kari kicked the ball, as hard as she could, past Joe's unmoving legs and into the net. Everyone shouted hurray and then Joe left his post for a moment to grab his daughter around the waist, lift her high and swing her round and round as she laughed and the others cheered.

"This has to work out. It just has to," Joan said to herself as she headed into town.

Sarah sat at the kitchen table. She felt as though she'd been shot out of a canon and was still in mid-air. She was ecstatically happy that Joe was alive and had come back, but she was so angry at him for disappearing, for causing her and the children such anguish, that she didn't know if she ever wanted to see him again. If she were a man she would hit him and kick him blow by blow until he was crumpled and silent. She didn't want to hear his excuses. She could hardly believe that her husband, the man she'd loved so completely, could have cut her and the children out of his life for an entire year, and then arrive unannounced at the new home, the new life she'd created, and assume he'd be welcomed back.

She remembered an experience she'd had years before at a sauna, remaining in the heat of the wood-slatted enclosed room until she felt that her mind as well as her body was melting into sweat, and then climbing down a ladder into the ocean, cold beyond belief, and remaining there until her limbs felt as though they would never move again and she would be forever frozen in place. Now, she was traveling between her passion and love for him, her gratitude that he was alive and well, and the horrific cold of her anger that he could have left her and the children for any reason whatever.

Chapter Sixty

WHEN JOAN RETURNED from the movie, the house
was silent but some lights were on. She found a note on the
kitchen table. 'Hi Mom, Joe and I are talking in the living
room. Please tell Sam when you come home because I
promised him you'd say good night. Love you.'

Joan went up to the boys' room. The light was on, but
they were both asleep. Sam had Joe's oboe case tucked under
his arm as though it were a teddy bear. She thought of trying
to rescue the oboe and put it somewhere easy for Joe to find
if he wasn't spending the night, but she decided to let Joe
and Sarah work that out. She turned off the light and tiptoed
out. Then she looked in on Kari. Kari slept on her side with
Bruce curled behind her knees. Joan had to stop herself from
picking Bruce up and carrying him to her own bed. She gave
Kari a quick kiss and tiptoed out. Then, she quickly used the
bathroom and closed the door to her room. She didn't want
to be visible when Sarah and Joe finished their conversation.
She wondered if she had interfered too much already.

Joan's room, actually Emily's, had a drafting table with a stool in front of it. Joan sat down at the table and began a letter to Oscar. Very quickly she realized that this was going to be impossible. She drew pictures of stick figures with clothes on—Oscar and her holding hands with Yeni and Eloina on either side, and Juan next to Eloina. Below she wrote, 'Mi família magnífica.'

Then she drew another group of stick figures holding hands and labeled them Sarah, Sam and Kari. She hesitated a moment and then added Paul. Then after more hesitation and realizing she was somewhat superstitious, she drew Joe holding Kari's hand. Beneath this group she wrote, 'También mi família magnífica.'

Then she drew a large valentine around both sets of stick figures. At the bottom she wrote, 'Te amo Oscar, Juana.' She sighed happily as she got into bed and not until she was almost asleep did she realize that she hadn't heard Joe or Sarah come upstairs.

Joan was up early, but not before Joe. She noticed his folded quilt and pillow on the edge of the couch. She found him sitting on the steps of the side porch. He looked very cold in his black suit. She unfolded the quilt, putting it around her shoulders for warmth, and joined him on the porch, slowly lowering herself down beside him and putting part of the quilt around his shoulders. They stared at the street and the bit of brown lawn between themselves and the driveway that would sometime soon be covered with snow. Two squirrels were playing in the neighbor's red maple. No neighbors were in sight.

After a few minutes of silence, Joan said, "I hope you're not sorry I brought you up here."

"No matter what happens, absolutely not, not ever, Joan."

"It was wonderful seeing you with the children."

"I'd forgotten how much fun they are. I hadn't forgotten for an instant how much I loved them, but I'd forgotten how much fun they are."

"Did you and Sarah have a good talk?"

"She heard me out, but we didn't really talk. The problem is that neither of us can really understand why I left. At the time it seemed like the only thing I could do. It seemed as though I was being the good husband and father protecting my family from horror. But seeing it through her eyes, I realize that I must have been made half insane by the shock of being told I was about to relive my mother's painful death. I have no other way of explaining it."

"What I don't understand is why you didn't call us from Mexico when you began to get better. I so wish you'd called me."

"The strange thing is that it never occurred to me that I wasn't dying. Even as time went by I just assumed it was around the next corner. In a sense I felt as though I had already died and I was just marking time until my physical death caught up with me."

"But you were working, playing music for people and all."

"Yes, somehow the music goes on by itself; it seems to have a life of its own. You're right. I should have recognized that I was feeling better, but in a way I had already cut myself off from my body—not wanting to know what was happening to it."

"And when you decided to go to Nicaragua?"

"Being told I might not be dying right away woke me up. It was like warming up after a long period of frostbite—it hurt a lot. That's when I decided that I might be better off being 'cannon fodder,' as the priest put it, than returning to Sarah and the children where I had messed up so radically."

"Surely the priest didn't agree to let you go to Nicaragua to be 'cannon fodder.'"

"No, I told him I wanted to be part of the 'human shield' of Americans living there so that Nicaragua would be less likely to be bombed. Just like you were doing."

"Yes, perhaps, although I didn't think of it that way. You're right though, even if I couldn't spread the word about what was happening, at least I was there, one more American. I very much look forward to getting back. I miss it already. Not only Oscar and the children, but the country itself. What will you do now, Joe?"

"That will depend a lot on Sarah. She says it's painful to have me here because she's lost her trust in my 'common decency' as she calls it. But I'm not sure she really wants me to go back to Nicaragua or somewhere else far away, partly because of the children."

"Yes, it would be terrible for them to lose you again." Joan realized then that she had nothing to suggest, so she said, "Do you want some coffee?"

"Yes," Joe answered, "I'll come with you." He helped her up and then held the door as they went back into the house. In the kitchen, Kari was carefully pouring milk from a little pitcher into a bowl of cereal while Bruce was sitting on the counter next to his half-full bowl of food watching her.

"Want some cereal, Dad?"

"No thanks, Hon, not right now. Where's Mom?"

"She's working."

"So early?"

"She's at the bakery."

"Who takes care of you in the morning?"

"Mom leaves me cereal. The boys walk me to daycare before school."

"Where's the bakery?"

"I know how to go. I'll show you." She quickly ate some cereal and then went to get her jacket.

Joan watched them set out, hand in hand. She couldn't hear their conversation, but they were clearly catching up.

When the boys came down a little later, they let Joan make scrambled eggs and bacon for them, which they wolfed down. Then they thanked her and went across the street and around the corner to their school.

Joan took a shower, put on her jeans, and headed over to the post office to mail her "letter" to Oscar. When she passed the bakery, she looked in the window and saw Sarah, who beckoned her to come in.

"Hi, Mom, were you okay last night?"

"Sure; I'm glad you and Joe had a chance to talk."

"Yeah, well, we're going to try to talk some more this afternoon. I asked him to pick me up here at two when I get off. Could you pick Kari up at daycare at three? That way, if I'm crying or something, she doesn't need to see it."

"Sure, and Kari and I will go shopping and make supper. So, if you two want to be on your own this evening, that's fine."

"Well, we'll see. Right now, I don't like being with him at all. Anyway, I loaned him fifty dollars to buy some warm clothes at the consignment shop before he takes you out for lunch. I know you don't care how he looks, but I do. I mean, I think I do. People are going to know he's my…he's the children's father. Oh, Mom, I wish I'd known he was coming. Joe told me how you tried to call from Miami. It's so hard. I love him and hate him all at the same time, and I have to think of what's best for the kids."

"I'm really sorry I didn't warn you. The truth is that I didn't think of anything when I saw him but how to hang on to him."

"Maybe you should have let him go. I don't know. What if the cancer comes back? Then what'll he do? He acted so crazy. It's hard to believe. I mean I know he's telling the truth, but his truth is so crazy."

"Well, maybe he could get a job in the neighborhood so you two could get to know each other again."

"And live where?"

"And live somewhere. Close enough to share the kids, but not with you until you know what you want."

"I don't know how I'd explain it to the kids, but that's a good idea. He's awfully thin, isn't he? But he's got to have clothes and a car in order to find a job and a place to live."

"As soon as I go back to Nicaragua, he can have my car."

"Oh, Mom," she almost wailed. "We still haven't talked about you. Do you have pictures of Oscar and his kids and the house and everything?"

"Yes, all of that. I have film that can be developed into slides as well as photos. I'll go to the drugstore to see if I can get them developed. Things like that are so much easier here. I'll pick up Kari and make supper. I'll see you when I see you and love you with all my heart. You know that. Bye."

"Bye, Mom, and thanks."

Joan walked to the post office and mailed her letter to Oscar with a quick prayer that all was well there. Then she walked back to Sarah's to dig out her film. There was no sign of Joe. She left him a note on the kitchen table. "Joe, dear, Hoping to have lunch with you. I should be home by noon. Love, Joan"

Then she set off again, this time heading for the drugstore to leave her film. She noticed the clock above the drugstore. It was only ten-thirty. What did she want to do? She decided she would buy presents to take back to Nicaragua.

She thought of the stores she knew on Main Street: a book store, an art supply store, a toy store and two gift shops.

What should she get Oscar? It was a surprisingly difficult question. Here was a man who had almost nothing, and could buy almost nothing in his own country, even if he had money. She wanted to bring him everything. Joan planned to send to Malpaisillo some of the furniture from the Ipswich house. But now, she wanted to get something new for Oscar, something personal, specifically from her to him. She headed down the street looking in windows, and realized that beyond the movie theater, there was a new store selling musical instruments and sheet music. She went in.

They had lots of electric guitars and some drums, and then she saw a wall display of instruments for children. Plastic recorders! She had learned how to play a wooden recorder as a child in camp. She didn't know if she could still find the sharps and flats, but on a bookshelf nearby were booklets describing how to play. She looked at one of them. It had lots of illustrations, so many that she thought one could find all the notes without knowing how to read English. At first she thought she'd ask about wooden recorders, but then she realized it was probably safer to get plastic ones. The heat in Malpaisillo might make the wooden ones dry out and crack.

She bought tenors for Oscar and Juan, an alto for Eloina and sopranos for herself and Yeni. She bought 'how to' books for each size and a book called 'Classical Trios Made Easy.' Then she wondered why she'd never thought of teaching Sarah or her children how to play recorder. She decided to ask Sarah if she were interested. She might be worried about bothering her neighbors.

She carried her packages back to Sarah's, pleased with her presents, but knowing she'd have to hide them from Sam and Kari, who would assume they were for them. She could hear Joe practicing the oboe as she turned on to Sarah's block. After stowing her purchases under her bed, she took a novel to the side porch. Bruce joined her there, jumping up beside her on the swing seat and then curling himself into a comfortable position to sleep. Joan opened her book, but instead of reading, she leaned back with her eyes closed and enjoyed Joe's practicing. It was something ornate, the kind of piece that shows off technique. Perhaps that was why Joe was playing it, in order to have an audition piece ready, should he get the chance. He did not play it very well yet. She heard the fast runs again and again and again as he tried to smooth them out. She thought of Angelica, how she and Angelica had tried to smooth things out between them again and again. Angelica had enjoyed taking her mother to galleries to show her the paintings she liked and those she felt should have been thrown away. But often on these out-ings, the two of them would hit a snag, usually something one of them said casually and, as they went their separate ways, both of them would be grateful that they had different homes to go to. But within the week, Joan would call her daughter and invite her to go to a favorite restaurant or to a movie and the two of them would try again. Joe seemed to have found further difficulties with his piece, but he was amazingly persistent, repeating the phrases again and again and again.

Chapter Sixty-One

SHOWERED AND IN corduroy pants, a flannel shirt and a down vest, Joe woke Joan up by giving her shoulder a gentle shake and saying, "Was my practicing so dull? That doesn't bode well. Can I take you to lunch? Sarah said I was not to let you cook for me because you'd want to reorganize her messy kitchen. Don't look at me like that. That's what she said. I know that's not one of your desires."

"My only desire" Joan said, still half asleep, reaching out her hand so Joe could help her out of the swing seat, "is to undo Angelica's death. No, that's not true," she continued, now standing upright facing him. "I have a huge desire that you and Sarah can join forces again. And also, for my marriage with Oscar and my new family, for both my families. You will be a wonderful bridge between us all, because of your knowledge of the country as well as the language."

"How do you always manage to make people feel better about themselves?"

"You know that's not true. I made Angelica feel worse, almost always. She told me so many times. As for Sarah, I don't know…I think she's still angry that…"

"That's my fault, not yours. God, isn't she beautiful? And the children are so happy and good natured. She never tried to turn them against me for leaving and she never told them I'd died. She's amazing, your daughter."

"Let's go to lunch," Joan said. "I'll wash up. You look very handsome in your new clothes."

"Thank you. I'll wait for you here." He sat down in the swing seat and began to rock, humming some of the music he'd been practicing.

Joan went in and washed her face and found a jacket. The sun had been warm, but she'd gotten a little chilled when she fell asleep. When she returned to the porch, she put out her hand to help Joe out of the swing seat, but he bounced up on his own and they descended the steps to the street.

"My favorite place is the Bookstore Café," she told him. "And I found a music store this morning where you can get sheet music." As they headed downtown, Joan grabbed Joe's hand for a minute—it felt so wonderful to have him there beside her, after a year of praying for his well-being and return. "Do you want to tell me anything about your talk with Sarah?" she asked.

"Well, she's terribly angry of course. When she's near me she can barely move, barely speak because of her rage. She can't believe I could be so wickedly stupid as to think it was better to leave than to talk."

"Did you tell her about your mom?"

"I reminded her of all that, but she knew about it before; it doesn't seem relevant to her." They walked on for a few minutes in silence.

"I think she feels that if she takes me back now," he continued, "I could walk out again just when she and the children become dependent on me. She's made a good life for herself and the children without me. I can imagine that in some ways I would be a fifth wheel, especially in the beginning."

Joan didn't say anything as they walked on. Then Joe added, "But the children, Joan, the children are amazing. They seem to have completely forgiven me. They've asked no questions at all."

"You wouldn't want Sarah not to ask questions would you? That would be really spooky, I think."

"You're right of course," Joe agreed. "I wouldn't want her not to ask questions, but I would love it if she didn't pour scorn on my answers."

They turned in at the Bookstore Café. Richard had his back to them when they entered. He was squatting beside a bookshelf, while an older woman, no longer able to squat herself, was telling him about a cookbook called, "Fun Food for the Over Fifties." He straightened up a little stiffly, pushing with one hand against the bookshelf, and with the other holding a book that he handed to the woman saying, "It sounds wonderful, Muriel. I'm sorry that we don't have it. Perhaps you'd like to look at this one. People say that the dessert recipes are to die for."

"Oh, I forgot my pen and paper," she almost moaned. "Wouldn't you know."

"Here you are," Richard said getting a legal pad and pen off his desk and handing them to her, "Let me know if you find something really scrumptious. Maybe Sage will want to try it upstairs." As the woman headed for the table with the book, Richard turned and saw Joan. "Why, welcome home, Joan. How good to see you. Sarah said that you would be coming back soon. Did you bring your fiancé?" He looked a little quizzically at Joe.

"Hello, Richard. It's good to see you too. No, Oscar couldn't come. Not this time, but soon, I hope. This is Joe, my son-in-law. He came back with me from Nicaragua."

"Hello, Joe. It's very nice to meet you." Richard shook hands with Joe and then turned back to Joan. "I didn't know you had another daughter in Nicaragua. I just knew about the one who…who lived in Boston. I am so sorry Joan for your loss."

"Thank you, Richard. I don't have a daughter in Nicaragua. Joe is married to Sarah, but he's been in Central America for over a year now."

"Well, how interesting. I mean, you must have had an interesting time of it. Are you with the government?"

"No, I mean, not the American government. I was in the Nicaraguan National Band."

"Joe's an oboist."

"Well, that sounds splendid." He turned to Joan. "Would you both consider giving a talk at the café about Nicaragua?"

"Yes, I think I could do that with Joe's help. He knows a lot more than I do, of course. I'll have some slides from the trip. They're being developed now. Do you have a projector?"

"I'm sure Sage can borrow one from the school."

"Okay, let's talk about it when the slides come back."

"Terrific. Well, it's great to meet you Joe. I'll tell Sage."

"If she's upstairs, we'll tell her ourselves. Joe is taking me out to lunch here."

"Best little place in town. She is here. She'll be really happy to see you. Go on up. We've got apple pie today. Truth is, I made it myself, and it came out okay. I'll talk with you both later," he continued as a customer came in. "Have a good lunch."

"See you later," Joan said as they climbed the stairs to the café.

"Oh, Joan, how wonderful to see you," was Sage's greeting. "Sarah told me you were coming, but I didn't realize how soon. You look wonderful. Aren't the children doing well? Did Sarah tell you about Kari's being in the all-county exhibit at the fair? Paul should have gotten in. His watercolors are becoming quite stunning. Did you know that I'm planning to retire from teaching in the spring? It looks as though we can make a go of this full time."

"That's wonderful," Joan said. "It all looks terrific. I love the paintings. Who's the artist? But before you tell me, I want to introduce you to Joe, Sarah's husband. We've just come back together from Nicaragua. Richard has been kind enough to ask us to give a talk and a slide show together on what's happening there. I must say I do like these paintings."

"Thank you. They're mine. Joe, I'm so happy to meet you. Sarah didn't… Well, in any case, I'm so pleased to meet you. And I look forward to your talk with Joan about Nicaragua. You know, Joan, we're thinking of expanding, building out a little into the back yard. We could have small concerts, a singer and a pianist, that kind of thing."

"That sounds wonderful. Joe is an oboist. He was part of the Tanglewood orchestra."

"Were you? My goodness. How wonderful! Perhaps you would be willing to play for us some day."

"Thank you. I'd like that." Joe looked truly relaxed for a minute.

"What am I thinking of, keeping you both standing?" Sage said looking at Joe. "Come, sit, anywhere you like. I'll get you some menus."

Joan chose a round oak table that was set for three. She hoped that if other customers didn't come in right away, Sage might sit down with them. She wanted people to get to know Joe.

They started by ordering cappuccinos. "Now this is something I haven't had in a long while," Joe said as he lifted his steaming cup.

"Yes," Joan said, "this is one of the few things, not counting people of course, that I'm going to miss. I think I'll try to have at least one every day I'm here, so maybe I can get tired of them before I go back."

"How long are you staying here?" he asked.

"Probably not long. I want to find renters for the house in Ipswich. When I go back to Nicaragua, you can have my car. What about you. Are you making plans?"

"I'm really up in the air. It all depends on Sarah. The one thing I'm sure of is that I need to see the children on a regular basis; I want to be someone they can count on. Seeing them, after all this time away, makes me think of my father. I don't know why he never came back to the states or even wrote to me. I hadn't realized, until now, that I'd been imitating him unwittingly. I think his disappearance, and the way my mother died, convinced me that there was something horrifically wrong with me that they'd found out. Anyway," he sighed, "I'm determined that our kids will always know that they are loved by both of us. But meanwhile, I've got to make some money. If Sarah doesn't want me living with her, I need to be able to pay for wherever I do live."

"Do you have money back in Nicaragua?"

"No, we were just living off the land as it were, begging for our food and shelter. Not so easy to do that here." Then he lowered his voice to whisper, "Did Sarah tell you to introduce me to people as her husband?"

"No, but she said we should go out to lunch together. Who else could I say you were?"

"Perhaps she wasn't thinking that far ahead. She's so generous, so beautiful, so extraordinarily wonderful in every way; I can't believe I was so stupid as to disappear like that. Anyway," he continued after a moment, "my plan, for the present, is to see if I can get some gigs, or just some kind of job that will put money in my pocket. The last thing I want is for Sarah to have to support me. If things don't work out here, I guess I'll go back to the city and commute here on weekends to see the kids."

Joan considered offering to support him for a while with the money she'd been sending Angelica, but some part of her knew the offer itself would make him uncomfortable, so she said, "I think you're right; just as long as you see the children on a regular basis, they'll be happy and know that they're loved. And I hope with all my heart that you and Sarah will be happy together as well."

Chapter Sixty-Two

AFTER LUNCH, JOE said he wanted to have a look around before he met Sarah at the bakery. Joan went to the public library to read up on Nicaragua. Then she picked Kari up from school and took her shopping for supper. When they returned home carrying their bags, Sarah looked up from the kitchen table where she and Joe had been drinking coffee and looking at the local newspaper. Bruce was in his spot on the counter by his food bowl, waiting for someone to notice it needed to be topped off.

Sarah got up to take the small bag Kari was carrying and put it on the counter next to Bruce, "Hi Kari, hi Mom. Did you have a good time? It looks like you bought a great supper," she went on as she began to unpack the bags. Then as Kari climbed into Joe's lap, Sarah said, "We found an ad for a live-in maintenance man to take care of an estate about five miles out of town. Dad and I are going to drive out and take a look at it. Would you like to come, Kari, and you too, Mom, if you like?"

"I think I'll stay home and cook supper," Joan said. "The kitchen looks wonderfully organized. When are Sam and Paul getting home?"

"They should be home around six," Sarah told her. "They're playing soccer. We should be back by then as well."

"Good," Joan said, "I'll have supper ready." She watched them walk down to the car, Kari bouncing with joy, holding hands with both her parents.

A little after six, Sam and Paul came in, ruddy and happy with their exercise. Sam looked a little wary when he didn't see his father. "Hi Gran," Paul said, "Those brownies smell good."

"Thank you," Joan said, trying to get used to his calling her that. "Your parents aren't back yet, Sam. They went with Kari to look at a possible job for your dad. They should be home soon. Why don't you boys wash your hands, have a brownie to hold you over, and then set the table for me."

"Ok, Gran," Sam said, and then, surprisingly, gave her a hug. "Thank you for bringing Dad back," he said into her ear, as Paul headed upstairs to the bathroom.

"I'm so happy we bumped into each other," Joan answered, not wanting credit for something she hadn't done.

"He's really happy to be home," Sam declared. "He said I had a good strong kick."

And then without any further question or comment, he followed Paul upstairs.

The boys were munching brownies when Sarah came into the kitchen. "Mom," she said, "How could you let..."

but then she glanced at the clock and changed her mind. "Have you helped Gran set the table?" she asked Sam.

"We're just about to," Paul said as he swallowed the last bit of brownie and headed for the silverware drawer.

"Where're Dad and Kari?" Sam asked.

Joan stopped to listen. Could Sarah have left Joe at the estate without warning Sam?

"They'll be in in a minute," Sarah answered. "Wipe your hands on the dishtowel, Paul, or you'll get the forks all sticky. And be careful, Sam, with that pile of plates. Sam, can you take the salad out, and Paul, will you take the glasses out? And don't forget napkins, boys."

As the boys left the kitchen for a few minutes, she turned to Joan and spoke quickly, "The guy said he wanted someone younger and stronger than Joe. So Joe came back with us." She shrugged as she continued, "I didn't know what else to do with him." Then she began to cry. Joan gave her a quick hug, and then Sarah turned toward the sink and washed a few dishes. By the time Joe and Kari came in after playing with Bruce on the swing seat, Sarah had wiped her eyes and they all had supper.

Chapter Sixty-Three

BY THE NEXT weekend, Joe was still sleeping on the sofa. On Saturday night, he and Joan gave a talk about Nicaragua at the Bookstore Café. There were about thirty people, and Joan was surprised by how much fun it was to talk to a group. It reminded her of how much she'd enjoyed teaching. She described how hard it had been for her at first in Malpaisillo and some of the mistakes she'd made, which got people chuckling. Then she showed her slides and talked about the wonderful teachers, health clinic workers and farmers she'd met, and told how the Contras, with the help of U.S. tax dollars, were threatening the villages. Then she turned to Joe, who was sitting in the front row with Sarah and the children. "My son-in-law knows a lot more about this than I do. He traveled from one community to another playing in the national band. He's going to play for you some of the songs of Nicaragua."

Joe stood up with his oboe, smiled a little shyly, and began to sing a liltingly melancholic yet hope-filled song.

Sarah was startled by how beautiful his voice was, remembering how she'd loved hearing him sing to Kari when she was a baby. He sang the song in Spanish, and then sang it again, translating it into English as he went. Then he played it on the oboe.

Then Joe asked the audience if they would like to learn the words to this song. Many nodded, and someone called out, "Yes!"

So Joe taught them the English words to a love song to Nicaragua written during the revolution. The song brought tears to some of the older people, while the young people sang with fervor, imagining themselves in the front lines of that war.

Joan felt as though she were in two places at once, upstairs in the Bookstore Café, and, at the same time, in Oscar's kitchen with Eloina and Yeni teaching her this song by singing the verses again and again as they rolled meat sauce into tamales.

After that, Joe told of some of his adventures traveling around the country and played some of the ceremonial tunes that the band performed. When it was over, everyone stood up as Joe took Joan's hand and they bowed together. The applause was loud and long. Later, as some of the audience left, others came forward to talk to Joan and Joe. About six people backed Joe into a corner and talked intensely while Sarah and Joan and the children helped Sage put away the slide projector and move the lunch tables out from beside the walls and put the folding chairs around them setting up the café for the next day.

As they walked home, Joe told them that he'd been offered and had accepted a job as music director at the Carleton Methodist Church. "I can almost hear the priest in Mérida chuckling over this," he said.

"Let's go now and find the church," Sam said.

"Good idea, Sam; let's see what it looks like," was Joe's quick answer. It was up a steep hill that Sarah didn't remember ever having explored, although the boys said that they'd had some exciting rides down it with their bikes. The church was white and small, hard to distinguish from the other houses on the street, except for the steeple and a small parking lot beside it. Paul spotted the plaque on the front door, 'Welcome to St. John's.'

"So," Joan thought with relief and gratitude, "everything is settled. Joe has work and can find himself an apartment if Sarah doesn't want him at home."

She was surprised by how quiet and strange Sarah was when they reached home. "You can put yourselves to bed, can't you?" she said to the boys. "Would you take Kari up with you? I'll be up in a few minutes to put her to bed. It's very late and I want your lights out in fifteen minutes."

The children were clearly surprised as well. There was almost always a story or at least a discussion of how the day had been.

"I can read them a story…" Joe said to Sarah as though it were a question.

"I'll be up in a minute," Joan said to the children's backs as they headed upstairs without their usual racing or shoving or arguing about how early it was.

Sarah was silent, until the children were out of ear shot. Then in a voice of icy control, she turned to Joe and said, "No, I don't want you to read them a story. In fact I don't know if I can bear to have you here any longer. It's too confusing for them."

Before Joe could reply, Joan said, "I'll just go up and say goodnight," glad of a reason to get away.

"Please don't, Mom," Sarah said, so sharply that Joan stopped with one foot on the stair. Then she added, as Joan turned to face her, "Don't you think you've done enough?"

The question "What do you mean?" came out before Joan could stop it. Because by the time it was asked, she knew what Sarah meant.

"But Sarah…" Joe began.

"I hate you both!" Sarah shouted and pushed past Joan as she rushed upstairs and slammed her bedroom door.

After a moment, Joe said, "Well, we know she doesn't mean that about you. But I don't know what…"

Joan felt exhausted and said, to stave off any discussion of where he should spend the night, "I don't know, Joe. I'm going to bed. Good night, dear," she added, trying to soften her departure, as she turned away and went upstairs to her own room. She thought for a minute of checking in on the children, but then decided to obey Sarah. They were her children.

Joan was reading in bed when Sarah tapped at the door. "Come in, dear," Joan called, having recognized her footstep.

"I want to apologize, Mom," Sarah said, rather quickly.

"That's okay, dear. Come on in," she added as Sarah stood in the doorway. She came in, closed the door and sat at the foot of Joan's bed leaning against the wall with her feet tucked up under her. In Joan's eyes, she looked about fifteen.

"You were right," Joan went on. "I have been kind of meddling. It's just that…"

"Mom, I just can't bear to have him so close. I thought he would give up and go away, go to New York or something, so the kids could see him once in a while. I never thought, not really, that he would get a job right in town."

"You know, I don't think he wants to…" Joan began, but Sarah cut her off.

"Don't, Mom. Don't stand up for him." She said it so loudly that Joan feared the children would hear her. Sarah must have thought the same thing, because she went on more quietly. "He's a fool. I don't trust him. I can't wait for him to move out of here, to get out of my hair. If you want to know, I don't think he's good for the kids either. They don't dare ask where he's been. What sort of relationship is that between father and child?"

"Do you think they're afraid to ask him questions?"

"Yes, I do. They think it might make him leave again!" Sarah responded quickly. "They don't trust him. They can't trust him. Don't you see?" She began to cry.

"Sarah, dear," Joan said, getting out of bed so she could sit beside her daughter and put her arm around her shoulder. "Sarah, dearest," she went on, "you've been so strong, so wonderful. You've created such a wonderful life for the children, including Paul. I'm so sorry to have brought this trouble down on you. I thought you still loved him. I thought you'd be joyous. I'm so sorry. I misunderstood…"

"You still don't understand," Sarah said turning to face her mother. "That's the point. I do love him. If I didn't, it would be easy. But I can't trust him. What if he disappears again? What would happen to the kids then?"

Joan had no answer, so she said into her daughter's hair as she hugged her, "Oh, my dear, I'm so sorry."

Sarah almost wailed, "Please help me, Mom! Tell me what to do!"

Joan hugged her daughter close. She remembered her as a four year old with painfully scrapped knees from a fall on roller skates, and as a teenager facing a test at school she'd forgotten to prepare for, and as the exhausted mother of a new born baby, exercising day and night to regain her figure for a part in a film. Joan had felt then that she could bring comfort to Sarah, give her good advice if not a helping hand. But now, in this situation, as far as she could see there was nothing she could do, and no advice she could give. Sarah and Joe would have to work it out on their own. "I don't know, dearest," she said. "I just don't know." It was a relief to say it. It was a relief to realize it. There was a feeling of peace as she recognized her limits.

"Oh, Mom," Sarah said, "I so glad you're here. I could never go through all this without you. And the kids too. What would we do without you?" With that, she gave her mother a kiss on the cheek, and left, closing the door quietly.

Chapter Sixty-Four

JOAN TURNED OFF the light, but she didn't sleep. She made plans within plans for how to convince Sarah to take Joe back. She had long conversations with Sarah in her head, about the children, about Joe's awful experience with his mother, about his absent father, about the importance of marriage, the importance for children of having their father nearby as a role model. She considered offering to take care of the children while Sarah and Joe visited Ipswich on their own, a second honeymoon. Or perhaps she should take the children to Ipswich, so Joe could start his job, but then what about the children's school? She went round and round, until finally, just before dawn, she fell asleep.

It was Charlie who she dreamed about, for the first time in many years. They were dancing together at a Valentine Ball held on the Boston Common with the moon shining brightly on the snow. The musicians were in the swan boats sailing round and round the little lake so the music swelled and then receded as the swan boats circled. Joan loved the feeling of Charlie's warm hand on the small of her back. The women were wearing low-cut gowns and high heels despite the weather. The men were in tuxedos. As the dance ended, the musicians got back onto dry land and packed up their instruments, Charlie whispered in her ear, "There's someone I want you to meet. He's one of the musicians. He plays the recorder." They looked toward the musicians who were heading over the snow in various directions. "Oh dear," Charlie said. "It's too late. He's gone. Maybe next year."

Bruce woke her up, jumping on her bed and licking her nose. When she got up and went downstairs, she realized it was late. The house was empty. There was a sealed envelope on the kitchen table that said, "For Mom, when she wakes up." Joan opened it immediately although her plan had been to drink some coffee before doing anything.

Good Morning Mom,

You were so sound asleep that I didn't want to wake you. I've taken the kids to the Mall in Albany. Joe is at his new church being introduced to everyone. We still haven't talked about where he's sleeping tonight! I really can't go on pretending we're a family. The kids and I worked so hard to let go of him. He can't waltz in here. Anyway, how did he think he could accept a job in Carleton without asking me first? Oh Mom, I'm so glad you're here. I couldn't go through this without you.

I love you, Sarah

When Joan finished the letter, she felt a little dizzy. She sat down, thinking perhaps her need for coffee had become extreme. But it wasn't that. She was frightened. Did Sarah really mean that she needed Joan? Did Joan need to stay on until she and Joe could resolve their lives? What if they never did? The kitchen felt airless. She got up, poured some coffee into a small pot to heat it. Then she went into the living room.

As she sipped the coffee and stroked Bruce, who had joined her on the sofa, she tried to clear her thoughts. How could Sarah say last night that Joan was meddling and today that she needed her? Did she need her? Was Joan really a help to her? Was it essential to get the children away while Sarah and Joe worked this out? What if Joan weren't there and Sarah asked Joe to leave and he agreed? She'd be losing the man she loved. And what about the children? Could Sarah take good care of them while she was going through so much anguish? Hadn't she sent them to bed without a story last night? But could Joan really help if she stayed, or would she just be meddling?

By the time her coffee cup was empty, Joan had made up her mind. She went back to the kitchen and called the train station. Then she quickly got dressed and stuffed her clothes and the new recorders into her backpack. She left her own note on the kitchen table, held down by her unwashed coffee cup.

Love to you all. I'm heading to Ipswich to pack my things. Thank you so much for taking care of Bruce. He seems completely at home here.

Mom, Gran, Joan.

It felt wonderful not to give an explanation.

But on the train to Ipswich, she realized how angry she was at Joe and Sarah, and at herself. Why had she run away? She had made the mess by bringing Joe home without warning, and now she was running away. But they were grownups, damn it; why couldn't they work things out? But what about the children? Maybe she should take the next train back. Maybe she should offer to take the children. But she didn't want the children. She wanted to concentrate on getting ready to return to Nicaragua. She wondered if she was the most selfish person on earth, preferring to think of herself and her romance instead of her daughter and grandchildren. By the time she arrived home in Ipswich, she was almost desperate. She kept thinking that she should return to Carleton, but even as she was thinking it, she was putting on the kettle to make herself some tea.

She heated up a can of soup, and drank her tea sitting at the kitchen table with the radio on for company. Suddenly she got up and turned off the radio; she had to think.

She'd made a terrible mistake. It felt as though she were waking up from a hallucination. Of course she couldn't go back to Nicaragua, at least, not now. She was needed here. Things were going to be hard for Sarah, whatever she decided, and Joan would have to stay here so Sarah could call her whenever she needed her. First thing Joan should do is offer to take all three kids for their next vacation to give Sarah some space. Clearly, Sarah wanted to talk with her mother about her decision about Joe. What was Joan doing in Ipswich? She was needed in Carleton. Or at least, if she wasn't needed at this moment, she should be on call for when the need arose. She should call Sarah right now and tell her that she could return to Carleton tomorrow if that would make things easier.

As she reached for the phone, she tipped over the cup she had just refilled with tea. It spilled on her lap, burning her legs. She began to cry. Angelica was gone. Nothing Joan could do would bring her back. Sarah was different. She had created a life for herself and her children. She may have needed Joan once, but she no longer did, not really. And Joe didn't need her either. He needed to build his relationship with Sarah and his children. They both needed only her prayers. She was free, free to hang out in Ipswich waiting for the phone to ring, or free to organize her life so she could move to Nicaragua, where Oscar and his children enjoyed her as she was, with no language to mask her fears and inadequacies. She felt accepted there with nothing to prove and everything to find joy in, more at home than she could remember ever having felt before.

She called Oscar. It was a bit of a production because there was only one phone in Malpaisillo. Luckily the mayor's office was open and his secretary said she would send someone to look for Oscar so he could call her back. After an hour or so of waiting, Joan decided to go to bed early, not having slept much the night before. She assumed the person who'd gone to look for Oscar, probably a child, had not been able to find him. She would try again in the morning.

Oscar's call woke her up. "What a lovely way to be woken, hearing his voice," she thought, but didn't have the words to tell him. Oscar told her that everyone in the family was well and looking forward to her return. Then he continued in slow careful Spanish. "You are not to worry, Juana, but there was a killing in Malpaisillo. Our soldiers cannot keep the fighting only in the mountains. We need more soldiers. Juan is leaving school to fight. I also may be asked to go to the mountains to fight. I cannot let my son fight without my help, if they need old men like me. Do you understand this?"

"Does this mean you don't want to marry me?" Joan responded, hoping her effort to speak Spanish would cover her despair.

"No, no my love. Only I want you to know. Will you marry an old soldier like me?"

"Yes, Oscar," Joan answered immediately. "I will marry you. I will marry you, my old soldier."

"Well then, come quickly," he said.

And they were cut off before she could respond.

As Joan hung up, she realized with wonder that she had understood every word.

An Epilogue in Letters

DEAR SARAH,

I haven't heard from you for months. I don't know if it's because you're angry that I left without warning, or if my letters to you aren't getting out of Nicaragua. The battles against the Contras make everything here very difficult.

Oscar and I got married two weeks after I arrived. We had the ceremony in his Evangelical church. (I had the feeling that Father McGinley was giving us his blessing even so.) The next day, Oscar had to leave for the mountains to fight against the Contras. His son Juan was already there and couldn't come down for the wedding. Three weeks later, both of Oscar's daughters left for the mountains as well. Eloina joined a brigade of women fighters and Yeni, at 15, cooks for them.

So, I'm on my own. I begin the day the way Juan used to, by sweeping the tile floors clean of the grit from the dirt road that comes in through the open door and windows and covers everything. I leave the door wide open when I'm home to let a breeze come through. It's very hot here. I don't try to cook. There's very little kindling and I'm not efficient with the wood stove. I walk into town and eat in the café. The walk is beautiful, in its way. As I go toward town, I see the volcano in the distance. It seems to be watching over us, guarding us, although it's famous for its destructive eruptions. On the way home through the square, I stop for a few minutes under the rare, and therefore precious, palm trees, soaking up their shade.

My Spanish is improving. I buy the local newspaper and read it while I eat breakfast, understanding enough to enjoy it. My neighbor, Tomaso, a retired journalist crippled by arthritis, is giving me lessons. When I asked how much they would cost, he said he was doing it for the war. "I'm too old to fight," he said, "but at least I can teach a fighter's wife how to speak." We have lunch together almost every day and he gives me a lesson in grammar. I'm also learning about food. The waitress used to serve me whatever was handy, and at the end of the meal I would hold out a handful of pesetas and she would take what she thought appropriate. Now, thanks to Tomaso, I can ask what's on the menu for the day and how much it costs.

In the afternoons, I read aloud to children in the library. Spanish is phonetic so I can usually pronounce words even when I don't know what they mean. When I make a mistake, the children make me repeat the word over and over until I get it right. There aren't that many children's books here, so some of them I almost know by heart. After reading aloud, we play a game they made up called "What is that?" We sit on the stoop in front of the wide library door and the children point to things on the street. I try to name the thing in Spanish and then they attempt it in English and we laugh at our mistakes.

After supper, I walk over to the Catholic Church for an evening prayer service. I can now understand most of what we're saying as I recite the prayers; we pray for the safety of the soldiers in the mountains, naming each one that we know; we pray for a peaceful resolution to the fighting; and we pray for rain and a good harvest. Then I pray for you and Joe and the children, and for Angelica, Aunt Marianne, and your dad.

In the evenings, I sit out on our patio with Guapo, our dog, at my feet; the chickens and pigs went up to the mountains with the men. I light candles as the darkness comes in, and write love poems to Oscar. I write them in English and translate them with help from a dictionary. They will be a surprise for him when he comes home, since there is no way for me to send them to him up in the mountains. I look forward to astonishing Oscar and the children with my proficiency in Spanish when they return.

My heart is filled with love and gratitude for you and your family and for Oscar and his children. May God keep you all safe, and bring you joy.

Love, Mom

Dearest Mom,

I wrote before, but I'm not positive the letter got mailed. We've moved and you know what that's like. Emily came back from Florence with a husband and two young stepchildren. Paul is thrilled, both to have his mother home and to have siblings. He reads Dr. Seuss to them, shows them how to do puzzles, and does finger painting with them on piles of newspapers. Emily's husband, Marco, is a pastry chef and he works with me at the bakery. We're expanding, in order to sell to restaurants.

They all arrived out of the blue, although Emily swears she sent a letter telling us of their coming. In any case, we knew nothing about it, and one evening as I was making supper, they all walked in. The kids shared my bed that night and we realized that we had to move double quick.

It was Joe who helped us out. He'd gotten a job teaching orchestra at a boarding school ten miles outside of Carleton. The job includes an apartment. So that's where we all, including Bruce of course, ended up the day after Emily arrived.

And, thanks in part to his sofa being so uncomfortable, it's all worked out. Joe and I are like before, only better. He goes once a month to an alternative doctor, recommended by Dr. Appleton, who says he's doing great. If the cancer comes back, we'll deal with it the best we can.

I can't tell you how much I love watching him with the kids. He's teaching Sam how to play the piano and Kari accompanies them on a miniature drum. He's teaching himself how to play the organ at the Church because the present organist is moving away. He's also leading the choir which I've joined. I sang a long ornate solo last Sunday. The kids cheered, silently, from the front pew.

You and Oscar and his children are in our prayers. I'm so glad you're in love. It's been a long, long time since Daddy died. Joe's begun to teach us Spanish to be ready for our visit to you as soon as the war is over.

We all send our love,

The letter was signed by each of them including an intricate squiggle by Kari.